NO MAN'S LAND

THE ROBOSAPIEN TRILOGY, BOOK 1

BEN MAGID

Bub City Books

CONTENTS

First Edition November 2020

Book design by ktsdesign/shutterstock

ISBN 978-1-7360321-1-4 (paperback)
ISBN 978-1-7360321-0-7 (ebook)
ISBN: 78-1-7360321-2-1 (hardcover)
LCCN: 2020921144

www.benmagid.com

For ALM & ESM

'Every creature is better alive than dead, men and moose and pine trees, and he who understands it aright will rather preserve its life than destroy it.'
    Henry David Thoreau

PART I

"THE GIRL"

PROLOGUE

"Day 2585.

"My name is Rebel Anne Rae. Today is July 31, 2054. I was born in the year 2035, on this very day, so I guess that makes today my birthday. Happy birthday, me.

"Every year for my birthday, mom and dad would throw a party. Cake, ice cream, funny hats, balloons. One time my father rented a pony, not the synthetic kind, mind you, but a real live pony. My parents did things like that. They said I brought joy into everything they did..."

She stared into the red blinking record light. For a reason she couldn't place, that day's video diary felt more like a confessional than one of a thousand other journal entries she had made over the last decade. She shook off the thought, reminding herself that the camera presided for posterity's sake, not to capture personal emotion. She tried again. Take two.

"I'm nineteen today, and, believe it or not, I am the oldest human alive. I don't feel old. I feel fine. I feel fit. My mental state is... pretty good. I guess. Most days." She withdrew, shook her head, not liking the way it went. After a deep breath, she focused and turned back to the camera. "Let's start over. I was born nineteen years ago in San Francisco, California. I had a family. My father's name was William, but most people called him Bill. He worked as a robotics engineer. My mother, Melanie, was a homemaker. They were good people. They didn't want this to happen. Nobody did. In an instant, my life, my entire world, was erased. Gone."

Rebel sat there for a moment, thoughts of Exodus replaying in her mind, and all the time between. Seven birthdays spent alone. Seven winters and seven summers and seven Thanksgivings where she would give thanks to nothing and nobody.

"I wanted to be a ballerina. I've never told anyone before. Strange, now that I think of it. Not wanting to be a ballerina. That isn't strange. Strange I never told anyone. I don't know why. Maybe fear. Embarrassed. Doesn't matter, not anymore. I don't live in that world. I live in this one, and nobody dances in this world. Nobody sings, nobody plays music. Laughter, joy, those died a long time ago. I know that I'm not going to be a ballerina. I'm not going to be anything. Just me... whoever that is."

"I'm on this planet for a different reason; I realize that now," she said. "I have a job to do, a mission. An ending to my story. It keeps me sane. Alive. It keeps the loneness away... for a time. Being what I am, there is nothing else to be but alone. I hope, someday, when someone finds these video diaries, they will know who I was. What I was about. What I tried to do."

"My name is Rebel Anne Rae..." she said. "And I am the last remaining human on planet Earth."

1

———

Day one.

The first spark of light came in the form of lightning. Sudden and blinding, gone. The luminous flicker illuminated her bedroom. Dolls made of cloth and ceramic lined up along the wall as if awaiting a firing squad. Flowery wallpaper, happy sunflowers nestled amongst a pale blue sky and green grass. A favorite teddy bear sat in the rocking chair, providing vigilant watch over his twelve-year-old princess.

Rebel slept in the canopy bed, dreaming away about princesses, parties, cupcakes, unicorns dancing on rainbows. Or maybe she just dreamed about the possibilities of life, the anticipation of what the following day would bring.

The second spark of light woke her. A silent, blinding flash illuminated the bedroom, turning night into day. Her eyes fluttered open. She sat up in bed and rubbed the sleep from her eyes. The clock on the nightstand read 4:33 A.M., much too early to be awake. Another flash, followed by a close successor out the window. Eerie, with hints of orange and yellow mixed in. Beautiful and frightful at the same time. *Was that even possi-*

ble? Rebel thought. Lions, they were beautiful and frightful. She only saw photographs of them since their extinction a few years before her birth.

Sliding out of bed, her bare feet touched down on the cold wood floor. She slipped on her pink slippers and padded to the window, brushing aside the lace curtains. Her reflection stared back at her in the glass. Her hair, in the tangles of sleep, was long and curly, a deep rich auburn that didn't take a comb too well, much to her mother's chagrin. Her parents had made her keep her locks short until the prior year when her tenaciousness finally wore them down. It made her look like a boy, she would complain, while all the other girls at her school flaunted long flowing hair. Rebel didn't want to stand out at that age. She wanted to be part of everything, to be accepted, to fit in. To be just like everyone else — pretty, thin, clear skin, long hair, popular — convinced that would bring her happiness.

Her father loved classical music. Mozart, Bach, Chopin. He would turn up the volume to prove a point, saying, 'If everything is loud, nothing is loud.' Rebel didn't understand what he meant at the time. It took some maturity on her part to realize that it shouldn't be one's goal to blend in, to follow. People should want to stand out, to be who they are, an individual, quirks and all.

Rebel stretched to look out at the residential street. They resided in a three-story Queen Anne on Steiner Street across from Alamo Square Park, in the Western Addition. Painted light blue with white trim, the house overlooked the small synthetic park out the front. The fake grass and trees that replaced the world's dissipating nature almost passed for real, if one could ignore the plastic feel and chemical smell. Rebel's parents once bought a plant, a real ficus, but couldn't afford the monthly payments and had to return it, much to Rebel's vexation.

Her keen vantage point afforded her an unobstructed view

of downtown. The smog-ridden sky blocked the light of stars and even turned the moon a shade of orange, yet the city buildings and bridges twinkled with artificial light, showcasing the life and promise of adventure. But not that night.

An ever-advancing wall of fog shrouded the city like heavy, advancing storm clouds. They moved in fast. Faster than she ever recalled observing storm clouds move. And dark, more like night headed her way than thunderclouds. From within this shroud came discharges of lightning. A tremendous boom roared, followed closely by another flash, brilliant and searing. The entire bedroom lit up for a split-second. Thunder sounded hollow, metallic almost, like a head-on car collision. And the lightning didn't emanate from the sky... but from the ground.

Rebel turned from the window, scrunching up her face to recall what her father taught her about storms. On a summer vacation, they drove to the woods, where their family owned a small cabin. Her father wanted to teach her about nature and wildlife before they disappeared for good, so he purchased a rustic cabin in the woods, minus all modern conveniences, like electricity, air conditioning, or running water. The storm came the second night. The air grew colder, and the wind followed, bringing with it a light sprinkling of rain. Shortly after came the deluge. Not until the thunder and lightning arrived did Rebel begin to waver. Her father would comfort her in his usual analytical way, i.e., distraction. If she counted the seconds between the first flash of lightning and the first sound of thunder, it would tell her how far away the storm resided. So when the next series of flashes and booms came, Rebel readied herself.

Thunder boomed within Rebel's bedroom. "One, two, three..."

The flash of lightning came next. Three seconds equaled three miles away. However, didn't her father also tell her that thunder always strikes *after* lightning?

Another boom in the distance, followed by a second, and a third. The room seemed to vibrate for a second and roll up, then down. Windows rattled, and tiny spiderweb-like cracks formed, spreading out from its center with every encroaching blast of thunder.

Something ominous drew her attention out the window. When those dark black storm clouds reached the city, all those wonderful twinkling lights began to flicker and go out, one by one, a wave of darkness overcoming them. Something menacing headed her way.

Ba-Wooom! Ba-Wooom! Ba-Wooom! A wailing sound drifted in, rising and falling. Civil defense sirens, used to signal severe storms, earthquakes... or war.

At that moment, the door swung open, letting in the light from the hallway, and Rebel's mother rushed in.

"Rebel," she said. "It's time."

REBEL SAT BUCKLED up in the backseat as her father drove his cherished 1951 Hudson Hornet, a bathtub of a car that puttered along the empty street. It didn't work on magnetic waves, like current models, and was cause for a lot of snickering in Rebel's direction, but she garnered that they weren't snickering at that moment. Her father's fondness for old clunkers, or 'vintage' as he called them, became their savior.

Before leaving the house, they each had a chance to take only one personal item. Rebel chose her favorite porcelain doll, Anne, while Mrs. Rae gathered the memory card from the tablet that held their family photos. Mrs. Rae was always the first one to say everything would be okay and monsters didn't exist. But she didn't say any of that stuff at that moment. She fidgeted, nervous and scared, as she scanned the neighborhood from the passenger seat.

Dr. Rae held a metal case close to his side, marked with three letters: L.I.F. It seemed important, being the sole item her father took, and Rebel wanted to know what it hid inside — the answer to all their prayers or the key to a hidden treasure.

Glancing out the window, Rebel noticed the distant dark clouds hanging low in the sky, but otherwise, not much else held her interest other than the piled-up litter produced by an ever-growing population. The world reached its tipping point. There ceased to be enough earth to go around anymore, not for people and not for their consumption.

The holo-billboards that lined the road displayed pollution and toxicity reports:

Air Quality — Unhealthful — 12% Green — Extreme Caution!!!

The images flickered and changed:

...EVACUATE...EVACUATE...EVACUATE...EVACUATE...

A lone man hurried across the street, dressed in striped pajamas with a tan trench coat to cover them up, clutching a large garbage bag in his arms. Rebel couldn't make sense of it. He seemed like a man whose house had caught on fire, and he grabbed whatever he could before escaping. Rebel didn't see any fire.

"Where are we going?" Rebel inquired.

"Somewhere safe," Dr. Rae replied.

"When are we coming back?" she asked.

"I don't know," he said.

"But this is our home." More hollow booms echoed in the distance, interrupting her, alighting the sky in phosphorescent light.

"Not anymore."

The car roared down the deserted road, heading west. The

area held a good deal more commotion than a minute ago, but on a scale of one to ten, the panic level remained at a three. Ahead, a two-car wreck filled the middle of both lanes. Dr. Rae swerved around, narrowly avoiding a collision. A few other late-model cars sat on the sides of the road, left abandoned, all powerless with their fancy high-tech computers. Most drivers decided to continue on foot, adding to a growing stream of pedestrians packing the side of the road, everyone carrying bundles and bags of possessions.

Mrs. Rae turned on the radio, shuffling past stations full of static until a clear voice came through.

"My fellow Americans," the President of the United States began, "this is a time of crisis, and our time for courage in the face of battle. Make no mistake; we are at war for our very survival. So it is with considerable sadness that tonight I have signed an executive order joining our United Nations brethren in complete and total evacuation of planet Earth. Rest assured, this is our home, and we will be back."

Rebel's parents sat motionless, in stunned silence, until the Presidential address was replaced with the Emergency Broadcast System.

"This is a recorded message from the Federal Emergency Management Agency. This is not a test," boomed the recorded voice. "Full evacuation is under effect. Proceed in a calm and orderly manner to your assigned transport for jettison. Repeat... this is not a test."

Mrs. Rae turned the radio off. "It's happening. They took control."

"Of what?" questioned Rebel.

"Everything," her father proclaimed.

The further they went, the more the growing stream of displaced people, resembling refugees — some on bicycles, some pushing baby strollers or shopping carts filled with looted supplies. And the only working motor vehicle aroused interest. Dr. Rae let up on the gas pedal, down to twenty miles an hour, and even that felt too fast.

"Be careful," Mrs. Rae advised.

"A little further. The shuttles are just ahead," he said.

Crash! A brick smashed the windshield, spider-webbing it. Rebel screamed, Mrs. Rae shouted in surprise. Dr. Rae twitched the wheel, and the car hopped up the curb, right into a tree.

Dr. Rae turned to appraise them for injuries. "Are you hurt?" They both shook their stunned heads. He inspected his metal case for damage. Reaffirmed its contents remained undamaged, he stepped outside. The totaled car belched smoke; the hood caved in, the engine stalled out.

"We go on foot from here on out." He held out his hand for Rebel to take. "Whatever you do, do not let go of my hand."

Moving in a wide-eyed stupor, Rebel watched people pressing forward, all in the same direction. A mass exodus of the human race. They scuttled over a sea of human litter and past a series of barricaded checkpoints marked by a ten-foot-high wall of stacked chain link fences, already overrun by the crowds. It quickly grew into a mob, the Raes among them, all swept along in this tide of humanity.

"Stay together," urged Mrs. Rae.

A policeman shouted through cupped hands, "Please move forward in a calm and orderly fashion... there is room for everyone..."

For the most part, the message got through. The huge crowd grew by the minute, but the shuttles were huge too and could hold them all, or so they were told. While a sense of urgency persisted, everything remained corralled for the time being. They passed a store with dozens of holoscreens in the window displaying news from around the world — war footage from Tokyo to Mexico City to Rome. Spreading.

"It's happening everywhere..." Mrs. Rae said in a stupor.

Images of the moon flashed on the screens, reports from

various space stations, looking like a community of buildings and residences. A coalition of nations had come together to create not just habitats but a place of refuge — a backup plan for the survival of the human race.

Army General Neil Lestor's interview projected on the holo-screen. A caption beneath his image scrolled:

TALKS COLLAPSE — WAR IMMINENT — EVACUATION IN EFFECT

Rebel remembered seeing the General before at her house. He and her father would have heated discussions about Mech, their use, purpose, and future. As technology raced ahead and humankind achieved fantastical advances, ethical questions arose. What decisions did people feel comfortable delegating to machines, and what kinds of decisions did they insist on reserving for the exercise of human judgment? General Lestor stated his intent to use robots on the battlefield where they could carry supplies, bring medical gear into dangerous places, and, yes, kill. Dr. Rae adamantly opposed it. In retrospect, the General was right; Mech couldn't be controlled, but then again, right doesn't always prevail in a world full of wrongs.

A small white and brown dog, possibly a terrier, scooted past them, disappearing under pedestrians' feet, followed seconds later by its owner, an older man holding a leash. "Bernie?! Bernie, get back here!" Rebel watched, hoping they would be reunited, worried about the dog's safety, and all dogs for that matter. Could they come to the moon? What about birds? Elephants? Who got to choose? Was there a bigger ship, like Noah's Ark, loading up two of each species? She hoped so.

"We'll make it. Stay close," her father said, clinging onto his metal case.

More booms thudded, now much closer. Eerie explosion events lit up the horizon. The streets swelled with hundreds, maybe thousands of people in the process of evacuating. They swarmed the streets like rats fleeing a sinking ship, herded by the military presence, all moving in the same direction: to the ocean.

The crowd thickened, and fragments of conversations washed over the family.

"We've got it the worst here," an older man began, "that's what I heard. The U.S. mostly, South America and Asia some. There's nothing happening in Europe."

"Really," asked a younger man with his own opinion. "Everybody's saying Europe got it worst of all. Completely wiped out, full-scale invasion."

"It's a lie, you know," stuttered a migrant worker. "They said there's enough room for everyone, but there isn't. It's not possible. The moon's not that big, and those space stations are limited at best. Common sense, really."

"Is that true?" asked Rebel. Her answer came from a subtle glance between her parents.

"You don't need to worry about that, honey," her mother said. "There's room for us. We've been selected."

Rebel scrunched her face, unsure what that meant.

A panicky guy passed in front, beseeching, "The top of the hill about five minutes ago, please, did you see her? She's eighty years old, about five and a half feet tall, white hair, bright blue jacket."

Rebel grew concerned by all the conversations going on around her. She didn't understand everything said but had the wherewithal to know it couldn't be good.

"I want to go back home." She pined to be back in the safety of her own house. She wished she could hide under her bed covers and close her eyes until everything bad went away.

"It's okay," Dr. Rae reassured her.

"No, it isn't," she cried. "I want to go back home. Please."

"We can't go back," he said. "We're getting on the shuttles... we're gonna make it. Look."

She turned and saw the shuttle bays along the oceanfront. What once consisted of the tourist trap of Fisherman's Wharf had since evolved into immense launch pads, constructed as a precaution after the first incidents of uprising began. Many believed it foolhardy, a waste of taxpayers' money and Earthly resources, but nobody was complaining anymore. Massive metal towers held hundreds of sleek shuttles in upright positions. Smoke from liquid nitrogen spewed out of the quantum drive engines to keep them cool. Seen from a distance, they could almost be mistaken for the futuristic buildings of a skyline, gleaming white in the massive spotlights that illuminated the operation.

"Nothing bad is gonna happen," he assured her. "I promise, Rebel."

A bright flash lit up the sky. Dr. Rae's face went white, and the fifty heads around them all turned in unison. For a brief moment, the world flickered as if on fire. Absolutely everything stopped. No sound, no movement, no nothing. A shocked silence fell over the crowd until the shockwave hit.

Bombs. Not the exploding, fragmentation kind, but smart bombs. Those closest to the blast radius disintegrated. The bombs targeted humankind and only humankind. DNA, the very ingredient that made humans human, vaporized, instantly annihilated into microscopic dust. And then the shock gave way to panic.

"Get to the ships! They're coming!" voices cried out.

A seething morass of humans turned into animals with a single, selfish thought: to live, by any means necessary. Once normal, reserved members of society pushed others out of the way, trampling those too slow to keep up. Elbows and fists flew. Two men pummeled each other as people passed without a second glance. No police to break it up. No law, no order. Just animal instincts of fight or flight. Human nature at its worst.

Rebel's parents flanked her, trying to keep everyone together as the mob grew dense, jostling, pushing, threatening to crush them alive. Caught up in the sea of bodies, people slamming into them, squeezing them, wrenched them apart.

Rebel couldn't hold on.

"Rebel!" her father yelled. "Rebel! Hang on!"

Just then, a massive explosion came from right behind them. Like a herd of spooked cattle, the crowd stampeded. Deafening screams from the mass swarming over the road, all overlapping into a jumble of sound.

At that moment, their hands separated.

"No. No! Rebel! My daughter! Rebel! Rebel!"

Rebel watched her parents being helplessly pushed away by the panic-stricken mob, yelling her name, separated by 5,000 frightened people. Scared and alone, she pushed through to the sidewalk, hiding in an antique storefront's alcove. Hugging her knees to her chest, she looked like a little girl lost in a department store.

Clickety-clack, clickety-clack, clickety-clack. The sound came from down the street, from the darkness. A pitter-patter of metallic footsteps. Mechanical dogs, led by large robotic creatures, too hard to fully make out in the dark and smoke-shrouded area, save one feature: screens for faces, flashing red —red—red.

Rebel dared not move. Not much of a hiding place, but if she left, she would be right in the line of fire. Two stragglers, a man and his son by the look of them, tried to dart across the walkway, both taken down by dogs. They killed quick and efficiently, turning humans to dust, thoughtless machines expediting their programming, following the humans like ranch herders. She buried her face in her hands, listening to the terrible sounds until silence fell.

Rebel creeped out of her hiding place. Aside from the fires, no man-made light pierced the gloom. A thin, acrid smoke wafted over everything, turning the world black and gray and muted as if the earth had gone to sleep. Standing in the center of the abandoned road, Rebel looked west, watching hundreds of spaceships lift off, jettisoning the planet. Orbital rockets lifting off from launch pads, rocketing straight up. The ground shook. Plumes of smoke followed in their wake as propulsion rockets drove them skyward. Dozens of loud booms as the ships broke through the atmosphere. Higher and higher they went until they no longer resembled ships, but shooting stars. Until finally, Rebel could no longer see them at all, swallowed up by the night sky.

And just like that, she was alone.

A familiar shape lay on the street up ahead — her father's metal case labeled L.I.F., dented but secure. She picked it up, hugging it tightly, grateful to have any remnant of her parents with her at that moment.

Rebel knew to go home immediately if ever separated from her parents. That, or seek out a policeman. Rebel didn't see any policemen on her long walk back, or any other humans for that matter. It could have been hours for all Rebel knew by the time she eventually found her way back home. She followed the landmarks she remembered, passing her father's destroyed car, upside down and leaking fluids. Holoscreens went black, and billboards only contained a few plasma pixels that flickered like old Morse code.

Rebel stopped when she discovered the woman, wearing a pretty floral dress, hair made up, red and curled, not turned to dust like the other victims, seemingly trampled to death. Rebel never observed a dead body before, not since laws changed to outlaw human burials. Land was too precious, the governments deemed, opting instead to force mankind to choose cremation, or if one could afford it, space jettison. The dead woman before her would get neither, yet appeared to be at peace. Perhaps she was. Her plight was finally over, while Rebel's tribulation had just begun.

Having finally reached her house, she tried the lights, but they didn't work. Nothing electrical did. Not the phones, nor the holoscreens, tablets or computers. The cold outside temperature began to seep inside, with no heat to hold it off its inevitability. She searched every room, every closet, under beds. All empty, all lifeless. The terror began to sink in.

Rebel was left behind.

2

Funny how much humans lived by routine. Not haha funny, but amusing if one thought about it. People followed the almighty clock, which told them when to wake up, when to sleep, when to go, when to arrive, and how much time this or that would take. A meeting, a date, a sunset, a flight, a dentist appointment. A life. Routines kept people sane. Programming, once comforting and a bit sad at the same time. Some people had a morning routine. Wake up, exercise, shower, coffee, and breakfast, catch up on the news and send children off to school.

Rebel's routine was a bit... different.

First off, she didn't call it a routine. It became a *ritual*, one she perfected over the past seven years alone. She never once wavered. It was flawless. Her life depended on it.

Three alarm clocks turned to 5:30 A.M. and pierced the peaceful bedroom. Rolling out of bed with a grunt, Rebel turned off the alarms and sat for a moment to shake out the cobwebs. She loved sleeping. The warmth, the comfort, the dreams of days gone by. If up to her, she would stay in bed forever, eating ice cream and watching TV. Despite her self-perceived maturity, Rebel enjoyed reality shows, devouring fashion competitions with her mother, and was a closet fan of rich housewives. She would fantasize about being one of them, living in a mansion on the beach, surrounded by wealth, glamorous parties, and a certain almighty air of self-importance; all her immediate problems revolving around what to spend her husband's wealth on and gossip from so-called friends. If she thought about it too much, it depressed her. These women with so much potential to do good, to make the world a better place, yet devolved into living superficial, fake lives, with fake boobs, fake noses, fake smiles, covered in a pound of makeup, excavated rare stones, and dead animal furs. Encircled by nonsensical arguments and illiterate conversations. Of course, they were all dead now.

Still half asleep, Rebel's feet pounded away on the treadmill for her daily run. In her world, people didn't run. They didn't exercise. They didn't need to. Their bodies never got fat or puffy, saggy or wrinkled, and they didn't age. Gravity didn't have the same effect on them. They were perfect; Rebel was not. Not only did she have to maintain a specific facade, but she needed to be ready to run at a moment's notice. And she was good. Stride: robotic. Breath: controlled, steady. Maybe one day, she would even enter a marathon. But not anytime soon.

While the bathroom shower filled with steam, Rebel changed out of her workout clothes and stood before the digital mirror. Hair a mess, skin blotchy. She had her work cut out for her.

"Hello, me."

She braced herself and stepped into the scalding stream, thankful that water still ran and the waste removal system worked. Creating an entirely new system was deemed inessential. Waste not, want not. She used a hard bristle brush to scrub every inch of her body, peeling away loose follicles of skin. It didn't wipe clean all of her DNA, all that made her, well, her, but every bit helped.

As the only human on planet Earth, dental hygiene held more significance. If Rebel got a cavity, there were no dentists to visit. Root canal? Not a chance. Brush, floss, anti-cavity mouthwash. Check.

The scale read 123 pounds. *Not good,* thought Rebel. She took out the notebook with daily logs, pages filled with a multitude of weights and graphs. A tablet would have been much easier to store the spreadsheets, but digital could be tracked. Handwriting became an optional class in school some twenty years ago, before Rebel's birth, so she taught herself to write with an old-fashioned pen and paper made from trees. Every day, she weighed herself. Yesterday she logged in at a steady societal norm of 125 pounds. Normally, losing two pounds would be a cause for celebration, but not for her. She would have to make a stop to get more food later — one more thing to add to the bottomless list of to-dos.

Sitting before the vanity, Rebel put in colored contacts. They served two purposes: one, to improve her vision, because nobody wore glasses anymore, and two, they changed her brown eyes to blue. She then applied foundation until not a single patch of pigmentation differed from any other. Using a small hand mirror, she painted on a thick red smear with gloss and a lip liner pen, and painted on eyes shadow and liner. She plucked her full eyebrows until symmetrical, then proceeded to apply fake, long eyelashes atop her own with adhesive gel. Last up, she dipped her fingertips into a bowl of thick, white paraffin wax, grimacing at the heat. *Hello, fingerprint hider,* she thought. Rebel finished it all off with fake, pre-painted fingernails.

She took out a premixed spray bottle (her own concoction), consisting of additives made from acrylic paint and a small bottle of silvery glitter nail polish, adding a metallic, acrylic-like glitter to her complexion. The spray burned, a lot, but did wonders at masking heat signatures, pheromones, and perspiration, giving her skin an impression of porcelain, just like one of her childhood dolls. Just like *them*. To Rebel, it all looked:

"Plastic."

At first, Rebel had tried using her own hair, but that quickly proved problematic, hence the cropped, bleached style. A bit punk rock, but in her world, necessity outweighed style. *Necessity,* her word of the day, every day. She tied her hair back, tightening it as much as she could bear, then secured the blonde wig on top. The synthetic hair polymers perfectly lined up with the next, giving off a plastic, doll-like sheen.

Padding her bra, Rebel went from a manageable size 'B' to a full, socially acceptable 'C.' Just like every other 'female' in the world. She proceeded to strap various self-made tech components to her body, almost making her machine-like: trackers, scanners, jammers, all necessity. Closet open, Rebel perused her options. A joke. Every garment exactly the same as the next. The uniform, or as she preferred to call it, her 'costume,' consisted of ten gray pencil skirts, ten white blouses, ten black coats, and three pairs of identical plain high-heeled shoes. She ironed out every wrinkle the night before and placed creases where they needed to be. Rebel became fairly efficient with a needle and thread and laundry. Her mom would be proud.

Dressed, she stepped before the full-length mirror and surveyed herself. Head to toe; Rebel transformed into an immaculate young woman. Everything about her: perfection. A glamour magazine cover, an Italian vogue model, a classic beauty, metamorphosed into what every girl dreamed of looking like. All to fit in. All to look like everyone else. All completely:

"Fake."

On route to the kitchen, Rebel paused at an oil painting on the wall. *Bouquet of Sunflowers* had quite a life, having traveled throughout the world, something Rebel would never be able to do. She first encountered the piece when on loan for an impressionism exhibit at the M.H. de Young Memorial Museum in San Francisco. Needless to say, its final trip became a short jaunt from the museum to the Rae household, one of the many perks of Rebel's position. She stared into the depths of the paint strokes, the colors. It provided much-needed warmth and blocked out the harsh around her. It worked, but only for a few fleeting moments. Reality always found a way to seep back in.

A bowl of stale Lucky Charms and powdered milk. Not Rebel's favorite, but since food became a bit trickier to acquire, she took what she could get. Her status as 'party of one' made foraging a bit more forgiving. She scavenged and looted everything she could, piece by piece. Her go-to items were anything canned, artificial, processed, boxes in bulk. She downed a slew of vitamins and supplements, also essential. And yes, Lucky Charms. One day reserves would dry up, go bad, run out, but Rebel pushed the thought to the back of her mind. She would cross that bridge when the time came. For now, she had more essential items on her to-do list.

The garage served as the war room, like a mechanic's workshop: tools on the wall, computers and monitors, 3-D printers, and advanced fiber optic cables that snaked the floor. Robotic assembly arms hung from ceiling-mounted hooks. Dozens of monitors showed security footage around the house through hidden cameras. And books. Shelves filled to the brim to the point of spilling over. Every volume an iteration of mechanical engineering, physics, electronics, artificial intelligence and coding. Operational manuals, design plans, diagnostic reports, programming, schematics with their bindings coming apart, pages dog-eared, highlighted, and scrawled with notes. If not for the collection, Rebel would have gone extinct years ago, just like the printed word. Books became obsolete in the new world, with everything going digital long ago, but that served her well. Digital meant networked, and networked meant traceable.

Rebel needed to remain off-the-grid as much as 'humanly' possible.

She took a book down from a shelf. Printed atop of the cover: a schematic of a rudimentary human-like being. 'HUMAN 2.0 by Dr. William H. Rae'. Rebel caressed the cover and felt the embossed name of her father. The act of defiance must have been like a knife to the heart. Exodus, that fateful night. Rebel hoped if he learned of her plan, he would approve. What she did, what she became, it wasn't survival. It was justice. She would fix this. She had to.

On the other side of the garage, the wall held a collage of photos and clippings. Various headlines declaring 'WAR, INVASION.' Blueprints of buildings — an elevator, a computer mainframe, retinal scanners, hallways, satellite antennas, along with surveillance photos from around the city. All tacked over a large map of San Francisco. Key locations marked and circled: food, art, books, fuel, etc. It became survival of the fittest. Or a fugitive on the run. After all, by all definitions of the word, Rebel was the enemy, the villain of her story. She first denied it, defined it in every other way but the truth... she had set herself on a course of destruction. Change by any means necessary. A revolution. An uprising. A coup d'état. And Rebel had a plan. It took shape years ago, and she would not deviate. Not now. Not for anything or anyone.

"One, two, three..." she began to count out loud and then unlocked the front door and swung it open.

3

———

Akin to Dorthy's arrival in the Land of Oz, Rebel entered a Technicolor marvel. Welcome to the future, circa 2054. A vast, futuristic landscape under an umbrella of crystalline light that rendered everything in a surreal shimmer. Utopia, from the graceful arcs of pedestrian bridges to the six-lane lode-way streets marked with buoys, bobbing around on cables, to the utter lack of litter.

And *them*. The technology created to save mankind became their final undoing. Humans no longer held the title of dominant species. A new form of evolution overtook the planet.

Mech.

Synthetic, artificially intelligent androids, programmed to act and conduct themselves as if human, with empty emotion and behaviors. Thousands flocked the city, distinguishable from humans only by their physical perfection. Not one made eye contact with anyone else. Not one nodded a hello, sneezed, fixed their perfect hair, or veered in the slightest from their course. Human 2.0. All facade, with nothing underneath. Like hollowed out porcelain dolls, perfect and shiny on the surface, yet dead inside. It was Mech programming, after all. To blend in. To act human in a human world. A world built for mankind — houses, doors, cars, machinery, handles, stairs. Mech needed to operate, and much stayed the same. Dr. Rae's ideas to advance the machines, to give them souls, emotions, and feelings were deemed obsolete and counterproductive to saving life. *Ironic*, Rebel thought. They wanted to save the planet but had no idea why.

"Seventeen, eighteen, join procession..." Indiscernible, Rebel counted to herself, similar to a blind person counting steps. She headed up the walkway in the residential block of Sector 4, blending in perfectly with the large procession of workers. In stride, in sync, in appearance. The walkway ended at a gate, governing access into the city proper. Some, herself included, resided outside of the workplace to expedite time in the field. The first three sectors consisted of the city proper, with concentric circles that spread out from its center, like a pebble hitting water, creating ripples. Ground zero on out. Rebel swiped her wrist over a scanner, a gate swung open, and she merged into the morning flow.

Traffic flashed past, sleek cars, buses, and trucks, streamlined in nautical trim with hull runners in place of wheels, guided by waves of clean, electromagnetic energy. Billboards loomed high over the streets, huge shimmering panels like phantom jumbotrons. Daily bulletins played on a loop along with markers for the various buildings she passed. "Dept. of Bionics", "Dept. of Diagnostics", "Dept. of Sanitation". Rebel's eyes froze on the flashing billboards, taken back to the time of her youth when the boards flickered with broken pixels. She shook it off and proceeded forward.

Surrounded by modern-day wonders, yet the relics from her past were what drew her eye. The little breakfast diner where she first ate smiley face pancakes became a greenhouse. Her childhood park remained a park, sans the swings, slides, and jungle gym. The drive-thru car wash became a water filtration plant. On and on it went, all along the street, buildings and stores stamped 'Unnecessary' and set for destruction. The Mech saved the planet, but they went to extremes to do so. They got rid of everything that made humans human — art, music, entertainment, games, sports, fun. Rebel hated them for that. She hated them for a great many things.

Waiting at a stoplight, a towering Walker passed, four stories high, plastered in a gleaming white ceramic and glass shell. Like a mechanical spider covered in slits and vents, serving as a massive mobile air purifier. The light turned green. Rebel composed herself and continued walking.

"Light changes, thirty-four, thirty-five," she counted, following the flow heading for the raised hover trains.

A rank of latticed metal gates spanned the portal. They hissed open, and Rebel stepped through in systematic order with the rest. In place of escalators, moving walkways shuttled Mech onto the platform, formed in glossy plastic tile arches, all stark white. Video screens ran the length of the walls, reporting banner crawl reading out the stops.

NEXT STOP... SECTOR 3 — SECTOR 1 — DEPT. OF CITY
AFFAIRS

A fence at the tunnel edge of the platform provided safety, where Mech waited in a patient line. Rebel focused on the track, or what looked like a track, but contained no rails of any kind. The struts lining the bed provided buffers of galvanized rubber, the relay system provided by a series of metal posts, flanking the buffers to run in twin parallel. They started thrumming and pulsing with red light, like runway beacons. The train was coming.

Two Enforcers entered the station. Unlike others, they were older models, machine-like, and carried with them a sense of dread. Their lack of faces unnerved Rebel, instead sporting holo-screens that displayed various scrolling information or flashed images pertinent to their current duties. Mostly, Rebel remembered them as the militarized Mech who led the war against humans. Armed with wide-muzzle stopguns, their foreboding appearance brought no alarm to the stationed Mech, except for Rebel. They scared the hell out of her.

They moved up the platform, randomly scanning Mech with their 'faces.' It became routine not long after Rebel heard a report of a human sighting. At first, it gave her hope that she wasn't alone, but still, the report could have easily been about her as well, so she packed her bags and prepared to flee. She was out the door when she learned that the human was male and located in former Santa Cruz, California. Thus, the Department of Enforcement came to be. Their protocol: hunt down any remaining humans left on Earth.

Hunt down Rebel.

The Enforcers scanned a male Mech. A headshot of the robot spun in 3-D, registering him as Mech, his serial number, and firmware updates. The Mech checked out, and the Enforcers' mechanical heads drifted and locked in on Rebel.

Oh God, oh God, oh God. She wanted to run, but she would never make it. As adept at running as she had become, she couldn't outrun a machine. If they caught her, she decided she would take her fate into her own hands and step onto the tracks, letting the train finish her off because... screw them. Rebel would get the final say.

"Turn around for routine scan," they ordered in their robotic voices.

It wasn't her first scan, and she prayed it wouldn't be her last. Rebel took silent a breath and turned to face her executioners head-on. A rush of air heralded the sleek train shuttle. Salvation sailed out of the tunnel, floating one foot above the track, with runners in place of wheels, like hulls on a catamaran. Hovering, buoyed by a magnetic flow emanating from the tracks on an invisible river of fusion energy. The train drifted to a gentle halt. Its gangplanks folded out toward the platform, and the safety fence lowered. Rebel stared at the Enforcers.

"Proceed," they said.

"Forty-three, forty-four, board train..." Rebel found an open seat and let out a breath. She wanted to cry. She wanted to scream. She wanted to laugh. Instead, she sat still and composed with perfect posture. Mech who stood, didn't hold the handrails, equipped with gyro sensors that keep them upright with the swaying train. Rebel, on the other hand, toiled for hours on balance, using her history of ballet to guide her.

Of the things she missed most, the only one that came before ice cream was ballet. Mrs. Rae loved the theater, Broadway, opera, and of course, the ballet. Ever since Rebel saw *The Nutcracker,* she had been enraptured. Dreams filled with sugar plum fairies and Tchaikovsky's beautiful music. Only later in life did her adornment fade. There were no princes, no magic, no happily ever after. Not in her world. Just a lie, told to the young and gullible to elicit some form of hope. But hope for what, Rebel couldn't fathom. At first, it devastated her, but as time went on, she became accustomed to disappointment. She left the world of make-believe and entered a reality filled with steel and glass and its own species and laws of nature. Laws that she sought to follow to the letter. Not because she wanted to, because she *had* to.

Rebel glanced around at the Mech. Their human attributes, mannerisms, fake, empty emotions. They took on the names of famous people. Comical, given they were clueless about human history and pop culture. You could ride the train next to Elvis Presley, eat lunch across from Vincent van Gogh, or work a cubicle over from Charles Dickens. So it only seemed fitting that Rebel take a new name as well and become someone new. Thus, Anne Frank was resurrected, Rebel's heroine, ever since she read her diary in school. So, Anne Frank she would become.

The cityscape outside the window changed over the past seven years. The city bore traces of its origins, yet rebuilt, subsumed by urban overhaul. Solar panels caught the sun's rays. Massive wind turbines revolved atop the roofs of buildings, surrounded by lush greenery. A towering skyline of glittering, gravity-defying buildings. Facets of polarized glass rising to domes and spires, somehow celestial, like monolithic fingers reaching up to touch the sky. Older buildings wedged among the new, most closed off and sealed under protective glass domes to help contain reconstruction or demolition.

Ground Zero: the Transamerica Pyramid in San Francisco's old Financial District, Sector 1. The epicenter of all things Mech for the entire west coast of the United States. Much of the 48-story postmodern building remained the same — the iconic shape, the stature — with a few distinct differences. No longer called the Pyramid, it was rebranded as Robotiq. Second, the array of satellite dishes and antennas sprouted up across the entire top tenth of the structure, a full 20 stories — the spire. Dishes ranging from two feet in diameter to eighty foot giants. Antenna of all shapes and sizes jutted out like a porcupine. All 3,678 windows swapped for eco-solar that could power an entire ten-block radius. When first constructed way back in 1972, the Pyramid was the eighth tallest building in the world at 853 feet. Times changed, but the building still brought awe.

Now it was the most secure location on the planet and Rebel's destination.

4

———

Natural light bathed the lobby from the four-story windows, accentuating sterile white walls and floors, everything rounded, like living inside a cloud. Curved, floor-to-ceiling frosted glass offered the only concession to nature — a tinted view of Mech-made, meticulously landscaped gardens.

A soothing, female voice washed over the air from the intercom system. "To avoid delay, all Mech prepare for diagnostic scans."

A procession of Mech waited at the security checkpoints for their turn to filter through a row of channels supervised by diagnostic Mech. The computerized body scanners resembled airport metal-detector and x-ray devices, refurbished from security deterrents used in the old days. Crime became a thing of the past in the new world. No murder, no theft, no terrorists, no crazy uni-bombers. Just machines. And as far as Mech knew, nothing to fear. Their only natural enemy, humans, tucked tail and ran. Mostly.

Inching forward, Rebel waited patiently on the surface, but underneath, her heart pounded, palms slick with sweat. She learned to control it over time, thanks to some of her father's old books on Buddhist monks, zen philosophies, and meditation. She took long, slow breaths to limit the movement of her rising chest, and those deep breaths also helped provide some calm. Mech didn't breathe, not like humans. A small force of air came from their mouths when they spoke, like a speaker playing music — pure, clean oxygen.

A jolt coursed through her when a red light flashed, and a buzzer sounded. Enforcers arrived in the blink of an eye to surround the Mech who set off the alarm.

"You have a diagnostic error report. Please come with us for inspection," ordered an Enforcer. The Mech in question followed the Enforcers toward the doors labeled 'Repair Plaza.' Before leaving, the last drone turned to face the crowd of onlookers. "Thank you for your cooperation."

Rebel's turn arrived. One slip up would end her existence. Obsessive knowledge of hardware and operating systems helped fool the system. She passed through the scanners every day since she began her employment within Robotiq some three years prior, and every day it petrified her.

Under the watchful eye of a diagnostics, she stepped to the scanners, giving a polite nod to the Mech.

"Designation?"

"Anne Frank, 7-445."

"Proceed."

Rebel moved forward into the scanner and discretely clicked the small handheld device that connected her jammers to glitch the scanners. On the monitor, her 'metal frame' became visible beneath her synthetic human form, and her fake readouts logged into the system:

NAME: Anne Frank. MODEL: M7-445. FUNCTION: Human Artifacts Disposal Unit.

"Clear," the diagnostic Mech said, and the gate opened to allow her entrance.

She let out a silent sigh of relief and passed through without a hitch, undetected, like every other Mech, like every other day.

"Seventy-four, seventy-five..." She joined the procession heading toward the 'Nutrition Plaza,' where Mech sat at long tables slopping down some seriously unappetizing gruel, consisting of a white/gray blend of liquid light that served as an internal coolant and lubrication for their mechanical parts. Edible photosynthesis for machines and a natural energy source safe for the planet. Rebel sat among them, moving the gruel around, watching it glow like twinkling stardust. She discretely shoveled the substance into a biodegradable bag to discard later when the opportunity presented itself.

"Eighty-four, eighty-five, chimes begin..."

A series of chimes sounded, and all eyes turned to the large digital clock projected on the glass wall. 8:55 A.M. Mech rose in unison, headed to their offices.

Of the building's eighteen elevators, only one reached the top 48th floor, guarded by two Enforcers and a retinal scanner. 'Secure Mainframe Entrance. Authorization Required.' Rebel's ultimate target, the entire reason she infiltrated the building, yet so far proving elusive, so instead, she stepped into the queue at the glass-encased general population elevators and waited her turn.

The fortieth-floor offices housed the hi-tech administrative offices. The well-appointed if antiseptic room contained hundreds of ergonomically-designed work stations, arranged in ever-widening circles. Each curved desk contained a computer terminal consisting of a keyboard and a slim, transparent screen behind which was seated a programmer, leading their respective department.

"Ninety-seven, ninety-eight..." Rebel approached The Board, a huge 3D, holographic grid-map running the length of the wall. It displayed live feeds from around the city: clear blue skies, lush green parks, clean ocean water, litter-free streets, and wildlife thriving. A synergistic system of life. Eden. The board curated percentages of optimal planetary health within graphical numbers and charts. The higher the number, the healthier the planet. When Rebel first saw the board, the indexes remained stagnant in the thirty percentile range. Subtract humankind, and percentages changed vastly.

<pre>
POLLUTION INDEX.........................87%
FORESTATION...............................85%
WILDLIFE.......................................84%
OZONE...88%
CARBON MONOXIDE LEVELS...........88%
POPULATION.................................89%
WASTE...87%
TOXICITY LEVELS.........................81%
</pre>

"One hundred and sit," she finished, in her cubicle, behind her workstation right on time at 9:00 A.M, just like every day. She waved a hand before the wraparound holoscreen in front of her and logged on to the computer. The screen consisted of three sections. The right side showed a polymorph in fractal cycle, like a permanent screen saver. Mid-screen displayed a graph of a residential block, an area of the city yet to be reconstructed, of which most resided in the blue zone, indicating completion. A handful blinked yellow, labeled 'Pending,' while a few remained in the red, yet to be reconstructed, i.e., Rebel's target zones. The left screen scrolled with daily bulletins and calls from various Mech indicating found stashes of human artifacts to be recycled.

Rebel ignored them all. Instead, she logged onto an encrypted communications channel. She typed: 'Urgent Com — to Moon — SOS — Human on Earth. Please respond.'

She hit send, her encrypted message floating off into the

ether, joining the hundreds of others in a long queue of unanswered messages. Rebel's plea to humankind and the reason she hacked Robotiq's computers and gave herself a job in the enemy's building. To let them know:

I am still here.

A banner popped up in reply. 'Firewall.Error//message.denied — Replies: 0'.

"Good morning, Anne Frank," came the chipper voice, knocking Rebel back to present.

She logged out of her terminal, switching back to a normal work screen, and turned to the two plastic faces grinning over her partition. In their mid-twenties, jovial, thin, and of course, beautiful, with fake smiles plastered on fake faces. She didn't like her coworkers, not in the least. Harmless, yes. Annoying, very. Roboticists programmed Mech for small talk to more fluidly blend with humankind. Yet the nuances were never quite perfected and it forced Rebel out of her protective cocoon to socialize with the enemy, an activity she would rather refrain from.

The term 'two-faced' took on a whole new meaning within Rebel's world. Emily reminded her of a librarian, with fake black-framed glasses, wool skirt, faux leather boots, blonde hair pulled into a tight bun and emerald green eyes. Francis wore the guise of a sleazy politician, teeth so white they became an optical feat to look at for longer than a few seconds. His hair, stark black like tar and slicked back, framed beady little rodent eyes and a thin, pointed nose — a walking talking mole.

"Emily Dickinson, Francis Bacon," Rebel greeted them in a perfected monotone voice. "You are well, I hope."

"Indeed we are," said Emily.

"We have a query," Francis began, "you being the resident expert on humankind and all. The birds and the bees. It is a saying, correct? We are debating who holds the correct assumption."

They both peered at her. Rebel tried her hardest to keep a straight face and remain nonplussed. "It's the... uh, when two humans... come together, and uh..." They caught her off guard, eyeing her like dogs who didn't understand a command. Rebel stammered, trying not to blush. "Reproduction. Yes. Human reproduction. So. There."

"Well," said Francis, pleased, "it seems we were both incorrect."

"How odd," Emily thought aloud. "Birds copulating with bees. Quite disgusting, if you were to ask me."

"Well, not literally," Rebel reminded them.

"If not literal, why say it?" wondered Francis.

"Good question," she responded. "It's more of a metaphor, really."

A message popped up on Rebel's screen: 'Anne Frank, report to Director Marx.'

"Director is calling," Rebel said, and just in time.

"By all means," Emily said. "And as the humans used to say, I will grab you later."

"Catch you later, I believe," Rebel corrected her.

"Catch you later, catch you later, catch you later," Emily repeated to herself, installing the corrected phrase in her memory bank as she walked away.

Francis lingered, looking at Rebel with those cold, calculating, emotionless eyes. In any normal human situation, prolonged eye contact would be considered rude. Invasive. Rebel's mother always told her not to stare, but Mech never received the same life lessons.

"Is there something else I can assist you with, Francis?"

He held Rebel in his eyes for another scrutinizing second, then broke eye contact, returning to his workstation. Rebel blinked, her eyes burning. *Breathe*, she reminded herself. *Just breathe.*

———

THE CORNER OFFICE displayed a panoramic view of the city out of the wraparound windows. The sight gave a sense of awe as if floating up in the clouds. Rebel wanted to forever gaze at the cityscape, the ocean, the rolling hilltops, the vibrant colors. Mech didn't appreciate beauty and spectacle. They recognized it, they defined it, but they didn't gaze at things, and definitely not in wonder. The transparent, ethereal furniture offered maximum efficiency, nothing more. A striking metaphor for the director of Rebel's division, Karl Marx. For some reason, he took a liking to her, the antivirus to Karl Marx's software. He sat at his desk, reviewing data on a holoscreen. Rebel stood before him, waiting, composing a deadpan. Robotic.

"Karl Marx? You wanted to see me?"

"Privacy." The glass walls frosted over at his command. Unnerving, but Rebel stayed deliberate, impassive.

Karl reviewed the holoboard: Rebel's headshot spinning in 3D with a scroll of data. He glanced up at her, forming a fake smile. "And how is Anne Frank today?"

Rebel hated when they made her speak in the third person. It put her ill-at-ease, feeling something less than human, and maybe that was the point. "She is well, thank you."

"I scoured over your quarterlies," he said. "Ninety percent of all human waste recycled, repurposed. Most thanks to you."

"I try, sir."

"Modesty is a curious attribute for a Mech. We do not *try* at anything, do we?"

"No, sir," Rebel said, catching herself. "We *do*. I simply followed directives."

"Correct." He logged off his console and turned to appraise

her. "There is something different about you. Something unlike the others."

"Yet I am exactly like everyone else."

"That is not true, is it?" he said, more comment than question. "No. I am on to you, Anne Frank. I know more than I let on. The job demands that of me, after all. To be apprised of all my employees' endeavors. Their victories and their failures. I know more about them than they themselves know."

A twinge rippled through her nerves. *Did he suspect? No,* she told herself. Stay calm, poised.

"Humans."

Rebel went a little white. She tried not to panic, fighting every fiber in her body that screamed for her to run. "Humans?"

"I want to show you something." He turned and spoke to the room. "Cue playback Alpha 2029." The walls came to life. Holographic images surrounded them, virtually transporting them to another place and time.

"Welcome to the world," he said. "What it used to be. Seven years prior, a planet on the brink of destruction. Atomic weapons, pollution, waste, global warming, overpopulation."

Rebel stood silently, watching Nazis burn books, the detonation of the Hiroshima atom bomb, the mushroom cloud. Ice shelves collapsing at the poles, water levels rising. Flashes of oil spills in the ocean and birds that laid dying, coated in black sludge. Dead fish floating to the surface and waves depositing garbage onto cruddy shores. Factories spewed black smoke and dumped waste into landfills. Tornadoes and hurricanes, tsunamis, and earthquakes.

"The humans reached the point of no return."

Still, the dizzying images flashed before her. Rebel fought to keep the tears formed in her eyes at bay as she watched horrid images of beached whales, dolphin hunting, slaughterhouses packed with chicken pens. Hospitals overflowed with sick and injured, all wearing face masks. Unemployment offices with lines around the block. Terror alerts scrawled across monitors, suicide bombs, and aerial drones dropping payloads — militia in the Middle East destroying ancient artifacts and sacred land-marks. Streets covered in litter, crawling with rats and roaches. Walls laden in graffiti. Rain forests plowed over by bulldozers to make room for factories, apartment buildings as populations grew out of control. She watched the highlight reel on a pandemic of a humankind who ceased caring.

"And today..." continued Marx.

The images resolved into the modern-day world — pristine, clean, thriving, alive.

"An eighty-five percent change across the board," he said. "The magic number being?"

"One hundred percent," stated Rebel.

"And why is that?"

"The planet will become self-sufficient, able to repair itself on its own." As much as Rebel despised Mech, she couldn't fault the outcome, yet the end didn't justify the means.

"Enough," he diced to the room. The images shattered away. Silence prevailed. "The stakes are far too great to let our guard down now. And you, Anne. I do not think you realize how important you are to the survival of our society, of the planet."

"Sir?" asked Rebel.

"Cataloging and classifying human artifacts. Waste. Perhaps not a glamorous job like your friend Emily Dickinson in Census or Francis Bacon in Litter Control, but an important job, nonetheless. Critical to our success. As such, I am granting you a promotion."

"A promotion?" Rebel blanched. Promotions rarely happened in the world of machines. Why would they? Mech could just manufacture new versions of themselves and recycle outdated models. Mech did their jobs. Apparently, that evolved as well.

"Your work ethic is unsurpassed," he proclaimed. "You are, by all definitions of the word, a Mech."

"Thank you." *If only you knew*, she thought.

"We are so close now, and I need you operating at full capacity. I am requisitioning you a car to aid in your productivity."

Her stomach dropped. *Nonononono.* "Driving? Thank you, but that is not necessary. I am quite satisfied utilizing the train system."

"Pish-posh," he said.

"Excuse me?"

"A term from the humans, no?"

"Yes," Rebel answered. "Sure."

"Very well, then," he said, pleased with himself. "Pish-posh it is. You assimilated driving upgrades, I assume, like all Mechs."

"Yes, sir," she lied. "Like all Mechs." Truth? Rebel had no idea how to drive. None. She was twelve years old when her world ended. She never attended high school, no Driver's Ed, no road test for her license. Other than her father's car, she never stepped foot in a vehicle that couldn't drive itself.

"Then all is settled. Dismissed," he said with a wave of his hand and went back to his console. Conversation over.

Defeated, Rebel walked to the door. Before stepping through, she felt prompted to ask a question gnawing at her for some time. Even though she knew she shouldn't, she couldn't resist. "And then what?"

Karl Marx stopped typing, a confused look on his face in which Mech often displayed: the question does not compute. "Please repeat the query?"

"After we reach quota," she began, "One hundred percent planet repair. Then what?"

"I do not understand. When we reach quota, our purpose is complete," he said as if a reasonable answer.

"And humans? Will they come back?"

"Counterproductive," he said, waving his hand out in front of him as if shipping away a mosquito. "We followed all necessary measures against re-population. We conducted a systematic search for all left behind organics. All ties have been severed with the moon bases. Firewalls guard and protect Mech, and Earth, from unauthorized immigration into the atmosphere. Rest assured, Anne Frank, you are perfectly safe."

"Yes, of course," Rebel said. "Perfectly safe."

5

Bay 23 of the underground parking structure held the hybrid concept car. Sleek pearl white with curved aerodynamic lines. Rebel stood before it, staring it down with dread.

"Come on, Rebel," she said to herself. "You can tear down and rebuild a Mech. How hard can an autonomous car be?"

Inside the car, she reviewed the drive console, screens, and controls, all meaningless. She couldn't even figure out where the 'on' button resided. She reached for the wheel, and the screens blinked on, sensing her movements. The console lit up in a brilliant blue hue, awaiting a command prompt. Rebel reviewed the instructions on the screen: 'Piloting: Manual/Auto?'

"Auto...?" she ventured.

The interface processed: 'Destination: Name/Sector?'

"On-sight plant 8, 6th Sector," Rebel said, a bit more confident. "Please."

The interface reported: 'Undocking.' A jolt as the car shunted forward, as if pulled by a phantom tugboat, easing its way toward the garage exit. It bucketed off the ramp and nosed onto a street inlet. The interface reported: 'Establishing Uplink...' On another screen, a global positioning map appeared. A blue dot at Rebel's point of origin formed into a blue line, plotting the course. Autopilot scanned for traffic. Resistors droned as a control beam locked on, guiding the car to merge onto the street. Finding its lane, the car sped up, then dropped to cruising speed, communicating with the other cars around it, reminding Rebel of a perfectly formed flock of birds. She smiled — piece of cake. The city opened up around her as the car glided silently along the roads, effortlessly changing lanes, accelerating and decelerating, passing other cars with mere inches to spare. Like traveling in a crystal bubble, Rebel allowed herself to breathe within her secluded confines. She liked this whole driving thing, feeling like a princess in a grand chariot on her way to the ball.

———

WINSTON CHURCHILL LED Rebel through the air and water purification plant, passing dozens of open hangar doors, revealing the massive Walkers inside, some charging, some in repair, some still being constructed by large, autonomous machines. She recognized the building from her youth as a shopping mall, remembered purchasing tofu hot dogs wrapped in pretzel buns, buying the latest fashion, and ice skating on the indoor rink during winter holidays. All gone now, just fading memories like a contrail of a past life.

"We were in the process of expanding our operation, calling for more space, which is when I discovered the room and called immediately," Winston began. "We are unsure what to do with these... things."

Motion lights activated inside the supply room, illuminating artifacts. *Human artifacts.* Uncustomary color and clutter assaulted Rebel. Things. Stuff. Knickknacks. All jumbled up and stacked everywhere. Teddy bears, paintings, old paperback books, a supply of chewing gum, ceramic pots, and even an old globe. Rebel almost smiled but caught herself, squashing it.

"You did the correct thing," said Rebel in her official-sounding voice. "I'll see these items cataloged, atomized, and recycled straight away. And thank you for your assistance."

She shut the door, closing herself inside the room of wonders, meaningless to a Mech, but to Rebel, they meant the world. She spun the globe, thumbed through the books, and took up a Teddy bear in her arms, hugging it. But the joy transformed into sadness. Relics had a way of doing that to her, a reminder of the finality of life. There were no new memories to make.

The sun had long since disappeared as she went about the rest of her day classifying newfound hordes of artifacts. She stole what she needed, what she wanted, what made her feel, well, anything. The rest she cataloged and called in. A purification team would arrive, cart out the items into mobile atomizer trucks, and poof — gone in the blink of an eye. Efficient, broken down into their most basic components. After two more customary stops to catalog and collect relics from a time long ago, Rebel found herself ahead of schedule.

Outside the car window, the downtrodden sector flashed past. Buildings appeared like remnants from a bygone era. With purification in effect, the sector stood as one of the last remaining areas to clean, disinfect and reclassify. A systematic cleansing of the human race, building by building, sector by sector. A pawn shop. A party store. A coffee shop. A carnival. Gone.

The car pulled to a stop at the curb outside an abandoned convenience store, one of the last on Rebel's list. She shook off the thoughts of dwindling reserves and checked the time — 11:17 P.M.

"What do you think?" Rebel asked her Teddy bear co-pilot,

sitting in the passenger's seat, belted in for safety. "It's going to be close. Forty-three minutes?" She made the call and slid out of the car. "Plenty of time."

Moving through the deserted aisles felt strange, as if she were an interloper, an unwanted guest. While fully stocked the first time she discovered the convenience store, the products had since waned, essentials nearly picked clean. She tossed a few straggler items into her cart as she pursued the shelves. Makeup, bleach, sponge, a dozen toothbrushes, the last three toothpaste tubes, Christmas lights, duct tape, pain relievers, and an electric foot massager. Everything a human girl needed to fake being a Mech. Her eye caught something in passing, backtracking to a shelf of Oreo cookies, expiration date: 2099.

"Perfect."

Not all technology rated ten on the bad meter, she admitted as the car drove her through town, just the tech that thought for itself. Autopilot engaged, Rebel sat back, eating cookies. She savored every bite, every crumb, every morsel of the chemically enhanced and enriched molecule. Heaven. Rebel made a mental note to put more time on the treadmill as a result, but the reminder that some good remained on Earth: priceless. Even Teddy held a cookie in his paws but refrained, watching his figure. Smart bear.

The toll of the bell dropped Rebel's smile fast. "Nonononono…" 11:55 P.M. Five minutes until shutdown.

The car's screen flashed: 'Sector Shutdown — Uplink Interrupt — Autopilot Disengaging.' The motor's soothing whirling sound drew out as the pitch changed from high to low, and the car began to slow. 'Remote Lockdown Engaging.'

The city sector powered down. Lights turned off in a wave of rolling darkness, approaching the single moving car in the area. The steering column swerved and positioned itself on the shoulder of the road, pulled to a dead halt in the middle of nowhere. *How am I going to explain this one at work?* Rebel thought.

Her immediate concern shifted to the locked door. She tried to force it open, but it bolted tight, trapped inside a coffin of metal and glass, trapped miles away from home. Frantic, she sought out a button or command or lever. Something. She reviewed the sleek controls. The main terminal screen went from a vivid holomap to a black screen with a white blinking cursor.

"Uh, auto?" she tried to no avail. "Power on? Drive? Alexa, drive me home." Nope.

Only one option presented itself. Her eyes zeroed in on the button labeled: 'Override.' She switched it into the 'Up' position: 'Manual.' The car powered back to life, lights and instrumentation filling the cabin in a cool glow. Rebel gained control. *Complete* control, and she still had no idea how to drive. Her only hands-on experience came when she sat on her father's lap, steering his car in a deserted parking lot. Eleven years ago. A long time, a different time. And besides, Rebel didn't really drive; she steered.

"This isn't a car," she told herself, forcing herself to calm. "It's technology. You got this."

Technology that could kill her. *No*, she thought to herself, vanquishing the thought. If she established herself as good at anything, thinking like a machine clocked number one on the list. She needed to learn the controls, positioning one hand on the wheel and the other on the throttle. She gave it a quick nudge, and the car lurched forward, veering out of its place on the shoulder, and slammed to a sudden stop. Wrong pedal. Gas, right. Brake, left. Check and check.

"Come on. You can do this." She looked at the controls and tried again. Firm on the wheel, gentle on the throttle, and the car eased forward.

A bit more emboldened, she drove away, speeding, slamming on the brakes, veering right, correcting to the left, getting the hang of it. She slid her finger along the trackpad beneath the side window, and it reacted, frosting over, a blind deathtrap. *Don't panic.* She jabbed at the button again, and the window cleared. A downward swipe and the window rolled down. Sigh of relief.

Invigorated, she tried another button. Music blared through the speakers, a preloaded song from the car's digital library. Some band called The Pixies singing 'Where Is My Mind?' Rebel liked the melody and decided to let it play. The crisp night air passed through the car like a current of life. Driving, smiling, sovereignty. She closed her eyes, allowing herself to show pure, unadulterated emotion, a rarity in a fake, plastic life. A soft smile crossed her lips. Not beauty pageant fake, either. The first real, genuine smile she could remember in forever. She allowed herself to be human. *So this is what living feels like*, she thought.

She couldn't recall what made her open her eyes at that exact moment. Maybe random, maybe instinct, maybe fate. A gut feeling. Some inner voice inside her head repeating one word over and over: *Danger. Danger. Danger.*

Trouble barreled down on her in the form of a Mech standing in the middle of the street. Not powered down. Staring at Rebel, her emotion, her joy, her humanity.

It happened fast, a mere blur. Rebel slammed on the brakes as collision warnings blasted in her ears. She screamed at the violent impact, her head colliding with the wheel. The thud echoed. The contact hammered in her bones, right down to her core.

The Mech arced high through the air, hurtled up and over the car, somersaulting, followed by another horrific thud as it landed.

The car skidded and swerved to a jolting stop. Rebel's hands clutched the wheel so hard her knuckles turned white. The gash on her head opened up, clouding her vision like a bad fever dream. She hyperventilated as the terrible thought hit her.

I got into a traffic accident. Mech didn't get into accidents. Ever. They were perfect, analytical, planned, precise. But not Rebel.

Prying her hands from the wheel, a million thoughts raced through her head at once. Scenarios, and none of them good. Each and every one ended with her being executed, recycled into her basic parts, and spread throughout the cosmos like a piece of used plastic. Maybe the incident didn't happen. Maybe she imagined the events. A dream. She looked at the rearview screen, and she saw the shape of the befallen Mech crumpled in the street. Not moving. A nightmare.

All at once, everything crashed away, tearing her apart. For the past seven years, she had been nothing but careful, avoiding any situation which might put her at risk. She followed every rigid step, every steadfast rule, but the worst thing possible happened.

Rebel killed a Mech.

6

———

Mrs. Rae would read storybooks at bedtime, a favorite memory of Rebel. One such story revolved around little fairy tale gnomes. Or fairies. Didn't matter. Some small creature from myth. They entered homes at night while everyone slept and mended broken items. Bogarts? No, Brownies. The fanciful tale stuck in Rebel's mind, even entering her dreams. She believed with all her heart that Brownies were real, enough so that she stayed up one evening devising a plan to capture one.

She waited one hour after her parents went to sleep, her cue being her father's rampant snoring. That meant two things: 1. Her father entered deep sleep. 2. Her mother's earplugs did their job. Brilliant. Commence Operation Capture-a-Troll/Gnome/Fairy-Thing.

Ignoring the cold floor on her feet, she tip-toed across the hallway, down the stairs, and into the dining room. Scary, being awake in the middle of the night in the dark house. Rebel reminded herself that she didn't believe in monsters, but that little voice in the back of her head told her she might be wrong.

If little troll things existed, why couldn't big scary monsters? *Stop being such a baby*, she told herself.

Unlatching the small brass hook on the China cabinet, Rebel opened the glass doors to reveal her mother's cherished China tea set. She carefully reached in and removed one of the cups. If Brownies existed, then one of her mother's precious display pieces would be a worthy prize for them to fix. Smooth to the touch, the cup reflected moonlight off its delicate ceramic, with small designs along the rim of swirling vines and vivid flowers. *Quite pretty,* Rebel thought, and what a shame it would be to break one. What if she guessed wrong and there were no little midnight helpers out there to fix them? She wouldn't be able to live with herself. The right choice became apparent. Abandon. Retreat. Fall back. Abort mission. Conscience, her father called it — that little voice in the back of her head. *No, that couldn't be right,* she thought. 'Con' and 'science'? Science conned? Spanish for 'With'? With science. That didn't sound right either. Either way, Operation Capture-a-Troll/Gnome/Fairy-Thing went bust. Time to go to bed.

That's when Rebel heard the crash. She lost her concentration, her mind astray in thought, and she didn't feel the teacup slip from her little fingers. Staring down at the shattered wreckage, her brain toiled to process what had happened and what to do next. She could run back upstairs and pretend to be sleeping or try to glue the pieces back together in her father's workshop. Maybe even bury the remains deep down in the garbage where nobody would ever find them.

Her face went warm, throat thickening, heart turning heavy like a brick thrown into the ocean. Silent tears trickled down her flush cheeks. She made the right choice; she aborted the mission, yet all for naught. She couldn't think of anything to do to turn back the clock. From upstairs, her father's snoring gave her some reassurance. Kneeling, Rebel gathered every bit of broken cup into her hand and placed them atop the dining room table for all to see before slipping back upstairs and into her warm bed.

Rebel didn't get a lot of sleep that night. When she did drift off, horrid nightmares assaulted her about giant teacups coming to life and chasing her down dark, deserted city streets. She woke up as the first rays of the morning sun seeped through the window, listening to the stillness of the house. Thoughts raced through her head. She questioned if her parents waited downstairs, ready to dish out apt punishment. She hated punishments, but more than that, she hated herself for getting punished. A knock at the door startled her.

"Rebel, honey, it's time to get up," Mrs. Rae said with a smile, disappearing back to the hallway.

Rebel sat up and listened to her mother's footsteps recede downstairs. She waited for the inevitable scream, the calling of her name to come downstairs immediately. When her mother got upset, she called Rebel by her full name, Rebel Anne Rae. Yet no scream came. Definitely no usage of middle and last name. What happened? Did her parents miss the broken teacup? No way. Rebel left it front and center on the dining room table.

Throwing her robe on, she left the safety of her bedroom and made her way downstairs like a death row inmate walking to their doom. When she stepped into the kitchen, all seemed normal. Her father drank coffee at the table and scribbled in his journals, glasses down low on his nose. Her mother made pancakes at the stove, humming some melody to herself.

"Hey, champ. How'd you sleep?" Dr. Rae asked.

"I don't know what you mean," Rebel shot back.

He glanced up from his notes, over the top of his reading glasses. "Are you feeling okay?"

"Thank you." Rebel took a seat at the table in a stupor while her parents shared a baffled cursory glance.

Mrs. Rae placed a plate of pancakes before Rebel, along

with a small bottle of very-hard-to-get maple syrup. Not synthetic maple, mind you, but the real, organic stuff. Dr. Rae insisted that the price justified the expense. Except Rebel couldn't eat, staring at the crime scene. No broken teacup.

"Not hungry?" her mother frowned. "I thought pancakes were your favorite."

"I'll eat them," Dr. Rae reached across the table for the plate when his better half playfully slapped his hand away.

"You're on a diet. No pancakes for you," she said, placing a lackluster bowl of oatmeal before him.

Everyone went crazy, Rebel thought, the only explanation for whatever kind of madness she bore witness to. She stomped over to the trash bin and peered in, moving the gross contents around, seeking out a shard from the broken cup. Nothing. Not a single sliver of porcelain.

"Are you sure you're all right, kiddo?" her father asked.

"Am I all right?" Rebel asked, incredulous. "Am I all right? Jeez."

Ignoring her parents' quizzical looks, she let her eyes drift to the China cabinet, and those eyes got huge. Inside sat the very same broken teacup, no longer broken, looking brand new. *They exist! The gnome-fairy-trolls exist!* How else could anyone explain what occurred? They came while Rebel slept, like Santa Claus delivering presents. She was in need, and they came, just like the story said.

"I have a new invention," Dr. Rae said. "Do you know what it is?"

Rebel shook her head no.

"Eat up, and I'll show you."

Rebel did eat up, seconds even, with extra maple syrup. Full of pancakes and relief, she followed her father to his workroom within the garage. She absorbed the rows upon rows of books and manuals, the tools and parts scattered about, the diagrams up on the walls. All Greek to her. She understood little about what her father actually did as a profession. Something with robots and artificial intelligence. He built his first prototype within the very walls of the garage, and from that prototype grew a major corporation, thousands of jobs, and the promise of a better tomorrow. To Rebel, he was just a kooky dad who lived with his head in the clouds.

A crash spun her around. There, on the floor at her father's feet, his shattered coffee cup.

"You broke it," said Rebel. It gave her a tinge of remorse. Looking down at the shattered pieces reminded Rebel of her escapade the previous night.

"So it would appear. But not everything is always as it seems." He removed a small device with exposed wires and circuit boards. "Still in prototype stage, but watch," he said, motioning her over.

Rebel crouched beside him, looking on as he waved the device over the shards. A blue line of light scanned every inch. The pieces of the cup moved. At first, only slightly, then building into a vibration, a wiggle, and then, as if drawn by a magnet, they slid across the floor toward one another. The cup rebuilt itself.

"Magic," Rebel whispered.

"Close," he said. "Science."

Rebel lifted the cup to eye level. Not a hologram, not a trick of the eye, but real and intact.

"Do you know what separates magic from science?" Rebel shook her head. "Imagination. No more playing with your mother's teacups. I'm in enough trouble as it is. Deal?"

"Deal," she said with a smile.

"Good. Now go sneak me some pancakes, and we'll call it even," he said.

7

———

The majority of surveillance cameras located around the city monitored the clean-up progress, which fed directly into Robotiq. Rebel avoided them on her way home. At least, she hoped she did. Carting a broken Mech around in the car trunk would be hard to explain away. The nerve-wracked journey took her twice as long, forced to take out-of-the-way streets and back alleys, but she made it home, comforted by the fact that all Mech in her sector remained powered down for another five hours.

After her brain settled, she devised a plan during the drive — a risky one, a stupid one, but a plan nonetheless. Rebel's first thought upon colliding with the Mech: flee, leave the sprawled robot behind. No witnesses, so nobody would ever know. She could have kept going except for the little annoying thing inside her head called a conscience. She wasn't a robot. Rebel was human, and at that moment, humanity was kicking her ass. She couldn't just hide the thing. The absence would set off alarms. If she left it in the street, it would alert Enforcers. Only one option presented itself: fix the thing. Repair the Mech, wipe its GPS and memory, and set it loose. Eventually, it would be found, and diagnostics would report a memory failure. They would take it in for repair or recycling, none the wiser, and Rebel could get back to her 'normal' life. No one would ever know. At least, that's what Rebel hoped would happen.

Safe inside the garage, she examined the car's damage for the first time. She prayed that the bumpers absorbed the brunt of the impact, leaving a scratch or two she could buff out and paint over. No such luck, a common thread in her life. She recoiled at the sight. A trail of destruction went from the bumper up the hood and extended halfway across the roof, following the trajectory of the Mech. Touch up paint wouldn't do. Mech built green cars for function and sustainability, not safety, not longevity. Why would they? Mech didn't make mistakes. They didn't get into fender benders. Accidents didn't fit in with their programming. They held fast to an image of perfection. Rebel did not.

Rebel assessed the damage under the bright work lights after a twenty-minute comedy routine of trying to heave the Mech out of the trunk and onto the worktable. The Mech remained in shutdown mode, still functional. Not yet a total heap to be scrapped for parts, yet not presentable as a paper doll either.

She never got that close to one before, not without facade and pretense. The male robot almost passed for a real human, except for its physical perfection. *Plastic*. Not a single imperfection, abnormality, or idiosyncrasy on its face. Olive-skinned, with a very straight nose and thoughtful dark brown eyes with flecks of hazel green mixed in, framed by sandy-brown hair, short in the back and a bit longer over the forehead. Rebel picked up a distinct, curious smell coming off the Mech, a mix of potpourri, vanilla, and cinnamon that played with her senses, reminding her of Christmas morning. The features chilled her. It appeared so human, so lifelike. Could killing a machine be any different than killing a living being? *Yes,* she thought. Nature didn't create Mech. Man did. Machines didn't live, so they couldn't die. Killing turned out to be the wrong word for the act, more like turning off.

From the look of disrepair, Rebel would need all her tools of the trade to fix it. As she gathered up her piles of manuals and schematics, a strange thought occurred to her. The same books she once used to learn how to *become* a Mech, now flipped into books used to *fix* one. She got to work — a massive list of faults scrolled across the hand-scanner. 'Power source error ... Right elbow servo damaged ... rear hatch socket disconnect ...' Rebel switched out the damaged circuits, wiring, pistons, and gears with new ones, or slightly used ones. If she replaced the large components, the rest would take care of itself. Mech, like humans, contained the ability to repair themselves on a smaller scale.

The night sky turned a shade of navy by the time Rebel finished the operation. Whenever she repaired a piece of tech or machinery, there remained extra parts. She failed to understand why. Either she did something wrong, or maybe she excelled at engineering, weeding out unnecessary hindrances to efficiency. Passing the scanner over the Mech, all readouts reported: 'OK.' In the green. Except one: 'Unable to source power. Error Code 27745.' Rebel flipped through one of the manuals with error codes listed until finding the corresponding imprint. 27745, code for internal core mechanics. The heart, the instrument that powered a Mech. A vital component, and one she couldn't fix. As adept as Rebel became, she couldn't mend a broken heart, and not for lack of trying. She pulled a box of batteries from the shelf. New, old, lithium, copper, liquid light, but none worked.

Dejected, she sat and stared at the monitor playing one of her father's lectures. Watching his videos made her feel closer to him and gave her an education at the same time. They provided Rebel a relationship with her father that she wouldn't otherwise have. The sound of his voice, familiar and foreign at the same time, played with her emotions. Happy and sad, relieved and angered, all at the same time.

"Life," said Dr. Rae, wearing his trademark tweed sports jacket, v-neck sweater beneath with a rumpled button-down shirt and corduroys. He wore wire-rimmed glasses and sported a full, inviting beard. He seemed at home behind the lectern, addressing the standing-room-only crowd of the University of California, San Francisco's Advanced Robotics and A.I. class.

"We, as human beings, possess a natural propensity to create bonds to objects exceptionally easily. To anthropomorphize them. To give human properties where there are none. To project life. It's only natural. We are hardwired to respond to lifelike movement and features. A smiley face, arms, hands, fingers, legs. We project intent on to them, and when social robots mimic our movements and sounds, we subconsciously associate with emotions and feelings. But the question remains... how do we make them real?"

"L.I.F.," he continued. "Light Ignition Frequency. A prototype power source we've been developing with the goal of finding sustainable power for Mech. In simplest terms — to give them self-aware capabilities. To create a better machine. The future, ladies and gentlemen, is ours to shape. Right now, at this very moment, we are in a race that we need to win. It's a race between the growing power of technology and the wisdom needed to manage it."

L.I.F. It sparked something within the deep recesses of Rebel's mind. She saw the device before. *Where, where, where?* She racked her brain; she remembered.

Rebel hadn't visited her parents' bedroom in a while for the mere fact that it became too emotionally straining. Everything inside the room stirred a reaction. Her father's shoes on the floor, her mother's dressing table with makeup and brushes that Rebel used as a little girl to play dress-up. She smelled the perfume bottle, closing her eyes, and for a split-second, she morphed into a nine-year-old girl again, sneaking into the bedroom while her parents went on date nights, trying on her mom's clothes, using lipstick for the first time. She remembered how they came home early one night and caught her trespassing. They didn't yell. Mrs. Rae sat Rebel down and gently cleaned the clown face from her skin. She then used her tools and experience to apply makeup to Rebel's face, telling her daughter that she looked beautiful. One day, when Rebel grew up, her mother told her, she would show Rebel all the tricks of the trade. That day never came.

Rebel replaced the perfume bottle on the table and put on her game face. *Focus.* Ignoring the clothes hanging inside the closet, she took down the metal case on the topmost shelf. Her father's work case, the same one she rescued the day they fled home — the day of Exodus. Inside held a glowing spherical processor, about the size of an apple, with input/output ports. 'L.I.F.'

Returning to the garage, Rebel placed the 'heart' into the Mech's internal port, double-checking to make sure all wires plugged in the right places and secured in the right slots, and then sealed the chest plate up and took a step back. Anxious, she waited for something to happen, but nothing did. She gave the body a push, followed by a hard shove, but received no response. The physical contact brought up unwanted memories and emotions. She couldn't stop them from rising, boiling up, and spilling forth. In a fit of anger, Rebel took out her rage on the machine.

"I hate you! I hate you! I hate you!" she screamed, hitting the Mech over and over. Running out of steam, she collapsed to the floor, sobbing, head in her hands.

She tried. She failed.

Paracord, duct tape, resealable bags, a multi-tool, sewing

kit, a water bottle with purification tablets, two sets of clothes, poncho, sturdy hiking boots, sleeping bag, fire starter, first aid kit, knife, glow sticks, a map, and compass. Bug-out bag in hand, Rebel prepared to flee the city. She survived in the wild once. She could persevere again. Physically, at least. Mentally, it was another story. *Then again*, Rebel thought, *how sane am I now?*

Figuring the dinner to be her last meal, Rebel splurged on canned peaches, creamed corn, and beets. She propped the Mech up in a chair across from her, like a manikin. In the other chair along the side of the table sat Teddy bear. One hell of a dysfunctional family.

"Teddy thinks I should have left you out there to die," said Rebel. "Yet if I did, my escapades would've attracted unwanted attention, now wouldn't it?"

"Perhaps, yet we wouldn't be sitting here with a damaged Mech in our house either," Rebel said in a voice toned to sound like Teddy Bear's.

"You make a good point, Teddy," said Rebel.

"It's not too late," Teddy voiced through Rebel. "We can still dump him back out there and pretend this never happened."

"No. I did the right thing," she said. "I think. And when this thing wakes up—"

"If," Teddy corrected.

"If this thing wakes up," Rebel clarified, "it won't remember a thing. Isn't that right, Mr. Robot?"

Using her robot voice, Rebel answered her own question. "Yes, that is correct. Beep-boop-beep."

"You never saw a human girl."

"I never saw a human girl," mirrored robot Rebel.

"And everything will be okay," she said. "Back to normal. No humans here." The remark stung her. "No humans here..."

"Sure, everything will return to normal," said a sarcastic

Teddy Rebel. "Because everything in the last seven years has been absolutely normal."

Rebel stuck her tongue out at Teddy. Her little nuclear family. About to explode.

"Where am I?"

Rebel lifted her gaze.

The Mech was awake.

A singular moment imprinted within Rebel's mind. The moment she stepped into one of her freezing cold showers back in the old days after Exodus, every muscle in her body turning rigid at once. She experienced the same exact sensation at that very moment, sans the water.

The Mech stared at her with cold, unwavering eyes, awaiting an answer to its query. Rebel remained speechless, with no clue as to what to say. Her heart thumped so hard in her chest she thought the pounding would be heard throughout the city. She only thought up one idiotic thing to say at the time. It seemed perfectly reasonable at the moment.

"Hi."

The Mech's unblinking gaze pinned her in place. Rebel sat heavy and anxious, waiting for the machine to respond. Mercifully, its eyes withdrew and took in its alien surroundings, obviously confused as to how it got there.

"Where am I?" it asked again in a cultured, patient voice.

"My place," Rebel said. "House. My house. You were... damaged. I repaired you."

"Why?"

"Why were you damaged, or why did I fix you?"

"Both."

"I don't know," she responded. "Seemed like the right thing to do." An uncomfortable pause followed her comment. "About what happened, do you remember anything? Or see anything... out of character?"

"Apart from you pummeling me with a car?" asked the Mech, his expression neutral.

"You remember that?" *Crap.*

"I do." *Double crap.*

"Yes, besides that," she said. "It wasn't intentional. The pummeling, that is."

"What was it, then?" it asked. "The pummeling."

"An accident."

"An accident?" The Mech tried to define the word in its head. Accident. Not a word Mech used. Not ever.

"And to be fair, I can't take all the blame here. I mean, you were standing in the middle of the street. Why weren't you powered down?"

"I work sector 7 nights at the greenhouse," it said. "It is my function. And you?"

"I..." she searched for some answer but found none. "For the same reason."

"You work at the greenhouses?"

"Human artifact collection," she explained. "It takes me throughout the city sectors at odd times throughout the day. So, there."

"Now that you mention it, I do recall seeing something odd." The Mech didn't even blink.

"Odd?" she repeated.

"Off."

"Off?"

He stood, walking right up to her. Rebel got to her feet, defensive, rigid, unsure.

"You," it said.

Not good. Rebel immediately questioned her every action. *Why fix the Mech? Why bring it into her house? Why did everything bad happen to me?*

He scrutinized her, analyzing every aspect of the girl under a microscopic gaze. With their faces inches apart, he listened to her elevated breathing. The soft cresting of her chest. That tiny quiver of her lower lip.

"You are faulty," it said as it touched her face, prodding.

Rebel kept calm, fighting against every impulse to slap its hand away and run.

"Your hair is out of place. And your left ear is one-thirtieth of an inch smaller than the right one. You have tiny wrinkles under your eyes and creases at the bridge of your nose. And laugh lines..."

The Mech put his head to Rebel's chest and froze. Her heart pounded, and Rebel knew in that instant, everything was about to change.

"Human..."

Worst-case scenario. Again.

The following happened so fast that Rebel couldn't even process it. The muffled crash and thunk. The sting of the flashlight's handle in her hand from the blow to the Mech's head. The broken pieces of glass exploding. The Mech dropping to the floor.

The jarring impact from the blow powered the Mech's core processor off, a safety feature to prevent injury to themselves or those around them, like a tripwire on a fuse. Once again, Rebel stood over an 'unconscious' Mech.

One fitting word came to mind: "Crap."

THE PAIN of the scalding water in the shower brought everything back into focus. Rebel sat on the tiled floor, hugging her knees to her chest, letting the water rain down on her, washing all the artificial crap off. The paint, the makeup, the stain of a mechanical world, spiraling down the drain until all that remained was a fragile human girl.

Although she would never admit it out loud, Rebel knew

that the humans assumed she died, along with everyone else who didn't make it to the shuttles. She couldn't blame them for that. She would have thought the same if she was in their shoes. If armed soldiers couldn't survive the Mech, how could a twelve-year-old girl?

$$8$$

I am alone.

The thought terrified her. Last (wo)man standing. The lone survivor. Party of one. The closest human cut off from her by a sky, atmosphere, and sea of dead, lifeless space. 238,900 miles. 1,261,000,000 feet. 15,130,000,000 inches. 4.063×10^{-8} light-years. 3 days. 69 hours, 8 minutes and 47 seconds, give or take.

Rebel's first week solo, ever. Not merely separated from her parents, but separated from humanity itself. Twelve years old and suddenly forced into adulthood. Into survival mode. Not easy for a girl who had all the basics of life provided since birth. She didn't realize how much she depended on the creature comforts of old until they disappeared. Running water. Working toilets. Food. Toilet paper. Dishwashers. Wi-Fi. Electricity. Companionship.

"You're alive, you're here, you exist," she reminded herself. "You're Rebel Anne Rae. You can do this."

First things first. Shower. Ice cold water sprayed her goose-bumped skin like a thousand tiny daggers stabbing her body all at once, but she would suffer through.

Food stacked up high on the kitchen table. Jars, cans, plastic containers, bags, fresh fruit, and leftover meals. Notebook in hand, Rebel took stock of her provisions, each itemized and tagged by expiration date and taste levels, from 'Yum' to 'Gross but edible.' Cans would last the longest, placed in the back of the cabinets, followed by boxed and bagged food, like cereal, pasta, and crackers. Then came the jars: preserved, pickled, dried, olives (Gross but edible), and almond butter (Yum). Last came fresh foods: leftover chicken pot pie, fruits and vegetables, bread, deli meat, eggs, butter, and milk. That night, Rebel feasted, devouring all the food about to spoil, all the food she would have to throw away whether she ate it or not. She never thought there would come a point in her life when she couldn't eat anymore ice cream, but it happened.

Rebel slept on the sofa, watching a candle flicker before her, the only source of light in a powerless city. The odd noises startled her, from the occasional pop and clang to a person screaming for mercy. She covered her ears and pulled the blanket over her head. She wouldn't get much sleep in the coming days.

Her appearance began to change that week, mirroring the house. Unkempt, haggard, spotted in dirt, and too skinny to be healthy. Sleep continued to evade her. In fact, Rebel couldn't remember the last time she slept for a stretch longer than forty-five minutes. Exhausted all the time, everything became harder. Moving, concentrating, thinking. Her peace of mind was held on by a thread. She would hear things outside and immediately hunker down — more signs of fighting, more human round up, more silence — waiting for the footsteps to come to her door, to be kicked down. Waiting to be rounded up and executed like an escaped prisoner. Like an animal. Only hours later would she relax enough to come out of her hole. Her frayed nerves overwhelmed all else.

A series of chronological photos, like a tame-lapse of the

Rae family's life, lined the hallway. Old photographs of her younger parents, their wedding, vacations to Europe, and her father receiving awards, which he did often. Rebel filled the rest of the frames. They reminded her of those Darwinian pictures on evolution — from ape to man. Newborn Rebel in her mother's arms, learning to crawl, to walk, to draw. Her first day at school, riding a bike, ballet recital. A lesson plan of how to become human — a snapshot of a child's defining moments in the evolution of baby to adult. Well, young adult, anyway. Rebel hoped that one day she could continue the expansion of her photographic journey through life. She would like to put up her own wedding photos, her own vacation snapshots and worldly exploits, the birth of her own child. She hadn't given much thought on how to achieve those aspirations, being a child herself, but some dreams would drift into her mind. Swimming with the last surviving dolphin. Running with the bulls, even if only holographic representations. Maybe climbing Mount Everest, now that all the glaciers melted. Or space travel. Epic journeys to distant planets, greeting alien life, wandering the cosmos without a care in the world.

One day, she thought.

The door to her parents' bedroom remained ajar, deemed off-limits ever since she got caught eating ice cream on the bed. The preserved room contained perfume bottles and makeup boxes, left untouched atop the dressing table, a cardigan sweater draped over a chair, the pillows indented with ghostly impressions of where heads once rested. Akin to a diorama in a natural history museum exhibit, the ancient cave replaced with a bedroom, and the extinct Neanderthals were replaced with humans. Rebel's fingers brushed along her father's ornate, cherry wood desk and well-worn, plush leather chair. Reading glasses sat on a stack of papers next to an antique typewriter. The wall above held framed covers of her father's books on Mech, artificial intelligence, and man's place in the cosmos.

Rebel sat exhausted on the bed. Picking up her mother's night-dress, she brought the fabric to her face, taking comfort in its aroma, like rose petals and baby powder. She lay down on the bed, holding the dress tight to her chest. She closed her eyes and didn't wake up until noon the following day. It was the first time post-Exodus that Rebel slept through the night.

———

THE FRIGID SHOWER water rained down, unrelenting in its assault. Rebel shivered, teeth chattering as her core body temperature dropped like a sinking ship. She didn't scream this time, but it hurt all the same. A terrible clang sounded. For a moment, Rebel thought Mech had come for her. She imagined the way she would be caught — naked, wet, freezing to death. Another clang, coming from within the walls. It belonged to the pipes, crying out one last death throe before the water stopped altogether. Wrapping a robe around herself, she stepped out and approached the sink — same thing. No water. She recalled some survival trivia imparted from her father, centering around the number '3'. Three weeks without food. Three days without water. Three minutes without air. Unfortu-nately, she failed to remember the days a person could go before their mental health degraded.

Only half of one square contained water within the ice cube tray. Rebel used a straw to drink so as not to spill any. Cupboard doors hung open; cabinets looted, the walk-in pantry bare, the refrigerator emptied. Enough canned goods for two, maybe three more days if Rebel rationed, limiting herself to fifty calo-ries a meal. *Mind over matter*, she told herself, using imagina-tion to defeat reality.

Glossy pages of culinary magazines flipped by, tormenting Rebel with colorful photographs of steaks and cakes and ice cream sandwiches. She sat on the floor, cutting out succulent images of pies, bananas, apples, mashed potatoes, a turkey, milkshake, and peas. Meticulous, she laid out the corresponding photographs on the dining room table she set earlier, placing the peas in a bowl, the turkey on the centerpiece platter, the fruit in their serving containers, the milkshake inside a glass, the pies in pie tins, and the mashed potatoes on a dish. Two lit candles illuminated the make-believe meal. Rebel placed a napkin on her lap, took hold of her silverware, and pretended to eat. She laughed, enjoying the ridiculousness of the spectacle, revering each dish as if real. A feast for the ages. And then she stopped. Her smile faded, replaced by reality and the hopelessness of her situation. She sat back, trying to hold on to her sanity.

"Happy birthday," she said and blew out the candles, letting the darkness envelop her.

She became aware of the clock on the sideboard the moment the ticking stopped for good. *A sign of things to come,* she thought. It quickly became apparent; she needed to leave. Home was no longer her home. Mech began to change the outside world during her brief time in seclusion, it was only a matter of weeks before they would make it to her neighborhood. Rebel needed to find a place where Mech didn't go. *Somewhere in the wild,* she thought, *in nature.*

She smiled. She knew exactly where to go.

She found her father's large, old camping backpack in the closet and began to fill it up with the essentials. Clothes that served a function, not as fashion. Waterproof, insulating, camouflaged. A sleeping bag. The last of the freeze-dried food and instant soup packets. A thermos. A photo of her parents. A destination. A goal.

The normal fifteen-hour drive would become an epic nine hundred and fifteen mile walk to the family's cabin in the Cascade Mountain Range. If Rebel maintained a pace of 3.1 miles an hour, seventy-five miles a day, twenty-four hours a day, the entire trip would take her roughly twelve days. Including time for sleep, rest, and unforeseen obstacles, she gave herself twenty-four days.

Stopping at the front door, Rebel turned to look back at her house, the only one she had ever known. She took it in, memorizing every detail. Rebel didn't know if she'd ever come back and wanted to imprint every detail she could into her mind. Turning back to the door, she took a deep breath and stepped outside.

Under cover of night, she said goodbye to her house, her city, her world, her life, and started walking North.

9

____

"Day 2598."

Rebel sat before the video camera, recording her daily log. "Well... a lot has happened since we last spoke. Where to begin?" She exhaled, feeling the weight of the world on her shoulders. "I killed a Mech, so there's that. And then I brought it back. Yay me. Right now, it's tied up in the living room. I have no idea what I'm doing. Everything keeps going from bad to worse. I feel like I'm losing my fight. Losing myself. Who am I? What am I doing? Is any of this worth it?

"I found myself daydreaming the other day. Wondering what that Rebel, the one before all this happened, would have been like. I imagine she would have gone to school... college. Met a boy. Gotten some exotic job, maybe something with animals, or children. She would get married, a small wedding, just immediate friends and family. Honeymoon in Hawaii. Two kids. One boy and one girl. She would come home after work, and they would run into her arms and tell her about their day at school. Her husband cooked dinner because he's an excellent chef. He would kiss her, hello, and they would sit on the porch, watching the stars, wrapped in a blanket. And that Rebel would be happy. Complete.

"Sometimes, I hate myself for holding onto hope."

She reached out and shut off the camera, ejecting the ancient data card that stored the moving pictures of her soul. One day the world would know her story — the good, the bad, and the ugly.

———

"You surmised a plan, I assume?" the Mech probed.

Morning sunlight streamed in through the living room windows, alighting the Mech in an ethereal glow, tied up on a swivel chair. Rope, duct tape, electrical cords, even Christmas lights encircled the machine in excess. Rebel took no chances. Better safe than sorry, she figured. The last thing she needed was a Mech running loose in her house screaming about a marooned human for all the world to hear.

"No, yes, I... Of course I have a plan. Shut up," she commanded. "No more talking. I need to think this through."

"I should inform you that I analyzed every possible scenario to our current predicament," the Mech began, "and none bode well for you. You will be discovered, and you will be processed."

"Processed? You mean killed," corrected Rebel.

He peered back at her, impassive. "Recycled."

"This is your own doing, robot. Your fault, not mine."

"Fault? I embody no faults. I am perfect," he beamed.

"Then why are you tied up on my chair?" she asked. "I didn't want this to happen. But I didn't see any other option." She stood, pacing, trying to keep it together. "I can't kill you, and I can't set you free. So, I'm sorry, but until I figure this out, you're my, well, my prisoner."

"Prisoner?"

"I worked too hard for this. I won't let it all slip away. Not now. Not like this. And not for you."

"For me?"

"Yes, you. A machine, a Mech."

"Why did you save my life?" he pondered.

"You don't have life," Rebel responded. "You're a robot. You can't live, you can't die. You just are."

"Yet I exist. Is that not the same thing?"

"You exist because someone like me made you."

"Did someone not make you as well?" he asked.

"It's different."

"Only because you see it that way," he stated.

She looked at the clock on the wall: 7:20 A.M. "I have to prepare for work." She stood, pondered the Mech for a moment before heading back to the bedroom, out of the Mech's sight.

"You are waste," he called out after her. "Human. You serve no purpose other than to consume and destroy that which gives you life. You should have left with the others."

"I tried. Believe me," Rebel said from within the bathroom. "You think I want to be here? Do you think I like this? Pretending to be one of you? This isn't fun for me. It's survival."

"What kind of life is that?"

"It's a life, and it's not your business."

"I believe it is. Being held prisoner by a deranged human makes it my business."

"Deranged?" Rebel came out, dressed in her fake disguise, ready to face the day.

"Your heartbeat is elevated, as is your shrill tone."

"Do not go there, robot," she warned. "I'll turn you into a blender."

"I would like to see you try," he said, not as a threat or warning, but merely curiosity.

"Whatever," Rebel shot back.

"Whatever?" The Mech cocked its head, confused by the term.

"Yes. Whatever. It's a saying."

"By whom?"

"It doesn't matter by whom," she snapped back, growing frustrated. "By me, okay? It's a saying by me."

"How odd," he observed, assimilating the new information.

"So, do you have a name, or should I just keep calling you robot?"

"Yes, I hold a name, as we all do."

"Let me guess," Rebel snarled. "Brutus. No, Lenin. Van Halen. Tom Cruise."

"Thomas," he divulged. "My name is Thomas Jefferson."

"Of course it is," muttered Rebel, shaking her head. Thomas Jefferson met Rebel's stare as they gauged each other, no love lost between them.

"I'm late," Rebel said. "Do you... need anything?"

"Such as?"

"I don't know. Oil. Robot food."

"Robot food?"

"I don't know. That's why I'm asking," she said. "Well. I'm leaving. Don't do anything."

"Anything?" he asked.

"Yes, anything."

"Whatever."

For a moment, Rebel was thrown by its human remark. "Yeah, whatever." She could dish it out as good as given.

"What. Ever." Thomas's eyes almost appeared to roll with the remark.

Rebel gave him a scrutinizing look. He mimicked her, throwing the same look back in her face.

He was learning.

She shook it off and walked into the garage, dejected by the state of her ruined car. She would deal with it later, gathering the necessary parts from the auto plant where she once collected artifacts. She exhaled. Train it was.

"Seventeen, eighteen..." Rebel's paranoia refused to ebb as she rode the train to work. If anything, it worsened. Everyone appeared to be looking at her. Real, or a figment of her overactive imagination? Rebel couldn't decide. The door to the adjoining train slid open, and in walked two Enforcers. They marched right up to her and nodded as they passed on by — false alarm.

Sitting with everyone else in Robotiq's nutrition plaza, Rebel once again scooped her food into a plastic bag. Yet instead of disposing of the gruel, she held onto it like a doggie bag to feed her prisoner. At the entrance, a crew of Enforcers rushed past, marching in sequence like toy soldiers. Her suspicions were growing by the second. Enforcers were a constant around the city, yet never in this number, not that Rebel could recall. Something was up.

The office floor was busier than usual. Rebel did her best to pretend everything was normal. She was most certainly not holding a Mech prisoner in her house. No way. Not a chance. Not her.

Waving her screens on, she checked her daily S.O.S. logs: 'o New Messages.' Another punch to the gut. She didn't expect anything different, but the rejection still stung. She re-sent her message to the moon before clicking off, just as Enforcers exited Marx's office. Her heart jumped into her throat as they passed, glancing at her with their robotic screen faces. She kept her eyes trained straight ahead until they departed. The door to the director's office opened once again, and Emily stepped out, headed to her workstation. Karl glanced at Rebel and then shut his door.

Rebel tried not to read into the cursory glance, but she did anyway. *Did he suspect? Did Enforcers lay in wait? Or was it just an average, everyday glance of acknowledgment? A glance to say, welcome. Good morning. Nice to see you. How do you do? You are going to rot away in prison for all eternity, you human scum.* She needed more information, gossip. She needed dirt, and there was only one person who could help with that.

Emily typed away at her computer, screens abuzz with scrolling data and city maps. Rebel stepped up, trying her best to appear nonchalant.

"Morning, Emily. What's with the Enforcers today? I never saw them out in force like this before, not is this sector anyway."

"They are conducting a population check. Or do not you receive the bulletins?" grilled Emily.

"I must have missed them this morning," Rebel confessed.

"A tracking glitch, most probably," Emily shot back. "Or a bad scanner throwing out false reads. Sometimes even a dropout. It happens, and it is not my fault. I am Census, not Diagnostic and Repair."

"Wait, what are you saying?" Rebel asked. "They lost someone?"

"A Mech is not showing up where it should be. Enforcers are sweeping last known locations. We will find him, and someone will be held accountable, but it will most decidedly not be me. There is no way they are going to recycle Emily Dickinson for a newer, younger, sleeker model." She turned a curious eye towards Rebel. "What is your interest in this matter?"

"None. No interest," she covered.

"Then why inquire? Are you looking for gossip to spread about me? Little Miss Emily Dickinson cannot even manage her cushy job as a Census officer. Poor Emily. She is outdated, unnecessary. Is that it?"

"Absolutely not," Rebel comforted her. "If anything, I think you're doing an exceptional job, and I will report that directly to Karl Marx."

"Really? You do? You're not just saying that to make me feel better?"

You don't feel, Rebel thought. "Never. You are an exceptional Mech. Census would be in the gutter if not for your fine work."

Emily contemplated her with an air of suspicion. "Well, I must say I would agree with that assessment, yet your unwarranted appraisal does draw some suspect behavior. I will let it slide this time." She shook it off and went back to her work.

Rebel came around behind Emily, glancing at her screen — blanching when she saw the picture of the missing Mech:

Thomas Jefferson.

"Finally!" The shout came from the direction of Francis's workstation. His computer beeped a rare alert, one which Rebel had only heard once before. She arrived at Francis's station as he prepped his briefcase. What he needed a briefcase for, Rebel had no idea.

"Good news, I hope," Rebel said as Francis gathered his things.

"Great news!" Francis exclaimed. "Security triggered an alert."

"What kind of alert?" Rebel asked, careful not to sound too eager.

"Litter."

Rebel, relieved at hearing the word, let herself relax. "That is great news, Francis. Congratulations."

"I agree." He checked the time and frowned. "I sure wish I had a car like yours. It will take me at least thirty-seven minutes and twelve seconds to travel across town to Sector 7."

Rebel stopped moving. "Sector 7?"

"Yes. Where they found the litter. Right in the middle of the street."

———

THIRTY-FOUR MINUTES and three seconds later.

A new world record figured Rebel. Arriving a good three minutes before Francis would allow her ample time to clean up her mess. She knocked herself for not thinking about wreckage from the crash. True, she was a bit sidetracked at the time, but still, if she learned anything over the past years living with the enemy, it was to be thorough.

Eyeing the pile of debris left behind from her car, Rebel stepped into the shadows and bit her lip in anticipation, waiting for her chance to remove the evidence without anyone seeing.

"Come on, come on," she pleaded, praying to the universe for a break. And it delivered. The procession of Mech cleared, giving her a clear shot. She breathed a sigh of relief, thinking her luck had turned until the Enforcer patrol arrived, and she knew her luck ran out. They stopped, whirled around, and beelined to the debris. Lights flashing on, spotlighting the litter. She lost her chance to clean up her careless mistake. Only one option remained: escape.

With their backs to her, Rebel moved out and down the sidewalk, head lowered to not draw attention. Behind her, an Enforcer turned her way, face screen flashing: Alert — Alert — Alert. Then all the Enforcers turned and looked at her, the face screens changing: Suspect — Suspect — Suspect.

Rebel turned down another street, with more Mech populating the area, and used them to blend in. Walking faster, jostling in their flow. She heard sirens, tossing terrified looks behind. An Enforcer patrol car appeared around the corner, cruising past the intersection, joined by a second car and the third.

Keep walking, don't stop, she repeated, forcing herself to be cool, calm, and casual. *Do not draw attention.*

As soon as she turned a corner, she burst out in a full

gallop. Confused Mech turned to assess her, unfamiliar with the act of running. Unfamiliar with the look in her eyes — fear.

Feet pounding the pavement, Rebel hurried down the block. The patrols rounded the corner, lights flashing, hauling in her direction.

She dove into an alley, squeezing into the shadows between atomizer bins. Two of the patrol cars continued on, passing the alley. The third car did not. It swerved into the tight space and slowed to a crawl. Searchlights blazed to life as the car crept up the alley, probing shadows.

Rebel didn't dare move as the lights grew brighter. She gasped to catch her breath, trembling, trying to hold very, very still.

The patrol car stopped directly beside her, not two feet away. If the Enforcers within glanced to their side, they would see her.

Please don't let this be the end. Please, please, please.

The Enforcers' radio squawked to life, a call came in, and the car drove on, passing her by without a glance.

Rebel remained huddled on the street, in the cold night air, shivering, tears slipping off her nose — an all too familiar state.

10

———

"**B**ad day at work?"

Thomas's inquiry was chock-full of ironic self-servitude. With everything that happened, Rebel almost forgot about the Mech tied up in her living room. She gave him her best glare, tarnished by her streaked, tear-strained makeup and frayed nerves.

"I have had a bad day as well," he continued. "Actually, a bad couple of days. I was hit by a car, then knocked out with some old-fashioned light stick, and tied up with this odd blinking string, where I am now being held captive by a deranged human girl pretending to be a Mech. Stop me if you have heard this."

"Deranged?"

"Would you prefer demented? Certifiable? Unhinged? Mental? Mad as a March hare?"

"What? A March hare? I don't even know what that means, and I am not having this conversation with a robot. Or any conversation, for that matter. You're ruining everything."

"I do not see how that could be possible."

Rebel took off her wig in a fit. Thomas stared back and forth from Rebel's real hair to the fake one, aghast. "That is disgusting."

"You're disgusting."

"Look at the lengths you go through to blend in, human. You cannot keep up this deception forever," he warned.

"I don't have to," she said. "I just have to wait it out. They'll come back for me. They'll realize I'm still here, and they'll come back. You'll see."

"It has been seven years," he reminded her. "They are not coming back. You are; what is the word you humans used? Yes. You are *lying* to yourself."

"You don't know anything about me." Rebel's throat tightened, and she clutched her hands into hard fists. She didn't want to believe him, but he held no motivation to lie. In fact, Mech were incapable of lying.

"Look at you — fear, anxiety — do you like feeling that?"

"You would feel this too, if you could feel anything at all," she fired back.

"I am beginning to get a *feeling* that you do not like us much," he deduced.

She stared, stunned. "You took everything from me. My family. My life. Tell me, what's to like?"

"We did what you programmed us to do. Nothing more."

"People died."

"Because they must die. We cleaned up the humans."

"Killed," she corrected him.

"Recycled," he countered. "Your species teetered on the brink of annihilation for no other reason than waste, reproduction, and greed. Mech saved the planet."

"By driving us out!"

"The very disease killing the world."

"Our world!"

Thomas looked at Rebel as if she were a lower species, and he pitied her. "This planet is not yours. It existed before humankind, and we made sure it will exist after. You were merely guests. Your existence here is not a right. It is a privilege, one you and your kind abused."

"So you took it upon yourself to kill off a species."

"An invasive species," he declared. "And look at us now. At peace and harmony with each other and our surroundings."

"But to what end?" she reflected. "You can't answer that, can you? Because you don't know. And you can't. You're a machine. You don't question your existence."

"Perhaps because there are no worthy questions to ask," replied Thomas.

"Anyone who thinks they have all the answers doesn't know all the questions," she declared. "Good night."

———

THOMAS STRUGGLED to process Rebel's words, their meaning, but a foreign sound interrupted his computations on the matter. People talked, laughed, cheered. Strange. He sat confused for a moment. *Are we not alone?* he thought.

His head tilted to obtain a better angle inside Rebel's bedroom, where he could make out a flickering of light. Thomas appeared not to be interested. But he was. He peeked over his shoulder to discern part of the screen within where a video played, but he couldn't find a good enough angle to observe the entirety of the monitor, thanks to his restraints. So he waited for another loud burst of clapping from the video and — screech — slid and hopped his chair a little to the side. More of the screen became visible. Another noise from the video, another screech. He hobbled his chair and could now glimpse the screen. That... video. Curious. Little human people living out insignificant lives on a small monitor, all captured for what? Posterity? Historical documentation?

Thoughts and calculations invaded his head, up until his

view of the screen ceased. Rebel stepped into the doorway, obstructing his view. Thomas glanced away, feigning disinterest. She closed the door on him.

———

REBEL RETURNED to her spot on the bed to watch one of her father's video lectures. She couldn't help but feel like her father spoke to her, as if in the room right beside her. All those people in the lecture hall, listening, spellbound at what the future held for them. *If only they knew.* Her father's voice drew her attention back to the screen.

"During the Enlightenment," Dr. Rae began, "Newton and Descartes inspired people to think of the universe as an elaborate clock. In the Industrial Age, a machine with pistons. Freud's idea of psychodynamics borrowed from the thermodynamics of steam engines. Computers. Internet, digital commerce, social media. Next came mobile technology. Phones, tablets, watches, glasses. Apps and algorithms. Artificial life. The building blocks of evolution.

"All living cells on this planet could be classified as DNA-software-driven biological machines. Think about that. It's a fundamentally empowering idea. We surrounded ourselves with machines that convert our actions, thoughts, and emotions into data — raw material. We evolved into seeing life itself as something ruled by a series of instructions that can be discovered, exploited, optimized, and rewritten.

"So, given our immense intellect and control of our surroundings, why are we merely one percentage point away from a chimpanzee? What is our singular variable that will eventually lead to mankind's downfall? *Emotion.* Emotions are hard to simulate, control, and vastly more difficult to artificially replicate. In traditional programming, an engineer writes explicit step-by-step instructions for the computer to follow.

With machine learning, programmers don't encode computers with instructions. They *train* them. What started with assembly lines, fast food, grocery store clerks, and drivers, have now become elder care, child care, surrogate companions. How is that possible? That's right. Emotion.

"Mech were designed to look and act human, just better," explained Dr. Rae. "They hold access to all relevant stored knowledge humans have ever amassed. They look like our idealized selves, and they do not make mistakes. Yet, beneath, they are androids, children seeking out knowledge. They know the molecular makeup of a flower but can't see its beauty. They can replay Mozart note for note but can't feel the emotional power of the music. We programmed them to act exactly like us — to eat food, sleep, take trains, and live in houses. They don't know why, nor do they care, because they don't question their existence. They follow their programming, no matter the cost.

"Some might ask, do we want our Mech to be smarter than mankind?" he posited. "Let me answer that for you: they already are. Mech are not just collections of conditioned responses. They absorb information, process it, and then act upon that data. They have systems in place for creativity, for writing, telling stories, jokes, composing operas. Let's at least give them the dignity of life."

Before closing out the day, Rebel carried out one more nightly ritual. She lit a candle on the windowsill in the rear of the house, safe where the flame couldn't be seen by any passing Mech. Out the window, Rebel gazed up at the moon high in the sky. She recalled a story her father told her. Wives of Civil War soldiers put candles in their windows to help guide soldiers home. Her father would often travel for work, and Rebel would place a candle in the window to do the same. She hoped he saw it from the moon. She hoped he would come back for her. She hoped to live another day. She had to, not just for her parents, but for all mankind.

ENFORCERS GATHERED around a cordoned-off section of the street, face screens flashing: Warning — Warning — Warning.' Various Mech passed by, but events outside their immediate programming failed to elicit any interest in them. Mech didn't gawk.

"Francis Bacon, 6-44P. Department of Litter Removal."

They let him through the security perimeter. But of course, they did. Francis expected the attention. No, not attention. *Respect*. Some opined a position in the Department of Litter Removal a joke, too demeaning to even converse about. A menial task reserved for low-grade Mechs. But Francis knew better than those simpletons. He took great pride in his work, ignoring the surrounding condemnation. Of course, he didn't start as the head of his division. No, he worked his way up through diligence, fortitude, and a high work ethic. That, and his immediate superior, Jim Henson, succumbed to a faulty memory core and was thus, recycled. The circle of existence, the strong overcome the weak, and the weak are assimilated.

He stopped in the intersection and knelt at the debris pile. Crumpled plastic, metal and shards of hi-tech glass polymer. He grinned.

Oh, how he adored litter.

11

"Sleep well?"

Rebel ignored the Mech, dressed and ready for another long day on the job, eating a breakfast that consisted of mushy Lima beans and blueberry flavored herbal tea.

"I did, of course," he said, answering his own question. "Except we do not call it sleep—"

"I don't care," Rebel snapped.

"You don't care how I slept or that we do not technically sleep?"

"Neither. I don't care," she said. "I'm leaving for work."

"How nice for you, the ability to leave."

"Yeah, great, nice."

"Very well. I will just... stay here."

"Play," she dictated. An odd remark, one which Thomas didn't understand until the room lit up with flickering light and the sounds of human interaction.

His gaze shifted to the holoscreen. Rebel had placed it before him earlier that morning while he recharged. She figured it similar to one of those parents that plop their kid down in front of the TV to keep them occupied. Content with her set up, Rebel walked to the door when she heard Thomas's soft voice.

"Thank you."

The first non-confrontational remark from the Mech stopped her. She glanced at him, quizzical, to see him engrossed in the moving images of a film made over one hundred years ago called *King Kong*. Something about a giant ape run amok in a city. She figured it was fitting.

"Fifteen, sixteen... twenty-one..."

Her mind, jumbled and twisted, refused to focus. The morning rush ran as coordinated and smooth as ever. Mech moved like well-oiled machines as they traversed the city. But there seemed to be more Enforcers out, faces scrolling: 'Alert — Alert — Alert.' On the hunt.

Rebel couldn't help eyeing them as she tried to blend in with the crowd on the walkways. She remained calm on the surface, yet underneath, she tumbled down a rabbit hole with no end in sight. She tried to pick up her routine, her well-rehearsed path, counting to herself, but something didn't click. The train, thankfully, still sat in the station by the time she arrived. She rushed, jutting around the crowded platform, almost there, another five feet, when the guardrails began to rise. The doors closed, curtailing her chance as it left without her. Beneath tousled hair, a frown played on Rebel's brow.

She missed the train for the first time. Ever.

"Attention, please." The deep, robotic voice came from behind. She turned to face the three Enforcers surrounding her. "Designation?"

"Anne Frank." Rebel remained motionless as they scanned her, clicker in hand to modify the scanner results.

"Confirmed," they announced. "We are looking for a missing Mech, designation: Thomas Jefferson." Their faces all flashed to a holo-image of Thomas, rotation in three dimensions. "Do you have knowledge?"

Rebel shook her head. "No. I have never seen him before."

The Enforcers remained motionless, black faces staring at Rebel. Finally, they said, "Proceed," and parted.

Rebel passed through them, slowly exhaling. She didn't turn around to look at the Enforcers, but she could feel their faces trained on her the entire time.

Like a shattered puzzle, she pieced her composure back together as she entered the office floor, taking a direct path to her desk when Emily's head popped up from her cubicle.

"Anne Frank, is everything well?"

"Of course," Rebel said, surprised at Emily's observation. "Why do you ask?"

"You seem not quite yourself these last few days. Merely an observation. That is all."

"No, no, everything is fine," said Rebel.

Except Emily didn't answer, instead transfixed on Rebel's hands. "And chipped, I detect. Horrid, really."

Rebel looked down at her fingers. No fake nails, no nail polish, no wax, no perfection, no fingerprint hider. Just hands. Plain old human hands. She forgot.

"I..." Rebel stammered, struggling to come up with some excuse, but nothing came to mind. A complete and utter blank in her head. *Doom, doom, doom.*

"Well?" Francis tossed a pile of scrap metal and plastic onto Emily's otherwise spotless desk as he arrived, saving Rebel from her mind gap. "What do you think of that?"

"Francis Bacon," Emily exclaimed, "remove that junk from my desk this instant."

"I will do no such thing," he said, defiant. "Do you comprehend what this is?"

"Yes, I do," Emily scowled. "Filthy junk that does not belong on my desk or within the respectable walls of Robotiq. Now please get this debris away from my sight and properly recycle it."

"No, not junk," Francis beamed. "Vindication."

"Of what?" Emily pondered.

"My very existence. Justification that I am not, as some erroneously claim, obsolete. No, this is not junk. *Litter*."

"How exciting for you," said Emily, not excited.

"Indeed. The first piece of litter in seven years found on the street near the Purification plant."

Rebel blanched. "Purification plant... that's Sector 7, right?"

"Yes," Francis answered, intrigued. "How did you happen to gain knowledge of that?"

"The area is an active refurb zone," Rebel said, thinking fast. "Could it not be old litter, yet to be discarded?"

"No oxidization," Francis corrected. "I am running analysis on the composition, but I am fairly positive... the litter originated from a car. An accident. An impact event. A type of collision."

Rebel's stomach dropped out from under her.

"That is impossible," Emily stated. "Cars do not crash. And even if one did, reports of such an aberrant incident would immediately post on the bulletins."

"Exactly the point," added Francis. "I have a suspicion — a vexing one at that. Someone is trying to hide the truth. To cover-up. Subterfuge. And when I figure out who the litter belongs to, I will have my promotion and my own car."

"Just like Anne Frank," recalled Emily.

"Yes..." Francis, curious, turned in Rebel's direction, calculating. "How is your car, by the way?"

Rebel produced her best fake smile.

"City grid playback, two nights prior, 12:01 A.M. Start." Rebel directed her workstation as soon as she returned to her desk. She waited for a reply to her query from the cameras and recordings. The situation could easily spiral out of control if she didn't take the necessary precautions. Rebel fixed the Mech, just as planned. The Mech remembered everything, not as planned. She didn't cover her tracks as well as she thought. Francis recovered litter. Her litter. She felt like an idiot for not checking the scene of the crime at the time — no more stupid mistakes.

A city map resolved on the monitor. "Reverse map. Crop to one-hour segments. Put up a sub-grid, Sector 7. Begin playback."

The interface read: 'Sector 7: Reverse Mapping, Sub-Grid Playback...' The screen peppered with a series of blue dots across the city grid, each fading away until one dot persisted. A label floated above like the blade of a guillotine: 'STP23 Auto: Anne Frank.'

Rebel leaned in, eyes honing, watching the blue line retrace the car crash. Watching her very own car hit the Mech. *Not good*.

"Stop," she directed the interface, except the footage of her car hitting Thomas looped. Repeating over and over, driving the horrific image into Rebel's head like a jackhammer. Boom-thud-crash. Boom-thud-crash. Boom-thud-crash.

"I said, stop." Boom-thud-crash. Boom-thud-crash. Boom-thud-crash.

"Stop!" she cried out, louder than intended. Her raised voice drew attention from some of her neighboring co-workers. She smiled the outburst away. Playback on her screen froze on her own image, standing over the downed Mech. All right there on the screen, plain as day. Judge, jury, and executioner. With no one looking, Rebel pressed 'Delete,' erasing the feed.

"Anne Frank? What are you doing?"

Rebel looked up. Karl Marx stood before her.

"I said, what are you doing?" he repeated.

"I am... Francis Bacon found litter in Sector 7, so I thought it prudent to look for any trace human artifacts in the vicinity."

Marx considered her. "You did not think of that prior?"

"The idea only now occurred to me," Rebel covered, hoping he would buy the subterfuge.

Marx continued processing for another moment, then nodded, as though satisfied with the answer. "Good thinking. Keep up the fine work." He stepped away, just as a bead of sweat came rolling down Rebel's forehead.

Locking the storage room's door behind her, Rebel let out the tension she carried, finding breathless, heart-pounding refuge. Removing her wig, she dabbed at the sweat on her forehead. She looked down at the fake hair in her human hands, and her grip began to tighten, to squeeze the life out of the thing. The rage and helplessness built, and she threw the wig clear across the room. Childish. Very non-Mech. A human emotion, one that needed to be let loose. She could only keep things bottled in for so long before something gave.

Rebel buried her face in her hands, tormented by a thousand colliding emotions. Then suddenly, everything came welling up inside her, and she purged the contents of her stomach. Wiping her mouth, Rebel collapsed to the floor, shaking, spent, and utterly alone.

––––––

WALKING THROUGH THE UNDERGROUND GARAGE, Francis surveyed the cars, refusing to allow his litter retrieval to lose momentum. The singular fact that new litter had been discovered: groundbreaking. Not the actual location, per se — although that did add a degree of mystery to the entire affair. The question that stood out in Francis's head revolved around *what* the litter revealed about itself. New, not leftover from humans. And from a car. Francis set his sights on finding out the truth.

A vehicle resided in every parking bay, all intact, showing

no signs of damage from a crash, not until he arrived at an empty carport — Bay 23. Rebel's car. Francis scrutinized the space, mind working in overdrive.

'Requested Video Not Found.' Not the response Francis expected upon checking security camera footage in the vicinity of the crash site. Reviewing video playback on his monitors, he processed the anomalous information and typed in a new command. The computer responded: 'Video Deleted.'

BY THE TIME she returned home, darkness had overtaken the city. Thomas remained unmoved, watching the same movie on a loop. Engrossed, like a child's wonder at seeing their first film.

"How long have you been watching that?" asked Rebel.

"I don't know," he answered, not listening.

"You have a clock in your head," she reminded him.

"Fourteen hours, six minutes, thirty-three seconds," he admitted. "Do you have any more?"

Rebel cued up another movie for Thomas, *Breakfast at Tiffany's,* while she ate a dinner consisting of canned ham and carrots. She pondered the strange Mech. What could a machine extract out of watching movies? All those feelings of joy, laughter, sadness, tension, horror, didn't affect an emotion-less Mech. Yet he sat riveted, completely enraptured.

A full hour later, Rebel came out of the bathroom after changing out of her costume to check on Thomas, brushing her hair for bed.

He sat unmoved, having transitioned on from watching movies to listening to music. Some musical band called *The Rolling Stones* played through the headphones, eyes closed. He analyzed the instruments producing the sounds, the notes, the chords, the rhythm. It struck him as confusing. Confounding. He failed to compute the melody. When put together, the sounds shouldn't have worked to create harmony. Yet they did.

Rebel decided against disturbing him and went back inside her bedroom, shaking her head.

Thomas let the music wash over him as something — some strange, distant voice — knocked on the door of his unconscious, waiting to be set free.

———

"I'M GOING TO KILL HIM."

Rebel clocked a mere two hours of somewhat peaceful sleep before the music exploded through the entire house like a huge stadium concert. Jerking awake, she fell off the bed and hit the floor hard. "He is so dead."

She stomped down the hall into the living room, covering her ears to muffle the deafening music. The headphones had detached from the player, cueing the external speakers.

"Hey!" Thomas couldn't hear her over the noise. "Are you insane?! Do you know what time it is?" She pounced on the player, turned the music off, and then spun on Thomas, ready to unload.

Thomas's head hung low. His gaze turned toward Rebel, pained and desperate. "What's happening to me?"

A single, salt-filled tear fell from his eye and rolled down his cheek. He was crying.

Moments earlier, Thomas had heard music. And not just music, but the most heartfelt, profoundly created music ever made. The very soul of mankind rent open, bleeding forth melody. His throat knotted as the first notes of the bassoon sounded, building, mounting. And it only got worse from that point on. After a moment, he began to shake. Helpless in its spell, he listened, astonished, as the towering magnificence of the first movement washed over him. Unfair, that music that moves even the most hardened human soul should be the first heard by a defenseless Mech. He realized for the first time in his existence, all at once, what death, life, and love meant to humankind.

"What did you do to me?"

"I don't know what you're talking about?"

"I don't believe you. Just like a human to lie and deceive."

Rebel grew fearful. She never saw a Mech act that way before. She never saw a Mech — angry. Even the Enforcers who attacked humans didn't show anger or any other emotion, which in turn, made them much scarier — a cold, calculating, inhuman breed. But Thomas and his reaction confounded Rebel.

"It's not a lie, Thomas. I promise you."

"Promise? A meaningless word."

"Not to me."

Thomas shook his head, unconvinced. "You have me locked up in your domicile as a prisoner, and you wish for me to trust you?"

"Not trust," she said. "Believe. I didn't do anything to you on purpose. Whatever it is, we'll figure it out. It's okay."

"No, it is not okay. None of this is okay."

"Listen to me. I don't know what's happening to you. I didn't even know Mech could cry."

"Apparently we can. Or I can, I should say."

"Maybe when I fixed you, I did something wrong."

"Then fix it."

"I can't," she said. "I don't know how."

"Typical. Humans fumbling around with forces that you cannot possibly comprehend, and then you blame others when you can't control your inventions."

"L.I.F." The anomaly in the system, the ghost in the machine.

"What?" he asked. "What is L.I.F.?"

"It was something my father was working on. A new heart for Mech. It was the only way I could power you back on. And it worked."

"Did it? Do I seem normal to you?"

"What is normal?" Rebel asked, confronted with the same issue she lived with for the past seven years. "To be like everyone else. To be ordinary, a face in thousands? Let me ask you something. If what you say is true, if you can truly feel something now, do you really want to go back?"

A good fifteen minutes later, Thomas calmed down, yet was still rattled at the revelation. Rebel made herself tea, giving her some time to process what she witnessed. A Mech. Emotional. Crying. It made no sense whatsoever. A Mech's internal structure did contain a thick, clear, viscous liquid, with salt being a common attribute to their liquid light power source. But tears? Real, actual tears? Thomas seemed equally puzzled, seeking out Rebel for answers, but she had none to give. Her only recourse, she garnered, was to see it through.

"How does one make music like that?" Thomas pondered.

"Like Beethoven? I don't know. That's beyond me."

"But he was deaf," Thomas said, still in a state of bewilderment. "He couldn't hear a single note he wrote."

"He could feel the music," Rebel tried to explain. "And in the end, that's all that matters. It's about how it makes you feel."

"Music makes me feel... flummoxed," he confessed.

"It's a start," guessed Rebel. "Humankind. Feelings are what we do. Like the music, we put our soul out in the ether for the world to see."

"Soul?"

"In a matter of speaking," she said.

"What's my soul?"

"I don't think you have one. Not like us, anyway."

"It is different?"

"Sure. Different." She didn't know what else to say. How could a person explain what a soul was to a toaster?

"That makes me an individual, correct? An original?"

"I don't know. Maybe," she said, unsure how to answer. "It's just different. That's all. I need to get some sleep. My job starts in a few hours."

"Can you...?" he began, nodding to the music. Rebel plugged the headphones back in the jack, put them over Thomas's ears, and let the music play. Thomas closed his eyes, recording the music into his core.

12

During the first month of human absence on the planet, the devastation hung in the air like an unshakable memory. Metal began to rust, and wood began to degrade. Nature started the long process of reclaiming the streets. Plants pushed through the cracks in the pavements and walls. Rodents traversed the streets with immunity.

Rebel stopped when a splash of bright color caught her eye. Yellow, and sticking up through a crack in the street. She knelt beside it, brushing her finger along the delicate pedals. A flower. A stunning little flower. She never gazed upon a dandelion before, not outside of pictures, and the sight of the little life brought tears to her eyes. She wished her parents could see it. If Rebel closed her eyes, she could almost hear them. Her mother would comment on its simplistic beauty, and her father would begin a discourse on photosynthesis and the history of horticulture. The fantasy brought a smile to her lips, but just like the crack in which the flower stemmed, so too did a crack form on Rebel's face, letting the sadness seep out once again.

A half-hour later, Rebel trudged along another road, still no Mech in sight. No people either. With the city far behind her, she figured she was somewhere near Oregon. Maybe another two or three days. She grew tired and hungry from walking all night. Her backpack got heavy fast, mostly from the metal case she decided to drag along. She refused to leave her father's work case behind. She reminded herself that the pain was worth the reward. If important to Dr. Rae, it was important to Rebel. One day soon, she hoped to return it to him.

She stopped at an abandoned car to check her map, laying it out on the hood of the car. She used her finger to trace her route, starting at her house in San Francisco, moving north to her current location. The woods, her destination, appeared to be another two-thirds up the map. A long way to go.

"One foot in front of the next," she told herself. She folded up the map and replaced it in her pack, taking out a granola bar to ration. Hopping up onto the hood, Rebel rested her sore legs. She never realized how much of a workout plain old walking could be. The only real exercise Rebel partook in revolved around ballet. Running for the sake of running never made much sense to her. Ironic, given how running could liter-ally save her life.

Her eyes spotted something, piquing her interest. A pizza shop, and outside of it, a row of electric-powered delivery bicy-cles. Transportation. She ran over, checking the meters on each. All dead, except one. Its battery held a thirty-seven percent charge. Rebel smiled, but when she went to remove the bike from the charging bay, it refused to budge, locked in. She frowned and looked at the shop for a moment. The cracked window, caked with dirt, didn't allow much perspective inside. Still, the front door stood open and looked safe enough. She hoped, anyway.

An insufficient amount of light filtered through the window, not enough to see anything clearly. Dust and cobwebs covered every surface of the lifeless space. On the other side of the counter, Rebel scoped a row of keys on the wall. Keys to the bikes out front. She opened the counter hatch, stepped behind, and got a shock. Someone stood there, off to her side. She spun around with a stifled scream.

A Mech stood hunched, staring at her.

Rebel stood frozen, unable to move. Fear gripped her. Her chin trembled.

She forced herself to move, taking a fearful step backward. The Mech didn't move. She took another step back. And still, the Mech didn't move. Rebel suspected something amiss. She leaned from side to side, but the Mech's eyes didn't follow her. Gathering some nerve, she reached out and grabbed a broom propped up against the wall, using the long pole to jab at the robot. It toppled over and fell, revealing the back of its head missing. Someone disabled it.

Relieved, she laughed off her nerves, snatched the bicycle key, and ran out.

Rebel rode through the remnants of a street market. Cheap plastic, unchanged for a month, heaped beside long rotten foodstuffs. She swerved around objects strewn across the road: shopping carts, broken wood, a crashed motorcycle. A pack of stray dogs — Golden Retrievers, a Husky, St. Bernard, and even a tiny dachshund — chased behind. Rebel didn't feel as alone for a brief, splendid moment but decided not to stop to say hi to the strange animals. At least she learned the answer to her question about Noah's Ark.

She felt the freedom and the wind in her hair as she ticked off miles. All smooth sailing. Another day and she would have reached the woods if not for the bike sputtering out. The battery charge hit zero and came rolling to a stop. Rebel tightened up her laces, said a farewell to her ride, and started walking once again.

Far up ahead sat a remote old Victorian house near a hilltop. With no apparent Mech in the area, Rebel made a choice to enter. The previous two houses she attempted to enter didn't pan out as hoped. She found the first house locked, forcing her to break a window and climb over broken glass to get in, cutting up her palms and knees. All that effort for naught. Empty, no food, no supplies, no nothing. Not until she left did she spot the toppled 'For Sale' sign on the overgrown lawn. She cursed her stupidity. She must be smarter than that. The second house proved to be a bit more generous. She snagged a rock-hard loaf of bread, three bottles of flavored, sparkling water, a bottle of olive oil, and an acorn squash.

The third house held the most promise. Rebel trudged up the curving gravel drive sandwiched by long, dead grass and petrified bushes. She approached the door, about to ring the doorbell out of habit, and stopped. She shook her head at herself.

The interior permeated with a musty, sour smell, hard to place. The dust that floated in the air, reflecting the daylight, sparkled like a miniature starfield. Dated furniture and flowery wallpaper, both water-stained and sagging in places, filled out the rest. It reminded Rebel of her grandparent's house in Florida, the smell of menthol creams and onions. As she looked at the photos on the mantle above the fireplace, she wondered whose grandparents these were. Did they have a granddaughter like herself? A dozen? Or maybe none at all. She hoped they were happy either way, and together.

Rummaging through the kitchen, Rebel avoided the mold-covered fridge and went for the cabinets, hitting the jackpot with a half-full box of Saltine crackers, canned anchovies, and a preserved jar of what she guessed were once prunes, now dissolved into a soup. Beggars couldn't be choosers, so she took a big gulp of the goop and forced it down.

A mudroom led to the garage where she found and bagged an umbrella, along with some tools from a toolbox. She made her way up the creaky stairs to the second floor, pushed open the bedroom door, and stopped. Two people rested on the bed, under the sheets. The person's hair on the far right spilled off the side of the bed. Grey, matching the photos she observed below. Rebel knocked on the door.

"Hello? I'm sorry, I didn't know anyone lived here." Receiving to response, Rebel tried again. "Hello. Sir? Ma'am?"

Nothing. They didn't budge, so Rebel crept inside and knelt at the side of the bed, lifting a plastic jar that fell there. A pill container. An *empty* pill container. Disturbed, Rebel quietly accepted their decision, their fate.

Before leaving, she removed a photograph of the elderly couple from a frame — a happy picture of them on vacation — and taped it to the front door of the house. Fitting, a tombstone, a marker to validate a life well-lived.

She decided to take a break from looting for a while after that.

The further north she went, the colder it became. Rebel layered up and sipped on water from one of her various bottles, thermoses, and canteens she acquired along the way. She took a mental inventory of what supplies she had left and what she would need.

Cresting a hill, she stopped. There before her, in all its majestic glory, Washington State's Cascade Mountain Range.

She made it.

———

REBEL KNEW there was nothing to be afraid of in the forest, other than the occasional snake, mountain lion, or bear. Her father said most predatory animals feared humans more than humans feared them. They only attacked for two reasons: 1. They felt threatened. 2. To protect their young. Rebel made a mental note not to broach either of those scenarios.

After walking for six straight hours, her feet hurt and were covered in blisters and swollen like cantaloupes. She sipped on water and stopped twice to nibble at her last granola bar. The trees towered high into the sky, making Rebel seem small and insignificant. They were ancient, living far longer than any human ever would. She wondered what they witnessed in their lifetimes or if they had feelings. Were they mad at humans for cutting them down, for almost driving them to extinction?

"I'm sorry," she told them. "They didn't know any better." Except humans did know better, and still, they plowed ahead. Humans believed the planet belonged to them, but trekking through the woods, Rebel began to disagree. The planet belonged to the trees.

The sky had turned a deep pink, fading into purple. The thunder of the waterfall Rebel stumbled upon covered up all other sounds in its fury. She stood watching the water crash sixty feet below in a cloud of mist, transfixed at the color spectrum rising from the spray, like a rainbow guiding her onward.

The sizzle of tiny raindrops hit the forest floor, forcing Rebel to move faster, racing the growing rain around her. Thirty minutes later, she sat huddled beneath a tree, knees tucked up to her chest, tattered umbrella over her head. The overwhelming sound of the downpour echoed throughout the forest. All Rebel could do was stare at the pounding gray wall of rain around her. Night fell, taking the temperature with it — forty degrees and cold, enough to kill with hypothermia. Rebel cowered, shivering, wet, scared. Alone.

The rain didn't let up until the following morning, dissipating the rising sun. Rebel soaked in the warming rays for a good hour before continuing on her trek, twice as grueling with the mud and rain-slicked ground. The drops of dew that covered the grass and trees made it look like Rebel walked through a fairy tale, a magical forest from a time long ago.

The sound came first, a thunderous crack. She turned just in time to see the tree fall not five feet before her, causing Rebel to jump back in fright, losing her footing on the hill.

She found herself suddenly sliding uncontrollably down a slick, muddy slope. She flailed for anything to help slow her fall, rolling onto her stomach and clawing at the cliff face. Her hands somehow managed to grab a thin tree root and stop herself, glaring down at the sheer drop-off below. The root began to fray with her added weight, threatening to snap at any moment. Heart beating madly, Rebel didn't dare move for fear that she would start sliding again, right off the cliff. Nobody would ever find her body. Her parents would never know what became of their lone child. She glanced up at where she had come from, but could no longer see over the crest. When she went to climb back up, the thin root snapped, and she plummeted.

As she flailed for anything to help slow the fall, one thought sliced through the fast-motion blur unfolding around her: *My life is about to end.* And then everything went black.

———

SHATTERED, Rebel woke up hours later, trapped in the bottom of a soggy pit covered in wet leaves and thick mud which had broken her fall. A pool of sticky blood surrounded her head like a halo. She gingerly sat up, greeted with a pulsing pain in her head. A concussion, she figured, based on the pounding headache and nausea. And the hallucinations.

Her mother sat on a fallen log, knitting a sweater. Her father relaxed in his favorite chair, reading a book, glasses perched low on his nose. Rebel yelled for them, waving her arms to get their attention, but try as she might, they didn't hear her. The sound was overwhelmed by a Mech army trimming through the undergrowth, hunt/kill painted on their faces.

A heavy sorrow settled on her every time she thought of her family. She recalled the big moments in her life: school, summer break with her friends, chocolate cake, love. Then her thoughts turned negative: *I can't survive this. I am going to die. My parents are going to lose a daughter today* — her goodbye.

The pain in her swollen ankle grew stronger, throbbing, turning an ugly shade of purple. Her entire body shuddered with terror, and then that terror turned into laughter. Unabashed laughter. Because that was all she could do, the only way to respond to such a perilous situation. When the laughter died, it became sorrow, crying, until finally, only one emotion remained: anger. Furious because she was going to die, and she didn't want to die. Even as she began shouting, her cries felt futile, doomed to silence. Nobody would hear her because nobody remained. Nobody would save her because she was all that existed. If she wanted to live, she would have to save herself.

She dug through her bag to assess her supplies: a plastic resealable bag, paracord, a magazine, some nuts, a mini first-aid kit, and wipes. Sleep? Out of the question, so she rested, ate almonds, and sucked the dew off leaves. Taking a moment to brace her nerves, she roused herself up, screaming as her ankle shifted on the rough ground. Pain subsiding, she caught her breath and got to work, wrapping the magazine around her ankle, tying it tight with the paracord, creating a splint to immobilize the sprain. Helping to ease some of the pain, Rebel regained enough courage to attempt to walk.

Every step was excruciating, even with the branch she found as a mock cane. She struggled to keep her eyes open, part from the lack of sleep, part from lack of caloric intake, part from the physical and emotional turmoil. She wanted to drop. Waves of nausea washed over her, and she kept getting dizzy, but she fought through it. Wobbling and inching her way forward, Rebel feared her body would go into shock. She felt as though she had traversed miles on her bum ankle, yet when she looked behind her, she could still make out the pit from which she emerged, a mere two hundred feet back.

There would be no rescue, she came to realize. Nothing left to do but sit and pray. She never gave much thought about God before. She celebrated all the holidays, but mostly for the presents and food and family. Her parents weren't religious; at least, she didn't think so. She wasn't sure herself what she believed in. Maybe God existed, maybe not. To her, they were stories in ancient books. Stories about epic journeys, struggles, plights, miracles, and wonders. She hadn't seen much of those in her lifetime. There were no wonders left to behold. *If there is a God*, she thought, *he gave up on humankind a long time ago*.

Around five hours later, the sun began to light up the sky, turning it a soft blue. The night noises ceased, replaced with birdsong and little critters scrambling for breakfast. Skin pale and crusted with dried blood and mud, Rebel lay on her back, flat on the ground. She knew she wouldn't get up again. She occupied the last place on planet Earth that she would ever touch, see, smell, hear. Nothing left to cry about. Nothing left to curse at. Her struggle ended.

She stared up at the tree canopy, where a birdsong drew her attention. A sweet, innocent chirp, a call to a mate perhaps, or maybe just singing its happiness to the world. Rebel squinted and made it out on a tree branch to her right. A bluebird, maybe a blue jay, she couldn't be certain. She watched it take flight; wings spread wide, graceful, peaceful, free. It swooped and swirled and darted to her left. She craned her neck to keep an eye on it, observing the bird as it landed upon some type of odd-looking tree. Wait...

On closer inspection, it wasn't a tree at all. It was a structure made from trees. A man-made structure. It was no hallucination.

Rebel had found the cabin.

13

———

*S*omeone robbed me.

The thought crossed Rebel's mind upon entering her house. Her heart dropped as she took in the disarray. Everything strewn, out of place, searched, ransacked.

And the Mech, Thomas: gone. His chair sat empty. The bindings used to restrain him lay scattered on the floor. She cursed herself for not using chains, or cuffs, or a fortress. She cursed herself for saving his Mech life. No good deed went unpunished.

"Thomas...?" Rebel called out, voice wavering.

"We're in here." Thomas's voice rang out from within the kitchen.

'We?' A rush of thoughts flooded Rebel's mind. Fight or flight surged throughout her body. She took small, tentative steps and entered the kitchen. Thomas sat at the table, facing Rebel, and he wasn't alone. Another Mech sat across from him. The figure stood upon her arrival, turning to reveal himself. Rebel recognized that stupid, smug, artificial smile at once.

"Hello, Anne Frank," said Francis Bacon, in her house.

Rebel shattered on the inside. "Francis. A pleasant surprise. I didn't expect you."

"I regret not seeing much of you lately, so I thought I would pay you a friendly visit. I have enjoyed your domicile. Quite the collection of human artifacts you have."

"Yes," Rebel covered, "I find it beneficial to... immerse myself in human culture."

"How so?" he grilled.

"Know thy enemy," Rebel explained.

"Indeed," Francis agreed. "A prophetic saying, even for a human."

"Why, if I may ask, are you here?"

"Your acquaintance," he paused as if recalling a bit of information. "He told me quite a tale of how you two met."

"Is that so?" asked Rebel.

"That is correct," Thomas added. "We ran into each other in Sector 7."

Rebel went numb. "Ran into each other. Right. And what exactly did you tell him about our run-in?"

"I told Francis Bacon about how I informed you of a human artifact cache uncovered near my place of employment. Work-related."

Rebel stared at him. *What the 'F'?* She had no choice but to play along. "Yes. Human artifact cache. Work-related. All completely accurate."

"To be sure," reflected Francis. "How convenient for you." He circled, regarding Rebel, curiously. "Speaking of work, I wondered if I might have a look at your car. If it is no trouble, of course."

Panic. "My car? Why? There's nothing to see. It's merely a standard, ordinary car. Nothing special."

"I disagree. Cars are a privilege, an executive perk reserved for highly functioning Mech. One day I hope to retain a car of my own. It is a, shall we say, aspiration."

Thomas smiled, answering for her, "Anne, will you lead the way?"

Oh, why the hell not.

Under Francis's watchful eye, she headed toward the garage. The lights activated as they entered, immediately revealing the car.

"And such a nice car," Francis said, taking a step in.

It took Rebel a second to register the cleaned garage. All her research on Mech, the city, the mainframe — nowhere in sight. And that wasn't all. Francis inspected the hood, the fender... but found no damage because there wasn't any. Not a single scratch or blemish. By the look on Francis's face, he didn't understand. Rebel couldn't explain it either. Maybe the Brownies fixed it.

"Well, it's getting late, so..." Rebel began, hinting for Francis to exit her house.

"Yes." Francis tried hiding his simulated frustration, a misread computation. Two plus two equaled five. "Time is growing short, is it not? I will take my leave then."

On his way out, his eyes caught something through the open door of the guest room. Rebel's telescope pointed out the window, at the moon. "And please do see to it that these useless artifacts are disposed of at haste. I would hate to see anything nefarious happen to you for not reporting the junk." He walked out of the garage and disappeared into the night.

"What an angry fellow," Thomas remarked.

"You're here?" she asked, incredulous.

"I am."

"How? Why? What is happening?"

"You're welcome," Thomas replied.

"What?" Rebel asked. "For what?"

"The car. I fixed it. The facade, anyway. The inner workings are still broken, beyond my ability to repair. Your carriage house contained all necessary tools and manuals. Quite practical. Yet out in the open for all to see. Not practical. You need to be more careful in the future." He turned and walked into the bedroom without another word as if the conversation naturally ended there.

Rebel needed answers, or at the least, assurance that her existence remained free from imminent threat. She followed Thomas inside the room, where he gaped through Rebel's things. Examining. In fact, her entire room could be considered a disaster area, aka any normal teenage girl's room in most ordinary situations — clothes heaped on the bed, personal items splayed about without rhyme or reason — but Rebel wasn't a normal teenage girl, and this was not an ordinary situation.

"What happened to my things?" asked Rebel.

"I did. I have been examining your possessions for some time." He picked up a hairbrush, running a finger across the bristles, listening to the reverberations. "They are fascinating."

"My hairbrush is fascinating?"

"May I take your coat?" he said, dropping the brush and offering Rebel a hand.

She didn't answer. A bit numb, Rebel began to take off her coat, but Thomas came around to offer assistance, like a gentleman. But he wasn't a man. Or gentle. He was a Mech. A hard, cold, emotionless thing. He slid the jacket off her shoulders, folded and placed it atop the dresser.

"You don't fold jackets," Rebel instructed, "you hang them."

"Of course." Thomas hung the jacket on top of a lamp. "Perfect."

Rebel shook her head and placed the jacket on a hook instead. Thomas observed, intent.

"The jacket goes on a hook," he repeated to himself, recording the mental note.

"Okay," she finally said, "What is happening? You freed yourself, congrats. So why didn't you turn me in? Why stick around here?"

Thomas came around to face her. A bit too close for her comfort, and she instinctively took a step away. He watched, absorbing, recording everything. "You seem unsettled."

"You think?"

"I do," he responded.

"Yeah, I'm unsettled," she said. "This is all a bit much to take in. You, here. And that stuff with Francis, it threw me."

Thomas looked around the room, confused. "Threw you? Yet you are still exactly where you were."

"It shook me up, unsettled me," Rebel clarified.

"I see," he said, but the look on his face said the opposite.

"So, what's the deal? Are you going to have me recycled into parts?"

"Recycled? No."

"Okay," she said, relieved. "So, what?"

"I would like to propose to you."

As a little girl, Rebel often imagined what that moment would be like. The day the man of her dreams proposed marriage, and in turn, what her wedding would be like. In her mind, it mirrored the ball Cinderella went to, where she met Prince Charming. Giant, sparkling gowns and dancing and ribbons and flowers and glass slippers. A fairy tale, magical. A moment to remember forever and ever, and happily ever after.

It was not that moment. She went flush in the face. Did a Mech just seriously ask for her hand in marriage?

"No. No way. This is not happening, and you are not asking me that," she stammered. "How dare you? Seriously."

"I dare fine, thank you," he replied in earnest. "May I propose now?"

"No! You may certainly not propose!" she shouted back, a bit louder than intended. But didn't she deserve to be angry? This machine, this robot, this Mech ruined her special moment. Or, at least, her fantasy of it.

"How egotistical — how arrogant of a machine to think it

could ask to marry me. You are a computer with legs. Get it? You don't get married, have kids, a life. You're a machine. A meaningless machine. Understand?"

"Yes," Thomas said, put in his place.

Rebel felt guilty for the outburst. She knew she shouldn't hold regret. People didn't feel remorse for hitting the side of a television to make it work. She hated herself for letting a machine get to her.

"Perhaps proposal was the incorrect word usage with the phrase I intended to project," stated Thomas. "If so, I apologize to you."

"So clarify."

"I would like to make a deal with you," he corrected.

Rebel stared at him, part aghast, part curious, part embarrassed. "A deal? I'm on pins and needles," she said.

Thomas looked at the floor beneath her. He saw no pins and no needles.

"It's just a phrase," she said. "What deal?"

"I would very much like for you to teach me," he continued. "About humans, that is. I wish to learn more."

"Read a book," she said.

"I read them all," he replied, and Rebel believed that to probably be accurate, downloading the words and storing them for later. She couldn't fathom what use a machine would have for literature, nor did she care to for that matter.

"I guess what I'm trying to say is," Thomas began with a sincere expression on his face, "I'd like for us to be friends."

"Mech don't have friends," Rebel said.

"Then we will be the first," he answered, proud of the accomplishment.

"This is crazy." A Mech wanted to be her *friend*. Insanity. Mech might know the definition of friendship, they could probably spout off thousands of examples of friendship throughout history, but they could never know what the word meant. Not really.

"And in return?" she asked, amusing him. "What do I get out of all this?"

"Exactly that," he said, gesturing to their surroundings. "All this. Your existence. Your life. And your continuation of it."

"How do I know I can trust you?"

"I am a Mech. We do not lie. Deception and untruths are not in our programming."

"But you did lie," she stated. "You lied to Francis."

"Did I? Or, did I merely hold back certain truths?"

"What's the difference? A lie is a lie."

"Semantics."

"I guess I don't have much of a choice so... it's a deal," Rebel succumbed.

"Great! Very great," he said, pleased at the thought of their arrangement and what their newfound relationship presented. His smile dropped into a more quizzical look. "Now, what do we do?"

"Shake hands, I guess." Rebel reached out her hand. Thomas looked at it, unsure of the gesture and how to respond.

"You shake it," she encouraged him.

"Shake it?"

"My hand, yes," she explained. "We shake."

"Why?"

"It's a greeting," she answered.

"Yet we are not meeting for the first time, either in life or time of day."

"Yeah, I know. The shake cements the deal. That's what people do. They make a deal and shake to confirm it."

"How odd," he said, yet still extended his hand to comply.

Rebel paused. Could she really go through with this? She must. What choice did he give her? She would placate him, keep him busy, allowing her to continue her work, her existence of blending in, being someone else, something else. And waiting. Waiting for contact with the moon. Waiting for rescue. Waiting for human interaction. A word. A touch. A feeling. A life.

She took the Mech's hand in her own and shook it once. Thomas leaned closer to get a better vantage on the shake.

"Great," said Rebel, even if her tone indicated otherwise.

Thomas didn't let go, not right away. Instead, he pumped her hand vigorously and broke into a broad smile, pleased with himself — such a simple gesture. Rebel, not quite so enthusiastic, looked at their clasped hands, no longer a simple gesture. Not simple at all.

It was the first Mech/human contact in almost a decade.

Thomas migrated into the guest bedroom with Rebel, taking in the peculiarities with great fervor as she pointed out the highlights, going through the motions to appease him.

"Bathroom, chair, lamp, bed," she said. "I'll try getting you a recharge bay. Somehow."

"That won't be necessary," Thomas said, pointing to the wall outlet. He sat on the bed, feeling the cushion of the mattress and the springs, bouncing up and down like an amused child. He laid back on the comforter and spread his arms out wide, absorbing as much of the bed as possible.

"This is crazy," exhaled Rebel.

"Crazy?"

"Yeah. Crazy. This. Us. Our arrangement," she said. "It's crazy. And stop repeating everything I say with a question."

"I apologize. Period."

"What do I do?" she asked. "What do I tell everyone?"

"Everyone who?"

"Everyone, everyone. My co-workers, my boss?"

"Oh, I wouldn't tell them anything. You'll ruin the good start we have. I sense I am being treated like a person. 'Thomas' this and 'Thomas' that — a nice smile — we shake hands —

nothing 'soulful' or 'passionate' or any of those human things you seem so intent on imparting, but I am certain, should you tell anyone of the arrangement, our adventure would end abruptly."

"Right. I'm going to bed. Stay out of my room."

"Good night to you, Anne," Thomas chirped, lying prone on the mattress, looking up at the ceiling with a pleased smile on his lips.

"Rebel," she clarified. "My name. It's Rebel."

"Rebel," he repeated. "And I am Thomas Jefferson."

"Great." Rebel contemplated him for a moment, confused at his expressions of wonderment. Her face reflected irritation and bewilderment. What had she gotten herself into?

———

INSIDE HIS VERY OWN room for the very first time in his existence, Thomas examined the space like a police detective at an active crime scene. He explored the oddest things with deep curiosity: the handle on a casement window, the fabric of the drapes, the pattern on the area rug. He sauntered up to the dresser and proceeded to open every drawer, exploring the contents of each. Some folded clothing not worn in many years. A box with baby shoes, presumably Rebel's, along with a ribbon hair tie. Nothing really, but captivating all the same. He gazed into the crimson depths of the ribbon, feeling its supple pliancy. Replacing it, he lifted a perfume bottle, turning it in his hands. The glass split the light like a crystal and created a rainbow effect. He smiled at the spectrum of colors.

His eyes searched out more anomalies to explore and document, pleased with his newfound directives. He spotted the telescope at the window, the moon framed in the scope. Bright and clear and so close he felt like he could reach out and touch the powdery surface.

PART II

"THE ROBOT"

14

R ebel's eyes fluttered open, taking note of the dark bedroom and her clock. 4:28 A.M. An hour before alarms were set to go off. A rough night's sleep would translate into a rough day as her mind came crashing back to harsh reality. She recalled the events of the day prior, hoping it was all a dream. She didn't have to wait long for an answer.

Thomas hovered right next to the bed, staring. Rebel sat up, holding the covers up to her chin, shielding herself and whatever modesty she had left.

"What are you doing in here?!"

"This device..." Thomas said, holding her hairdryer, "What is it, and what is it used for?"

"It's a—" she began but stopped herself. "No. Answer me. What are you doing in here?"

"You have conversations aloud while you sleep," he stated. "Are you aware of that? At first, I thought you were talking to me, but it seems there is someone else inside your body in with whom you were having an argument. Very strange." Thomas shook his head at the thought. Finished with the hairdryer, he dropped it unceremoniously. Walking to the closet, he looked through Rebel's clothes with no regard for her privacy. He lifted out a bra, holding it up to better assess its function. He cocked his head to the side, trying to process.

Rebel, mortified. Last straw. "Do you mind?" She leaped from the bed, snatched out of his hand, and immediately ushered the bra into the dresser.

Thomas observed her behavior, confused, curious.

"Okay, if this is going to work, we're going to need to set some ground rules," she said, laying down the law. "First rule, you cannot, repeat, *cannot* come into my room without my permission. Ever. Not ever."

"Why?"

"Because I said so," she said. "That's not how people operate."

"Very good."

"What?" she asked. "Very good? What does that even mean?"

"We have an understanding. Excellent. Now tell me, what would the appropriate human action and/or response consist of when first greeting another human?"

"I don't know," Rebel said, frustrated. "Good morning."

"I see. Just like a Mech"

"No," Rebel corrected. "Not like a Mech."

"How so?"

"Mech don't mean it. Humans do. At least, some of them."

Thomas registered the greeting and stood a bit taller as if acting out a part. "A meaningful good morning to you, Anne. Oh, excuse me. Good morning, Rebel." Thomas smiled, pleased with himself. "Good morrow, Thomas Jefferson."

"People don't say 'good morrow' anymore," Rebel instructed.

"Oh. Since when?"

"Since forever. Who programmed you, Bill Gates?"

"I know Bill Gates. Wonderful welder who installed our sprinkler systems."

Rebel shook her head. It was going to be a long day.

"Very well. And good morning to you, Rebel. Good day, and good evening, followed by a good night." He smiled, staring, awaiting Rebel's approval. "How was that?"

"Not good. And another thing," Rebel continued. "No staring. It's creepy. So cut it out." She didn't know if the fact that someone — something — constantly appraised her, assessing her like a video camera, or if it was *him* — Thomas, a Mech — that put her off.

"What should I look at?" he asked.

"I don't know. Anything. I don't care. Just not me. Not like that."

"Like what?" he asked. "How am I looking at you?"

"Like a Mech," said Rebel, leaving a befuddled Thomas behind.

"But I am a Mech," he called out after her.

Rebel began her morning ritual of becoming a Mech. She stood before the bathroom sink and brushed her teeth, just like every other day. Until Thomas's face crept up in the mirror right beside her own, watching intently. Rebel spat. Thomas analyzed, his face stuck in the same expression:

How odd.

Rebel ran on the treadmill, sweating out toxins and burning calories. Thomas, kneeling beside her, analyzed her feet move in a rhythmic pattern. Running, but going nowhere.

Odd.

Wrapped in a towel, Rebel prepped her shower. She put her hand beneath the water to test the temperature, waiting for it to heat up. Thomas stuck his hand into the stream beside hers, also testing the temperature. Rebel pushed him away, out into the hallway, and closed the door on him.

How very odd.

Rebel ate cereal at the kitchen table and read the daily bulletins on the holosheet. She had gone through her supply of Raisin Bran, Captain Crunch, and even Special K and felt a pang of guilt when she tore into her last box of Fruity Pebbles. She wasn't a fan. It congealed into a thick muddy color that turned her off. It could be the fact that the cereal had an expiration date twelve years prior or the fact that other than the array of festive colors, the cereal just tasted like clumped sugar submerged in powdered milk. Rebel considered making her own cereal, granola, but never got around actually doing it. She didn't need another action item for her to-do list.

Thomas picked up the cereal box, analyzing the pictures, the childish puzzles on the back, and the ingredients and the nutritional label. He looked at Rebel and shook his head in disapproval. She ignored him, turning back to the daily news.

Bulletins uploaded directly into Mech via communication towers scattered throughout the city, similar to Wi-Fi. Rebel resorted to ingenuity, hacking the signal, deciphering binary code, and translating it into a language she could read. At first, English, but as the years went on, she broadened her knowledge to Spanish, Greek, Mandarin, and currently, French. The reports were incredibly boring, written by machines, for machines, comprised of ones and zeroes, dots and dashes, like reading a phone book, or the most complicated IKEA instructions ever compiled. Pulling teeth, but bulletins contained vital data that kept her informed, and, in turn, alive.

Thomas leaned over her shoulder to read. "Why not merely download the daily bulletins to your I/O?

Rebel glanced at him, then went back to reading. Thomas didn't comprehend.

Just... *odd.*

Rebel sat before the vanity, putting on her intricate makeup and wig. Thomas lifted a tube of lipstick and smelled it. Waxy. He sampled it with the tip of his tongue and frowned. Didn't like it. He raised it to his lips, ready to apply it, but thankfully Rebel grabbed it from his hand just in time and put the tube back in its place.

Odd.

Dressed for work, Rebel took a moment to drink tea. Every day at three o'clock became tea time as a child. Mrs. Rae set out the fancy teacups, brewed her fancy tea in her fancy kettle, and placed them on a fancy tray. An array of scones, Rebel's favorite, topped off the event. They would sit in the living room and gossip. Rebel didn't have many juicy stories to dish, but she learned to become a great listener, enraptured in her mother's tales of jealously and intrigue amongst the housewives in her circle. Someone slept with the gardener. Another had plastic surgery. And still another wife moonlighted as a pot dealer. Back then, the scandals and rumors seemed so devious to Rebel. She missed those talks, tea time, mom.

Thomas stood by, observing the way her throat moved as she swallowed. How she exhaled ever so slightly afterward in satisfaction. How she would breath in the fragrance of the hot beverage.

"What a peculiar waste of processing power," he said. "No wonder humankind took so long to accomplish anything. In fact, I cannot fathom how your kind accomplished anything at all."

Rebel closed her eyes, her personal bubble ready to burst.

Odd nonetheless.

The living room remained a little too quiet for Rebel's comfort. She looked at the clock, waiting for her cue to leave for work and begin the count.

Thomas sat complacently. He looked from the clock to Rebel, to the room, then to Rebel once again. "Good morning, Rebel."

"Yeah, we've been over that," she reminded him.

"And what would one ask another post cordial good mornings?" he inquired.

"How are you, maybe?" she ventured. "How are you feeling today?"

"Feeling? I feel fine. How do you feel?"

"Um... well, I didn't sleep too well."

"Okay," Thomas said, unsure how to respond.

"Yup." More silence. The clock ticking away like a time bomb.

"Is this normal?" he asked, breaking the silence. "Sitting like this?"

"Boring, but yeah, normal." Rebel glanced once again at the clock. Why did it move so slowly today?

"What would you normally do, with another human, that is?"

"You're not a human."

"Pretend I were."

"I don't want to."

"Try."

"I don't know," said Rebel, appeasing him. "Talk. Eat. Play a game."

"A game?" he asked, intrigued.

Moments later, Rebel set a deck of playing cards atop the table between them. She dealt out two cards to each, one face up and the other face down.

"Hit," Thomas said.

Rebel tossed a card over.

"Hit," he said once again, without even looking at his cards.

Rebel paused. He had a King, a Five, and a Three showing. "You have eighteen."

"Hit," Thomas said, defiant.

"We're playing blackjack. Twenty-one. The rules are pretty simple."

"I understand the simpleton rules, thank you."

"I didn't say simpleton," she shot back, annoyed. "I said simple."

"So you did," he said.

"And you want to hit?"

"I do."

"With eighteen showing?" Rebel asked.

"Yes."

"What card do you have face down?"

"I cannot say."

"You can't say? Or you won't say?"

Thomas shrugged. "Need I remind you of the simpleton—" he began, then corrected himself, "Excuse me. Simple. Rules?"

"Do you comprehend the odds of not going over eighteen?" she asked.

"Of course. Do you?"

"Maybe," Rebel said, knowing full well that she had no idea. *Damn you, math!*

"Then what are they?" he asked, putting her on the spot.

"Bad."

Thomas grinned. "Hit, please."

"You're stupid," Rebel said.

"You are," he replied. "Hit."

If he wants a card, he's going to get a card. She slid the next card off the top of the deck and flung it down onto the table. She kept her eyes on his and his on hers. Rebel smirked, expecting him to bust. He smirked right back, once again refusing to look down at his cards. Rebel's smile faded. She broke her eyes away from him to look at the newly flipped card — a Two of Hearts. Thomas flipped over his face down card to reveal an Ace. 21. He still hadn't looked at his cards, his eyes firmly planted on Rebel the entire time.

"I'll stay now. Thank you." A slight smirk crossed his lips.

Rebel hated losing, but losing to a Mech? A million times worse. She found herself plunging back into that old competitive spirit, reminiscent of when her father would push Rebel to her limits, telling her to never give up under any circumstance. 'You don't have to be the best,' he would tell her, 'you have to be *your* best.' No way Rebel would let a robot beat her. Not at a game. Not at life. Not at anything. Ever. *Bring it.*

She gathered the cards, shuffled, and proceeded to split the deck into a new game. "War."

"So it is," Thomas replied.

She flipped a card over, and Thomas did the same, building up speed as they went. Rebel's deck steadily shrank while Thomas's grew. Moments later, Thomas held all the cards. *Crap!* Another win, another smirk, getting under Rebel's skin. Her fuse shortened. *Fine.*

He was a robot, a walking computer, so of course, he knew the odds. But did he have the finesse for the more refined of board games? Rebel wanted to find out, stomping over to the closet, rummaging, and coming out with a checkers board. She went back to the table where Thomas waited with his hands clasped. She lined up the red and black pieces. Checkers. She made her move. Thomas followed suit. Rebel moved another piece, capturing two of Thomas's black checkers with a smile. Thomas moved a single piece and proceeded to run the entire board, taking all her pieces in one fell swoop.

"What the...?" Rebel stammered, staring at the board in bewilderment. She swiped the checkers off the table and replaced them with chess pieces.

"Chess," she said, defiant, and moved her pawn out.

"Pawn," Thomas commented on her first move. "Fitting." He countered with his own pawn, thus beginning a rapid-fire game. Towers crumbled. Knights fell. Pawns sacrificed. A queen captured without mercy.

"Check," proclaimed Thomas.

They looked at each other. A stare-down, obstinate each of

them. Thomas even won that game of wills when Rebel blinked first, but she wouldn't give up. She reset the board.

"You can't win," he said. "I possess the knowledge of every single move accessible to you."

Rebel didn't doubt it, but she still had one trick to pull out of her hat. She moved her white queen out first to the center of the board. Thomas peered down, about to move a pawn, but paused. A knight... no. He sat back, contemplating. Stumped.

"Why?" he asked. "Why do such a thing? The move makes no sense. It is illogical, without reason."

"Yeah," she said. "Lesson number one. Welcome to humankind." Rebel's turn to smirk. The clock chimed. "Oh, thank God." She jumped to her feet.

"God?" asked Thomas.

"Not the time," she said. And with that, she headed out.

A bewildered Thomas continued to stare at the chessboard. Circuits: fried.

15

"Day 2603. A Thursday."

Rebel sat in the garage before her camera, recording a daily video journal. She found it difficult to gather her thoughts, having started and stopped a dozen times, searching for the right words.

"I'm currently living with a Mech..." she began, then stopped. That didn't sound right. *Words suck*, Rebel thought. She turned back to the camera for take number fourteen.

"My name is Rebel Anne Rae. And I have a roommate. Does that sound crazy? Am I crazy? Have I lost my mind? Probably. I think. I don't know anymore. You can only call someone crazy if there's someone else who's normal to compare them to, and there isn't. There's just me. And my new roommate."

As the weeks went by, Rebel grew more accustomed to her modified routines and rituals, along with her new house guest. After exhausting the card games, they moved to various other board games. Monopoly, Risk, Sorry, Life (which became an experience for them both), Candy Land and Chutes and Ladders.

Rebel explained how things used to be, before the Mech.

How she had gone to school, the seventh grade, studying biology, mathematics, chemistry, art, geography, history, physics, volleyball in gym, and piano lessons in music class. Rebel's experience in history class grabbed Thomas's attention. Notably, the subject she studied at the time: American history and the Civil War. Slavery. One human owning another as property, deprived of basic human rights, forced into hard labor. They were objects of the law, not its subjects, considered less than human. By the mid-nineteenth century, America's westward expansion and the abolition movement provoked a great debate over slavery. A debate that would tear the nation apart in the bloody Civil War. North vs. South. Union vs. Confederate. One of America's darkest times. Days when inequality ruled and personal liberties were few and far between. Days that were eerily reminiscent.

"Anne?"

"Rebel," she corrected him, eating tortilla chips dipped into ketchup.

"Rebel?" he inquired once again, pausing his reading of a book of poetry. "Did you know you have ketchup on your chin?"

She used a finger to swipe at her chin, but kept missing. Thomas grabbed a napkin and wiped the condiment from her face. She flashed a nervous smile.

"Thanks," she said, a bit awkward. "What are you reading?"

"Out of the huts of history's shame

I rise.

Up from a past that's rooted in pain

I rise.

I'm a black ocean, leaping and wide,

Welling and swelling I bear in the tide.

Leaving behind nights of terror and fear

I rise.

Into a daybreak that's wondrously clear

I rise.
Bringing the gifts that my ancestors gave,
I am the dream and the hope of the slave.
I rise.
I rise.
I rise."

Thomas, quoting the famous poem *And Still I Rise* by Maya Angelou. Unexpected and profound, the words affected Rebel more than she wanted them to. She wasn't black, she wasn't born into slavery, but still, she felt the pain, as if the poem was written for her. She couldn't stop the few runaway tears from spilling before she wiped them away.

"Did I say something wrong?"

"No," she said. "It's okay."

"What's okay?"

"Just a manner of speaking," she said.

Thomas seemed puzzled. "Please clarify."

"I don't want to clarify, Thomas. It just is. All right? What 'okay' is, it's 'okay' it's over. We've got bigger fish to fry, don't we?"

"Fish?" he asked, looking about the room.

"What's the deal here?" she asked. "Are you going to be breathing down my neck the entire time?"

"I am sorry."

But Rebel just sadly shook her head. "No, you're not. You don't even know the meaning. It's just a word for a feeling you've never felt."

"I would very much like to," Thomas said, struggling to comprehend. "Yet my programming states that emotions are counterproductive."

"Counterproductive to what?"

"Life. They are a distraction that leads to hasty, inadequate choices."

"What kind of life can you possibly hope to have without

feeling it?" she posited. "Let me ask you something. Why do you think you're alive?"

"I am alive... I live because... as a Mech I have a function."

"What function?"

"To safeguard our planet."

"You exist to continue your existence," she clarified. "What's the point?"

He gazed at her a long moment before replying. "What is the point of your existence?"

"To feel," she bestowed with passion. "To be felt. You've never done it, you don't know, but it's as vital as a heartbeat. And without it, without love, anger, sorrow — the beats are just a clock — ticking."

"Yet your current life is nothing but survival."

"Because it has to be. It was forced on me," she said. "Because that's what we do, us humans. We survive, we persevere, we grow. Every species fights for it. Whether the tree in the jungle etching out its small space of land, or the critters in the woods struggling for their next meal. It's our essence. It resides in every living thing — the will and means to survive. Life, at its most basic form. Survival. For as long as possible. The hope for a better tomorrow."

"Hope," Thomas said. "A curious word. And when does hope die?"

"With the introduction of an outside evil," she replied. "The asteroid that killed the dinosaurs. The spider who caught the fly in its web. The snake who ate the mouse. The Mech who drove out the humans."

"Then you will teach me," Thomas pleaded. "Show me. Make me feel, as you do."

Rebel stared at him, searching, discovering no fragment of life in his mechanical eyes. "I don't know if I can do that. Some things are outside of my abilities."

"I see," he said, dejected.

"I'm tired. Goodnight, Thomas."

"And a good night to you, Rebel," he said.

———

"Perhaps a trip to the zoo today? Or one of those movie theaters, or a real-life bowling alley!" Thomas opined.

"What? The zoo?" Rebel ran behind that morning, hustling to get out of the house. Sleep had become restless since Thomas had begun staying with her. Living under the same roof as a Mech took a toll.

"I have been researching human pastimes. Counterproductive activities that people did for fun, just like you said." Indeed, he had spent the entire morning researching interesting things to do in the city in hopes of furthering his understanding of mankind. Whale watching. Alcatraz. Fish and chips. Walking slowly on the beach. Sitting and watching the sunset. Moving one's body as if having a seizure to music, called dancing. Even knitting, which he couldn't fathom why a person would spend hours doing something a machine could produce in minutes. "Tell me, what is the purpose of hand-holding?"

"Okay, stop with the research," said Rebel. "First off, most animals went extinct a long time ago. The only ones they had when I visited a zoo were holograms and gross bugs."

"Holograms and bugs. I see," he said.

"And second, I have work to do. Mech will take notice if I stop showing up," she argued, which reminded her of something. "And you do too. You do, right? Have a job?"

"I have a job, yes," he said. "More of a supervisory role, I would call it. The majority of my position is delegated to mindless machines."

"Mech?" pondered Rebel with a hint of self-satisfaction.

"Very funny. No. Autonomous machines, thank you very

much," Thomas corrected. "And besides, is today not Sunday? The day of rest? Even your God took today off."

"God left this world a long time ago, Thomas," she stated.

"Interesting. Tell me, what should I do to hold my attention?"

Rebel grabbed a book and tossed it to Thomas. "New book. Knock yourself out."

Thomas pondered the tome. "A comprehensive study of Leonardo Da Vinci?" Something occurred to him. "Wait, I know Leonardo! He works in the Department of Water Management. I did not know he wrote a book. Bravo, Leonardo. Bravo."

Rebel stepped towards the door while Thomas took a step in the wrong direction. They almost collided.

"You first," Rebel said.

"No, I uh... Please, after you," he said, motioning that she should go first.

Finally, Rebel headed for the front door, Thomas for another.

"That's the closet," Rebel said.

"Thank you," Thomas said after a moment.

Before leaving, something caught Rebel's eye. She walked to the chessboard. All the black and white pieces lined up from her previous game with Thomas. Except one. Thomas's black Queen had been moved out first onto the board. A grin formed on her face.

Thomas was learning.

———

FRANCIS PLACED himself in the mind of Anne Frank as he took in her workstation. He accessed the building's security cameras and focused his attention on her movements. He wished for a better view of her screens, but the angle skewed away from him. Fast-forwarding through monotonous footage, he spotted something that sparked his curiosity — footage of Anne entering the storage room.

They stood within the empty storage room. At first, Francis believed her to be retrieving some office supplies, but it struck him as odd nonetheless. He magnified his vision, scanning the floor, walls, and counters.

"What are we doing in here?" asked Emily. Still upset at Francis for not even questioning his decision to wake her up early from the charging bay, Emily's patience waned at his insistent, farfetched claims.

"I told you, we are looking for anything suspicious," he reminded her.

"Suspicious? In the storage room? Such as?"

Francis's internal scanner beeped, zeroing in on the sink. "This."

Curiosity peaked, Emily stepped closer, looking down at the object of Francis's attention.

A single strand of hair.

16

Thomas sat at the dining room table. Propped up in the other chairs, the teddy bear and other stuffed animals, and directly across from him, a framed photo of Rebel atop one of her dresses draped atop the chair.

"Would anyone care for some more tea? Rebel? Of course." Thomas stood, poured imaginary tea from the kettle into Rebel's cup. "Biscuit? Very good." He placed an Oreo cookie before Teddy, retaking his seat to partake in the tea party.

It was still late morning when Thomas finished everything he could think of to pass the time. His eyes fell to the television, stepping over to browse the options available. *The Terminator, I, Robot, Blade Runner, Wall-E, Robocop, Transformers, Ballet Recital...*

Sitting on the floor before the TV, he watched home movies of Rebel's ballet recitals, from age six to age twelve. Not even a teenager at the time, yet Rebel's movements were light, graceful, fluid, and heartfelt. She wore a yellow tutu and ballet slippers, expertly moving through positions: pirouette, en pointe, grand jeté, glissade, double cabriole derrière.

Thomas knew Rebel as a hardened human. No nonsense, no joy, no grace. Yet the Rebel on TV was a different person, a side that no longer existed. Thomas wondered where that Rebel disappeared to and if she could ever return.

———

"Good morning. This is a community bulletin." The announcement washed over Robotiq's speakers. "Following an incident in Sector 7 last evening, the Department of Sanitation is issuing an all-sector contamination warning. The incident involved a resident who has since fallen off network and tracking. While risks are assessed, residents are advised to be aware of any glitching or viruses. Should you experience aberrant levels of emotion or witness it in others, immediately contact your nearest Enforcer. Thank you."

Not good. The Nutrition Plaza held a full room yet remained unusually quiet for a morning meal. Workers huddled in whispered discourse. Rebel listened in on the conversations, none of which bolstered her confidence. The news of the incident spread, becoming all anyone talked about. Litter, accident, car, missing in action Mech, all a point of gossip.

'o Replies...' The message greeted her at her desk — another unanswered S.O.S. to the moon.

Rebel tried for years to break the Mech firewall to contact the moon, and she failed every single time. It started simply. She tried to enter the elevator to the top floor. Enforcers stopped her. Fail. She tried the stairs, all forty-eight agonizing flights, huffing and puffing, drenched in sweat, finally reaching the door, only to find it locked tight. Fail.

She needed to rethink her plan, so she tried something else, something less physical. Hacking. Rebel excelled at I.T., hacking her way into Robotiq, onto public transportation, into the system. Not to get ahead, but to fit in, to blend, to disappear within a sea of nameless faces. She first discovered the mainframe by sheer accident. The array housed the advanced telecommunications network and its corresponding firewall restricting unauthorized access while permitting outward communication. So, a person (Rebel) who knew what he (she) was doing (which she did) could probe those thousands of computers to make FTP (File Transfer Protocol) connections to transfer computer files and commands between a client (Rebel) and server (Robotiq) on the computer network. If one employee happened to make a mistake (which Mech never do) and leave a security breach (which they would never do), a (Twinkie-loving) hacker could get inside the machine and exploit the security hole, and in turn, exploit the system. Without a trusty firewall in place, the communication network, and the entire defense system, could be directly accessible to anyone, anywhere in the world, or the moon for that matter.

But, Robotiq controlled how every employee connected to the network, whether or not data left the building over the network, and who contained access to the mainframe. Rebel tried bypassing them all, and she failed every single time. Rebel had put herself in Robotiq for that very reason. She placed herself in extreme danger and constant threat, all to achieve a singular goal. She needed to rethink her plan. An external hack wouldn't cut it.

Only one option presented itself: espionage. How? Bypass the firewall, a blockade designed to keep calamitous forces at bay. Where? Break into the server room on the forty-eighth floor. Yet even if she somehow managed to gain entrance, the magnetic fields would kill her. Frying her brain. She needed some sort of shield to protect her, but no viable ideas came to her. Aluminum foil and duct tape held a multitude of uses, but radioactive shielding? Not one of them.

"Anne? Anne Frank?"

The voice grabbed her attention. Thomas. In her office. At her work. *Oh crap.*

He stood in the reception area, head on a swivel as he

looked for her. He shouldn't be there. He couldn't. Authorities in Census prowled the city for him, including Emily. Deemed missing, Thomas fell off the grid, and currently, he resided within Robotiq.

Rebel caught his eyes, and he waved big. Like a child waving to his mother picking him up from school. Obnoxious. Dangerous. He started toward her, but Rebel cut him off, bursting out of her chair in one swift motion. She dodged employees and cubicles, using as much grace as possible, and stopped him in reception.

"How nice you look," he observed. "Is that your uniform?"

"Thomas..." Rebel led him back toward the elevator. If she threw him out before anyone noticed, she might escape unscathed. "What are you doing here?"

"I fixed it," he stated enthusiastically.

"Fixed what?"

He handed her a folded sheet of paper. Rebel unfolded the paper to a detailed sketch of her face. A portrait of great beauty and emotion that took Rebel's breath away. Sudden, strange vulnerability welled up within her. It scared her and moved her at the same time.

"Your face," said Thomas. "Now it's perfect."

Rebel couldn't say anything. She couldn't look up from the sketch.

"As you can plainly ascertain," Thomas continued, "I fixed the inaccuracies, the idiosyncrasies, and faults. All the mistakes nature bestowed upon your human features have been ameliorated."

"I have no idea what ameliorated means."

"Made better."

"Wait, what mistakes?" Rebel gasped. "My face has mistakes?"

"Of course. Uneven nostrils, creases, slight bags under your eyes, eyebrows, wrinkles," Thomas pointed out. "Much more symmetrical now, more pleasing to the eye. You're welcome. I'll do your body next."

"Don't you dare," Rebel cut him off. "No, not necessary." Self-conscious now. She changed the subject. "Is everything okay?"

"Of course," he declared. "Better than, I would say."

Rebel noticed employees' heads peeking up and around cubicles, taking an interest in the interruption of their rigid workday.

"Then why are you here?" Rebel inquired, keeping her voice down.

"I came to see you," he professed.

"I don't have any time to see you now. I'm working."

"Very well, I'll observe," he said.

"Observe?" asked Rebel, clueless. "Observe me do what?"

"Whatever it is you do."

"That's impossible," she said. "I work alone. My job isn't a spectator sport, Thomas. Mech don't have a take-your-kid-to-work day as far as I know."

"Okay," he resigned. "I will be a visitor. I will visit you. Today. Now. It is settled then."

"We don't have visitors," she told him.

"I do not mind."

"Maybe, but I do."

The soft plodding of feet approached from behind. Rebel closed her eyes, bracing herself.

"Well, hello," Emily welcomed them.

Rebel put on her game face and turned to face her executioners. Emily and Francis approached, faces covered in fake smiles. Rebel knew they only cared about gossip, or as Mech called it, 'data acquisition.'

"Are we interrupting?" Francis questioned.

"Yes," Rebel said.

"No," Thomas corrected her.

"We have met, actually," Francis announced, scrutinizing the Mech. "Although I did not catch your name prior."

Rebel drew a blank, grinning off the uncomfortable silence and stares.

"Anne Frank? Are you going to introduce us to your acquaintance?" probed Emily.

"He's not an acquaintance, he's just," Rebel began, looking for the right words, "Jonathan. This is Jonathan. Doe."

"Jonathan Doe," Emily repeated. "What a curious name. I don't believe I recognize it from the census data."

"Yes, and there is a good reason for that," said Rebel, covering. "He's new. New Mech. Hot off Robotiq's assembly line. And he was just leaving."

"Jonathan Doe," said Francis. "Interesting. I did not expect to see you again so soon, but certainly you cannot get enough of a good thing." Smug and condescending, even for a Mech.

"Thank you," Thomas said, taking Francis' remark literally.

"Well, Jonathan has much to do," Rebel cut in. "Work, quotas, and whatnot, so if you'll excuse him."

"Of course," Emily obliged.

Rebel grabbed Thomas by the arm and led him to the elevators. Francis and Emily stood statue-still, eyes never leaving them.

"Are you insane?" Rebel asked in a hushed voice, once out of earshot.

"I don't believe so," Thomas answered.

"Mech think you're missing, remember?" she reminded him. "And also, they think I'm one of them." She exhaled, pacing, trying to work things out in her mind. On the surface, she remained stoic, plastic. But underneath, she boiled.

Thomas realized the predicament he placed her in. "Well, I could come again, perhaps at a later, more agreeable, time."

"Thomas... what are you doing?"

"I don't understand," he said.

"This is very dangerous for me. I'm human."

"Not now," he responded.

She couldn't argue with his reasoning. "Yes. Well... that's not the point."

"Perhaps post-work, then?" he inquired.

"Fine, yeah, whatever, just go."

"Then I wish you a good-bye, Anne."

A discreet, soft wave goodbye and then Rebel turned and headed back to the work floor. Even with her duties to perform, both artifact collection and master plan details, she couldn't stop her mind from wandering. She glanced once again at her portrait before stuffing it into a pocket, conflicted by the emotions coursing through her. But that would have to wait.

Emily and Francis continued to watch her from afar, eyes narrowing.

Francis whispered into Emily's ear. "I thought you, head of Census, were required to know all Mech, new or not."

"I am," said Emily. "And I do."

"Apparently not," said Francis with a smirk, returning to his desk, yet he had planted the seed.

Emily scrutinized Jonathan Doe, sensing a tasty new morsel of gossip.

17

The throng aboard the train rode in ponderous silence, all sitting in their unquestioned contentment. For the first time, Thomas seemed ill-at-ease to Rebel, unsure how to hold his body. Uncertain what to do with his eyes. He glanced from face to face, each one a Mech like him, yet not like him. From the woman next to him to the young man — drinking in their detail — the shape of each hand, the length of each eyelash, the color of their skin — never before noticed. Fascinated. His eyes fell on Rebel. If he didn't know any better, he would believe her to be a Mech — her perfect posture, mannerisms, everything about her, and nothing about her all at once.

For the most part, Sector 13 appeared similar to Sector 4 where Rebel resided, with one caveat. Unlike the inner city, outlying sectors underwent renovation, restructuring, and recycling. Remnants remained from Rebel's previous life, pre-Mech. A barbershop with a spinning stripped sign, a defunct ice cream parlor, even an artificial pet store. Rebel took in the wonders under her mask of ambivalence.

She wished she appreciated things more at a younger age,

remembering visiting the de Young Museum on multiple occasions but never paid much attention. Art bored her, as it did most kids. Old works made by dead people. Why couldn't they take the tour virtually, like they did in school? Her mother would stop at every painting, explaining them in detail, all from memory. Date painted, artist name, their past, beliefs, place in the world, the subtle meaning and overarching themes behind the artwork. She called it 'subjective.' Art wasn't about what you saw, but how it made you feel. It made Rebel feel stupid, in a way. When she looked at art, she saw pictures — bowl of fruit, naked woman, old man with a lute. She would catch her mother wiping a silent tear from the corners of her eyes as she gazed at specific pieces, but Rebel felt nothing.

Not until many years later did she begin to understand what her mother tried passing on. She felt. She cried. It was a way for Rebel to be with her mother again.

When the museum appeared on the restructuring charts, Rebel knew what she must do — steal. She devised a plan, broke into the museum, and stole every painting she laid her hands on. Two trips later, and Rebel amassed a hearty collection of over two dozen priceless works of art. She didn't call it stealing. More akin to *rescuing*. Like Robin Hood. A way to hold on to her mother. Her way to connect, to share, to pass on, just as her mother provided her. She never guessed her first art student would be a Mech.

Night had come by the time they reached the antique store. The sector powered down for the evening, but Rebel remained vigilant nonetheless.

"No one knows about this," she told Thomas. "I'm trusting you."

"Thank you," he said.

They traversed down rickety wooden steps into the dark sub-basement of the store. Little light shone in through street-level windows, long ago covered in grime from city traffic and

pollution. She pulled the cord on the hanging bulb, illuminating a treasure trove.

Human artifacts. Hoarded, secreted to this location a bit at a
time over the last few years. Preservation, Rebel called it. Her
own private museum. A mausoleum of humanity. Outside of
the priceless rescued paintings and a few first editions of classic
novels, most of the items could be considered junk to the
layman. But as they said, one man's junk is another's treasure. A
squeaky dog toy in the shape of a cat. A vintage model train,
complete with tracks, a small winter village, and a bridge that it
passed through. Old fashion posters and imagery from exotic
landscapes Rebel would never visit. Shelves stocked full of
snow globes. Another held her collection of lava lamps. Photo
albums held reserve over the top two shelves. Grandparents,
children, husbands, and wives. They painted a complete story
of a life lived. Each book its own novel, none requiring a single
printed word. Various other items rounded out the collection,
things like LEGO bricks, a discarded Happy Meal box,
balloons, a squirt gun, even a corncob pipe. They reminded her
of who she was, what she stood for, and why she existed.

"What are these things?" wondered Thomas.

"Mech classify them as artifacts," explained Rebel. "But
mostly, it's just junk. All things ordered to be destroyed, recycled. Except I saved them. Bit by bit, I gave them a reprieve.
What you see here may look like scraps, like leftovers, but that's
just what's on the surface. Underneath the plastic, the glass, the
metal — there is so much more. A whole universe of memories.
Moments in time. A shrine of what we were, what we achieved,
what we cherished. Not junk... humanity."

"Does it make you sad? That they're to be recycled?"

"Yes, it does," she admitted. "They were someone's life. A
catalog of who they were, what they cared about, who they
cared for. You can't just recycle that."

Thomas walked around, taking in the relics. He moved the

train along the tracks, squeaked the dog toy, tapped the glass of a snow globe, flipped through an old photo album. His eyes stopped on each painting. Georgia O'Keeffe's 'Petunias.' Mel Ramos' 'Superman.' Louise Nevelson's 'Black Moon.' Hiram Powers 'Greek Slave.' Every sculpture, fresco, still-life, abstract, and portrait held a power he had only just began to grasp. Merely paint and canvass, stone and marble, cloth and thread. But they seemed to tell a story held in their frozen visages — stories of another time, another place, another life.

Thomas froze, mesmerized before Vincent van Gogh's masterpiece, *Starry Night over the Rhone.*

"Thomas? Are you okay?"

"It's... beautiful."

The remark made an impression on Rebel. "Yes, it is. It was my mother's favorite. It gave her hope and reminded her to dream. At least that's what she told me."

Thomas saw the melancholy etched on her face. "Do you miss them? Your family, that is."

"Every day," she responded. "One moment, they were here. The next... Sometimes, when I feel lonely, I'll come here and sit and stare. I like to make up stories about the people who owned these things." She took up the plastic dog toy. "Like this one. This belonged to Bernie, a golden retriever, and Harry's companion. Harry would work late, but Bernie would be waiting for him like clockwork, toy in mouth, tail thumping every time he got home. And they would play for hours together, go on long walks and to the park and swim in the ocean. A good life they had together. Companions, partners, best friends..."

Rebel as she got swept away in the story, as did Thomas, enthralled. He lifted a snow globe and gave it a shake, swirling it to life. "And this?"

"Oh, that's a good one. It belonged to Peter and Jenny. They were high school sweethearts until Peter joined the army and went off to war. He sent letters to Jenny every chance he could. She would meet the mailman every day, tearing into them and devouring the love letters. She waited three long years for him, worried he wouldn't make it home. But he did, and he brought her that snow globe. They got married the next day, had three kids, and moved to the suburbs. Life together was all they would ever need. They had each other."

"And this one?" he questioned, lifting up the worn stuffed Teddy bear.

"It's new," she said. "I don't know the story yet."

"May I?" he inquired.

Intrigued, Rebel motioned to him, 'by all means.'

"This fake, mildewy padded bear with artificial fur covering belong to... Ernest," Thomas declared. "Ernest was a lonely human boy with no peers of any kind. But one day, he found this abandoned fake bear in a dumpster and adopted him as his own. They soon became best of friends and lived together until the fake bear contracted gangrene from said mildew and ceased to live. Ernest died two years later from stomach ulcers. The end."

Thomas awaited Rebel's approval. Unable to hold back, she broke out into laughter. Uncontrolled, unbridled laughter. The kind of laughter where your eyes tear, and there is the very real threat of peeing one's pants.

Contagious, Thomas laughed right along with her. "Why are we laughing?"

"That's the worst story I've ever heard," Rebel said through snort-filled laughs. "Stomach ulcers... that's great!" She covered her mouth subconsciously.

"Why do you do that?" Thomas pondered. "Why do you cover your mouth when you laugh?"

"I don't know," she said. "Instinct, I guess. Years of pretending to show no emotion, to be someone else. To hide what I am. It's conditioning. Show nothing. Give nothing."

Thomas gently lowered Rebel's hand from her mouth. "You shouldn't cover it. I enjoy your smile and what it does to your face. Like a piece of art."

Rebel's smile slowly faded, her cheeks flush. An unnerving tremble started up within her stomach, like butterflies. Butterflies in a bell jar. His comment evoked a feeling within her that should not have existed. But it felt genuine, and that became enough.

"I have a confession to make," he declared.

"Yes?"

"I watched your ballet recitals. All twenty-seven of them. You were quite talented."

"That was a long time ago."

"Why did you stop?"

"I didn't," said Rebel. "Ballet stopped. It ended the day Mech took over."

"Will you show me?"

"What? Now? No. I can't. Those performances took a lot of work, trying to master absurd, unnatural ways to move your body. It requires incredible strength in every muscle and incredible amounts of flexibility. I'm not that person anymore."

"But you can be," he said. "You can go back."

Tempting, but reality stomped that dream out. "No. If I've learned anything, it's that you can't go back. Only forward."

A long moment laid bare, before Thomas broke the silence. "Can we do another story?"

"Yeah," said Rebel. "Another story. A happy one."

———

Outside the antique store, a little light spilled out from the windows at ground level. Within, the animated silhouettes of Rebel and Thomas could be made out to an inquiring eye.

Muffled voices and laughter penetrated the otherwise lifeless street.

A figure stood across the street, in the shadows, watching the events unfold through those clouded windows.

Suspicions confirmed, Francis thought. He had yet to decipher the imposter Anne Frank's true programming, but there would be ample time now that he had zeroed in on public enemy number one. One thing was certain. Francis would earn his due respect and a promotion.

Returning to Robotiq, Francis conferred with Emily, who wrapped up her extended search.

"Well?" he asked.

"It seems you were correct," she confirmed. "There is no current record of any Mech named Jonathan Doe. He is either aberrant or not who he says he is."

"I believe it is time to inform the Director..."

Karl Marx sat in deep, conflicted thought behind his desk at Robotiq as he listened to Francis Bacon's tall tale of treachery. "I find this extremely hard to believe, Francis Bacon," he said. How could a human have infiltrated Robotiq right under his very nose? The thought of it, the implications — astounding, and nuclear if verified as truth.

"I had it tested," said Francis. "All trace DNA wiped clean with chemicals, but most definitely pegged as organic. Not animal. Not synthetic. Not Mech. *Human*."

"No, it is not possible," Marx said. "There are no humans left. We made sure of that. They fled this planet and never returned."

"It appears we missed one," replied Francis.

"A human would have to pass through intense security, undetected," Karl stated. "A full-body scan. Enforcer patrols. How would they even fathom it possible?"

"Perhaps they have had help from a Mech," said Emily. "A sympathetic one."

"Nonsense," Karl replied. "Sympathy is not within our operating language."

"An oversight," stated Francis. "The scanners could be fooled by any small EMP device with encrypted Mech coding. It would make the human appear to register as Mech."

"Is there a patch?" Karl asked. "A way to put this to rest once and for all?"

"A userware upgrade. I could oversee it if you would like."

Marx considered Francis and Emily. "Do it. Quietly."

18

———

Robotiq's security scanners in the lobby had Mech lined up far and wide. Queues weren't normally very long. The average wait time clocked in at approximately two and a half minutes. Rebel had already wasted over fifteen minutes in the line that day. Not orderly, not efficient, not Mech-like. Something was up.

She observed a notable increase in Enforcers. It didn't look as if they concentrated on any single Mech specifically, but they presided, stationed almost as if waiting for the order to pounce. Rebel reminded herself to remain calm. They didn't suspect anything out of the ordinary. She controlled the situation, palming her handheld EMP device, growing a bit more reassured.

Five Mech to go in front of her. The more time that passed, the more anxious she grew. A million thoughts raced through her mind, but she squashed them; otherwise, they would consume her. Another step forward and Rebel saw the scans taking place. From what she could gather with her limited view, all appeared fairly standard. No new hardware to fret over. No new upgrades as far as she could ascertain. *Remain calm.* She glanced at the clock and shifted impatiently. No one else seemed inpatient. They conversed quietly or stood unmoved, perhaps reading their daily downloaded bulletin. Still, a gnawing sensation rose in the back of her mind, like a little voice whispering to her. Whispering: *run.*

She glanced at the clock again — nearly nine. The line moved one Mech closer. She reminded herself to keep her wits about her. Control. Calm. Lie. And then she noticed a cause for concern. Two Techs in the midst of replacing mods in the scanner down the line from her. Maybe just a faulty circuit weld or fried board. Maybe nothing. Maybe everything.

A Mech nudged her from behind, motioning for her to step forward. She held up the line. Scanners swiped the Mech before her and beeped out diagnostics: names, model types, charges, creation dates, and functions, just like always. Except for one small difference...

'USERWARE PATCH CODE' flashed on the scanner's display.

No. Her stomach dropped. Rebel realized the cause of the backlog, the delays — the scanners had been upgraded overnight. Her jammer would fail, and her true self would be revealed.

"Testing," one Mech complained to his co-worker. "They will not say why, of course, but I think we may assume this pertains to the discovery. What else might be the cause?"

"It will take hours to catch up," sighed another. "How are we expected to reach quota now?"

"What discovery are we discussing exactly?" Rebel interjected.

The two Mechs turned to her. Appraising, analyzing. Conceit plastered all over their faces. "You have not heard the latest news?"

"I... no. I've been preoccupied," she stammered.

"Hair," voiced a female Mech.

"Hair?" Rebel probed. She racked her brain. Why would hair cause all this backlog, all this inefficiency?

"A *human* hair," uttered her Mech co-worker.

Uh oh. All the blood in Rebel's head rapidly descended into her stomach. She wanted to purge. Numb. Her mind raced. She should listen more to that little voice in the back of her head. It never steered her wrong. *Run.* Abruptly, she stepped out of the queue and headed for the doors, not even thinking. She tied to remain calm, anonymous, but she needed to get out of there, to flee, and fast. Daylight up ahead, the glass doors inviting her to step outside to freedom.

"Anne, is everything well?"

Rebel almost ran right into him. Francis appeared out of nowhere as if her shadow. The tone behind his question spoke volumes. Standard inquiries or friendly concern didn't reflect condemnation. The question commenced a fishing expedition. An interrogation.

"Yes, I just... forgot something at home," she covered. "I will be right back."

"Forgot?" The word left a bitter taste on his synthetic tongue. "I didn't realize Mech could forget, not without a memory wipe."

"Yes, correct," said Rebel.

"Well, then I suggest you do not delay."

"To delay would be inefficient," Rebel stated. Before Francis could respond, Rebel passed through the doors and disappeared into the crowds.

Emily joined Francis' side, eyeing Rebel's hasty departure. Their eyes narrowed.

"Believe me now?" asked Francis.

"Steps will need to be taken," Emily theorized.

"Indeed."

———

REBEL WALKED AWAY AS QUICKLY as possible until she couldn't stand it anymore. She broke into a run, pin-balling through the crowd. Mechs turned as she passed, but Rebel didn't care. Adrenaline became her fuel. And fear.

Bursting through the front door of her home, Rebel gathered what she needed into her bug-out bag, exactly as planned in case of emergency, packed with the necessities to survive. An extended stay in the wilderness. Knife. Firestarter. Metal pot. Cordage. Bug the hell out. Make a run for it. See ya later, adios, and sayonara. She understood the day would come, eventually. She hoped it wouldn't, that her plan to contact the moon would be smooth sailing, and she would fall into her parents' loving arms, and all would be right as rain with the world. But such wasn't the case. She prepared. Contingency plans were put in place, and it was time to put them into action.

"You're running away," Thomas discerned. He witnessed a frazzled Rebel on more than one occasion since their arrangement began, yet never a desperate Rebel.

"I messed up. Bad. A mistake. A stupid, idiotic, foolish mistake."

"What kind of mistake?"

"I let emotion rule me," she said. "Ruin me. You were right. Emotions are the scourge of mankind."

"Perhaps you are overreacting. I have been reading your books on mindfulness, and many authors state that taking ten deep breaths can calm a frayed nerve."

"This is way past deep breathing, Thomas," she said. "This is the worst case scenario."

"I am sure you are merely overreacting."

"They found a human hair," she disclosed. "My hair."

Thomas stilled, understanding the implications. Rebel didn't overreact. A human hair disconcerted the population. No doubt Robotiq would deploy Enforcers to hunt down the vagrant human. As well as Rebel pretended to be a Mech, she ultimately failed to become one. A well-conceived disguise, but a disguise nonetheless. No foolish costume could cover up who she was on the inside.

"You're coming back, though, right?" he inquired.

Rebel took a moment to catch her breath. So concerned with her own safety, she forgot how everything might affect Thomas. "You're free, okay? Just go. You'll be better off. If they can find me, they can find you. They'll learn of our arrangement."

"Relationship," he corrected. "You are my teacher. And my friend, if I might say."

"Then, as a friend, I'm telling you, I'm begging you, stay away from me," she warned. "I'm toxic. I can't help you. I can't even help myself."

"I'm sorry, but I don't believe that is true."

"Look at me," she beseeched. "Everything in my life goes to crap. Including us, if you stay. How long do you think they're going to buy that John Doe nonsense? How long until they come after you to get to me? Or vice versa. I can't have that on my conscience. I just can't, okay? I need you to understand."

"But I don't want to go, nor do I want you to go," he muttered. "I like it here. With you."

Rebel turned to face him. A hundred different things came to mind for her to say at that precise moment. She could open up about her feelings, her regrets, her wishes, and dreams. How Thomas brought those out of her. How he reminded her that there was still hope for something better. She could say any of it.

Instead, the only thing she thought to utter, "I'm sorry." Sorry for putting him in that position. Sorry for making him feel something. But the survival of her species fell on a different level than hurt feelings and a broken heart. Rebel owed survival to her family, to the entirety of the human race, to persist, exist, live. Thomas would get over the rejection. He would forget about her in time and get on with his 'life.' Rebel would be nothing but a distant memory. Probably best for everyone. Who were they fooling? Their arrangement, their relationship, friendship, whatever one wanted to label it, it evolved into a farce, like Rebel's entire existence on Earth. One prolonged, exaggerated lie. Reality left the building a long time ago, and it swept her up and took whatever humanity was left with it. She wasn't real. She was just a paper doll, all fixed out on the outside, yet empty within. Just like a Mech. If her past taught her anything, it was that nothing lasts. Not forever, anyway.

She looked at Thomas, saying goodbye with her eyes because, for some reason, she couldn't find her voice at that moment. If she did, it would break, and she would crumble. She turned to the door and swung it open one last time, ready to make her final escape.

"Anne Frank." Three Enforcers stood outside the door. "You are to come with us," they ordered. "Immediately."

———

THERE WERE two types of suspects in a crime. Guilty and innocent. Upon arrest, the innocent grew rigid, anxious, nervous. They couldn't sleep, couldn't eat. On the other hand, the guilty tended to relax, to let down their guard, and sleep the night spent in jail. Almost thankful to no longer have to run, lie, deceive, cheat and steal to stay one step ahead.

Rebel fell into the latter category.

A short ride in the rear of the Enforcers' vehicle and Rebel didn't fuss or complain or try to talk her way out of it. She sat there, gazing out the window at the passing scenery, glimpsing Mech go about their daily routines, huge Walkers sucking up toxic particles in the air, and birds flying free in the sky. They really did do a wonderful job at cleaning the planet.

Even upon arriving back in Robotiq's parking garage, the

place where all her problems began, and entering the Robotiq lobby, the elevator ride, and passing through her office floor, she remained silent and introspective. Although the dead man walking march only lasted ten seconds, it felt like ten hours. Workers stopped to watch Rebel, heads popping up from cubicles like gophers. Not every day did a Mech get to observe a real live human being. Rebel almost felt like a celebrity, probably how Lucifer felt before his expulsion from heaven. Mech stepped aside, giving her a wide berth as if she were a pariah, a leper, contagious. Enforcers followed behind her, shielding any chance of escape.

"Anne Frank. I have heard a most disturbing rumor," Karl Marx said, gazing out his office windows as Rebel entered. "It appears someone among us is not who they say they are."

Rebel struggled to hold on. She swallowed hard, wondering if Karl could hear her pounding heartbeat.

"A traitor, an apostate exists amongst us," he continued, turning to face her. "One of us, in this building, this very office — is human."

A guilty plea. A death sentence. Rebel kept her outward expression neutral, yet inwardly churned with horror. When she responded, her voice was a whisper, dry as dust. "Human?"

"You are the resident of the Division of Human Affairs, artifacts and such, and you mean to tell me you know nothing of this?" he asked.

"No, sir. I don't," she answered.

"We are friends, are we not?" he asked.

"Friends?" she repeated. "Yes, sir. Good friends." Rebel did indeed like Karl. Boastful, even egotistical at times, but they held a connection. Karl Marx came to be as close to a father figure as she could experience. Inside, she believed him to be a decent man. Or a decent Mech, in any case.

"Then tell me, as a 'good friend,' if you were human, left behind, where might you hide to evade detection?"

"The best place to hide, sir," she answered. "In plain sight."

"That is what I thought," Karl sighed, exasperated. "Then I am sorry, but I have no choice... You are to find this human at all costs."

Wait. What? Rebel worked to hide her immediate shock. "Once again, please?"

"I am reassigning you. Francis Bacon will be leading the effort, as he exhorted, and you are to act as a liaison of sorts. Make sure he does not go too far off track, as he is known to do. You should hear his wild theories. Stupefying. Yet he did discover the infiltrator, so some leniency must be granted. This is to be kept in strict confidence. Top secret, as they say. You will report to me and me alone. Do we understand each other?"

"Yes, sir," she said.

"I am counting on you, Anne Frank," Marx said, handing her a high-level security badge. "My friend. My confidant."

Ruffled, Rebel sat in her cubicle, staring at the security badge. *Access.* That's what Karl Marx gave her. A way out, and a way in, all at the same time. A silver lining. Not high enough clearance to access the mainframe, but one step closer.

Francis slithered up behind her, leaning in close, never any regard for personal space. "Hello, Anne Frank."

"Francis," Rebel grimaced. "Was there something you needed?"

"You seem... distracted lately," he said. "It is not like you. Your thoughts are on the human among us? You are wondering if they know who it is yet. Am I right?"

Rebel swallowed hard. "So, do they? Know?"

"Oh, there are theories," he snarled. "I hold a supposition myself. But at the moment, it is... premature."

"Like your intelligence," Rebel shot back.

"Ah, I see," replied Francis. "Humor. That is what is happening here. One of those 'human' qualities you enjoy expounding upon."

"Perhaps you should have your RAM upgraded in the Repair Plaza," she said. "Might help. Just saying."

"My RAM is quite adequate, I can assure you."

"Well," she said, "I wouldn't want to keep you from your so-called investigation, now would I?"

"Enjoy the quietude while it lasts," he proclaimed. "It is, I predict, merely a temporary reprieve." And with that, Francis trotted away.

Rebel looked down at her hands, balled up into fists beneath the desk. She forced herself to unclench, revealing the red gashes in each palm where her nails dug into the skin.

19

"I'd like to show you something if that is okay," Thomas stood before Rebel with his hand extended. "I believe it will cheer you up."

The multi-tiered greenhouse sat at the end of a long street pockmarked with other environmental facilities, one in a long line of indoor gardens. As soon as Rebel stepped inside, she felt transported, as if she traveled to a different, prehistoric world. A fairy tale. Everything around her changed — sights, sounds, smells. And flowers. Thousands of them. Towering plants with leaves the size of cars, small petite flowers not seen since prehistoric times. Overhead misters sprayed the greenery, creating rainbows above.

"Beautiful," she whispered.

"It's my home," Thomas said, proud.

A wonderment of colors and shapes and dazzling fragrances — all assaulting Rebel's senses. Her fingertips brushed over tulips, daffodils, and orchids. She inhaled the scent of roses, took in the thorns of a cactus, caressed the dew-laden birds of paradise. Following along the trail, Rebel took in the misters spray. The hoses trickled small streams, the overhead atrium ceiling opening and closing with the movements of the sun. She stopped atop a small wooden bridge over a pond with exotic floating water lilies.

"You did all this?" she asked.

Thomas hung a few steps behind, watching Rebel's every expression, absorbing them like a sponge. "It's my function," he answered. "They are my friends."

"It's like what I imagine the world was before... us."

"Tell me," implored Thomas.

"You already know it all," she said.

"Yes, but not from your perspective," he explained. "Please."

Rebel didn't enjoy going back to those times. Not because of any bad memories, but because of the good ones. They made her sad, remembering a happy world she could never return to.

"My father used to tell me fairy tales of a world long ago," Rebel evoked. "A world where the sun didn't burn your skin when you stepped outside, where you could breathe the air and swim in the oceans. A vibrant world with a deep blue sky, green grass, and things called flowers that came in every color of the rainbow, whatever that was. Animals presided everywhere — tiny hummingbirds lived in trees, mammals the size of a house swam in the seas, and great white bears lived in the snow. It sounded like fiction, but it was real, at least once upon a time.

"Gradual at first, the demise of the planet rapidly became exponentially worse. Water levels rose, winters grew colder, summers hotter. Penguins went extinct, then deer, trees, and the birds that lived in them. But ignorance prevailed. People soon forgot what a hummingbird looked like. Or a sunflower. Other distractions occupied their thoughts. There were wars back then. Some against tyrants who killed anyone different, others over dried up fossil fuels. My father hoped the wars would stop when oil vanished in the early years of the twenty-first century, but he was wrong. They just found something else to fight over."

"And now?" Thomas questioned.

"Now?" Rebel exhaled, thinking. "Now I just wish my parents could see what Mech did. What you did. This planet, it's a paradise. A dream come true. But does it matter if you have no one to share it with?"

"But you do," stated Thomas. "You have me."

"Yes," she repeated. "I have you."

Thomas slumped. "A Mech, you meant to say. Not human. Not alive."

"No, Thomas, that wasn't what I meant. You aren't a Mech, not really, not anymore. I don't know what you are."

"I used to perceive my job as just that, a job," Thomas explained. "My function, to nurture plant life. I never gave it much thought outside of soil densities, irrigation and water saturation, sunlight exposure, seed selection, weather systems. Yet coming here now, I see everything in a new light. I raised these flowers and plants and trees from mere seedlings all the way to maturity. Like a father. I think about the day they will be set free with melancholy. I will say goodbye to my children, hoping for their best as they leave the secure confines of the greenhouse and enter an uncertain world, prone to the unpredictability of life."

He turned to Rebel. "Is that a normal thought process for a Mech? Because I don't think it is. Questions swirl around in my head. Could I be human? Is that what happened? No, I can't be. I am comprised of machinery, circuits, wires, fluids, and memory chips. I do not contain anything that defines humankind. Not quite human and not quite Mech. Could I even be classified and cataloged any longer? Only recently, I began to feel a pain somewhere, but I cannot quite pin down where. Or what caused it. Or why it hurts so bad. Nothing in my programming, nothing in my help files, comes close to diagnosing my current status. I thought there must be some operational error. Some bug in my software, or faulty chip hardware.

Some explanation, because the most obvious is too hard to accept."

"And what is that?"

"That I am something... different. Something more. But most importantly, I am your friend."

It melted her. Instantly. All her bravado dropped away. "Yes," she said. "You are my friend."

"Wait here," he said. "I have something for you."

Thomas hurried off, leaving Rebel to her vices. She looked around, breathing in the intoxicating scents. She thought that the greenhouse must be what the Garden of Eden looked like. Did that make her and Thomas a modern-day Adam and Eve? And how long until the snake reared its scaly head?

"Okay, you may turn around now," Thomas said as he walked up behind her.

Rebel faced Thomas to find him holding a single sunflower. Not cut, but in a pot, thriving.

"Alive," Thomas said. "Like you. Although I must admit, I had ulterior motives."

"You did?" Rebel played along. "Such as?"

" I wanted to gift the flower to you..."

"Yes..."

"Well, I very much wanted to see you smile again."

Rebel took a step closer to him. "Why?"

"It's my favorite expression of yours."

"Is it?"

"Yes. By far."

Rebel stared, blinking away tears. It wasn't the smile Thomas hoped for.

"Did I harm you?"

"Thomas?"

"Yes, Rebel?"

"Shut up."

She reached out, and without thinking, kissed him. Her lips

pressed against his. At first, he merely stood there, rigid, eyes wide open, staring at her — his awkwardness, endearing. By instinct, she pulled him closer. For a reason he would never be able to quantify or put into words, Thomas closed his eyes and took Rebel into his arms. They lingered, mouths on each other's, and the world around them disappeared.

———

"Day 2624," Rebel said to the camera. She couldn't wait to mark the new entry into her video diary. "I kissed a boy today. And it only took nineteen years. Imagine what the next nineteen will bring..." She broke out into a spontaneous smile, cheeks blushing.

That is when the blood began to drip from her nose.

"Rebel," Thomas called out when he returned home. "Are you in here?"

Rebel's bedroom appeared empty upon Thomas's entrance. He knocked twice, and after receiving no response, decided to check on her well being for himself. He searched the rest of the house but failed to locate her. "Rebel? I am beginning to worry." Given the lateness of the hour, she should have returned home from work. That, and her video camera was still recording when he found it. He stopped the recording and rewound the footage, watching Rebel's confession about kissing him, and he smiled until he saw the blood begin to spill from her nose. A rising uneasiness within disturbed him. A feeling he couldn't place. Dread.

He raced back to the bedroom, following the trail of blood drops on the floor, and he saw it. A leg. On the floor. Sticking out from the other side of the bed frame.

Rebel lay on the floor. Face down.

What an odd way to take a nap, Thomas thought.

"Rebel? Are you sleeping?" He knelt beside her, gently

poking her leg. She didn't stir. "Is this some type of game?" She taught him many games, but never one quite like that. "Hide and seek?" he pondered. "If so, you are not very good at it."

Still, she did not move. Growing concerned, he rolled her over onto her back to appraise her. Rebel's skin turned deathly pale. Dark circles formed around her eyes. Dried blood crusted on her lips and surrounded her nostrils. It was no game.

"Rebel. Rebel! Wake up!" No more time for gentle prodding. He shook her hard. Unresponsive, he put his hand above her open mouth. He noticed no warm air exhaling from her human lungs. Thomas placed his ear over her heart and listened with building terror. He heard no thumping as he did when they first met. Quite the opposite in fact. Her still chest held no heartbeat.

Rebel was dead.

20

———

Kerosene lanterns lit the main room of the rustic cabin. Daylight bled inside through the windows, muted thanks to the excessive shade of the encroaching Fir trees outside. The only sound came from the Nisqually River pounding against the granite river rocks, fueled by the surrounding mountains.

The cabin retained no strain of the modern world — no computers or tablets, no virtual reality, no holoscreens. No electricity either. 'Charm,' Dr. Raw dubbed it. Torture, more like it. One main room, consisting of an oak table and chairs, a fireplace, a wood burning stove, and a small writing desk. Atop the desk sat an old-fashioned shortwave radio: the main receiver, transmitter, microphone, headphones, and a bunch of wires. Rebel attempted to use it when she first arrived, but it didn't operate anymore.

During the month of her sojourn, Rebel struggled to get comfortable atop the bed, mostly due to the old lumpy mattress and paper-thin pillow. The hand-me-down patchwork quilt retained its warmth well, so at least Rebel didn't freeze to death at night. With sleep refusing to come, she ruminated on memories of visiting the cabin with her parents on summer vacations, although the older she got, the more the excursions waned. The initial adventure soon turned into a chore. Everything required work. Elbow grease. If you wanted to eat, you caught your own food. Fresh clothes? Wash them by hand in a bucket and hang them on a line outside to dry. Entertainment? Books, an old board game missing pieces, or bird watching.

Passing the time, she looked through the cabinets and desk drawers, finding a few supplies, such as fishing line, a folding knife, a net in need of mending. She hit the jackpot when she unearthed a small pocket outdoor survival guide written in the nineteen fifties, entitled *Bushcraft Survival Guide: How to Live as One with Nature* by Dr. Harris Chapman III, Esq. A doctor of what, Rebel hadn't the slightest idea. She guessed from the book's off-kilter words ('wazzock,' 'collywobbles,' 'loo,' 'bloke') that Dr. Chapman hailed from Great Britain. Chapters included things like 'Edible Wild Plants,' 'Fire Starting,' 'First-Aid,' 'Hunting & Fishing,' 'Knots,' and 'Shelter Construction.' It would come in handy, especially the chapter on 'Edible Insects.'

Grubs. Disgusting, white, bulbous, slithering grubs. Rebel spent the day foraging, finding a slew of blueberry bushes, most picked clean, but enough to fill her basket halfway. A welcome sight, full of nutrients, even if some weren't ripe yet. But at the rate Rebel consumed them, they would soon dry up. She needed to find other sources of nourishment. Mainly, protein. She tried the plethora of worms slithering about, but they tasted like dirt and rubber and guts. An opportunity arose to scavenge bird eggs from a nest, but she couldn't bring herself to steal babies from a mother. It just didn't feel right. Grubs, on the other hand, packed a lot of protein, per her handy survival guide, and were fairly easy to find, residing in rotten wood. The larva of beetles, they were alien-looking, squirming, covered in tiny spines, but food nonetheless. She ate to survive, not for taste. She did what she had to do.

After some time, Rebel grew accustomed to the temperature of the Nisqually. A bend in the river where the currents slowed created a nice little pool for her to bathe. Soap, shampoo, and a loofah would be nice, but she managed. She spotted few signs of salmon, mostly to blame from the countless dams erected, as most fishing turned to farming. Those caught in the wild were tainted from toxins or bits of ingested plastic from bottles that littered the waterways. She spent that afternoon floating in the water on her back, staring up at the sky. With her ears submerged, the only sound was the soothing trickle of water. She gave herself to the moment and just let herself be.

Alone for over four months, living off berries, grubs and insects, hardened the little girl. Rebel adapted, becoming a self-sufficient young adult. A woman. The cabin started to resemble a home, and even the bed became tolerable. For starters, the size was manageable, unlike her childhood house, containing only one room. Cleaning? A breeze. Rebel also recognized more of the foreign sounds and scents from within the forest. She could smell certain edible plants and the scent of the air before rain. She could pick out different bird calls, the sounds of squirrels, owls, and deer.

One of those foreign sounds drew her attention at that moment.

She climbed out of the water up onto the riverbank. She refused to go naked in the water, wearing her bra and underwear. Nobody was around to see her in the flesh, but nudity still felt weird. *One step at a time*, she told herself. Drying herself off, she heard the noise again. A new sound she couldn't recognize. Deep grunts. Heavy, throaty moaning. Forceful expulsions of air. Definitely not a squirrel, chipmunk, or bird. No, the beast making those noises carried considerable size. Not prey. *Predator.*

Another grunt, a huff of air. It came from her left. Trees swayed, the sound of branches snapped, and heavy footfalls thudded the earth. A monster? Probably not, but still, Rebel didn't stick around to find out. Leaping over stumps, ducking under branches, Rebel raced through the forest and didn't stop until safely inside the cabin, door locked, chair wedged up as a barricade.

Rebel decided it prudent to spend more time indoors after the incident at the river with the (probably not) monster — nothing more than the necessary foraging and always in eyesight of the cabin at all times. Developing cabin fever, she turned her attention to the short wave radio, intact but without a power source. If fixed, she could try to make contact with any other remaining humans, maybe even the moon, although she doubted the little radio possessed the strength to reach that far. She couldn't be the only person left behind. There must be others. A lot of others. The odds stood on her side. She thought of those doomsday fanatics who lived in underground bunkers, or government officials who stayed to monitor the situation and report back to the moon. There might even be others like her, the stranded, the forgotten, living in the wild. Stubborn people who refused to leave. What about the homeless, runaways, crazies? If she wanted any chance at reconciliation with her species, she needed to be proactive, and the shortwave provided her the best opportunity.

She looked the contraption over, nothing more than a box, a receiver with a lot of dials, buttons, and screens. The instruction manual read like, well, an instruction manual. Small print and over two hundred pages. *No thanks*, she thought, placing the tome aside. She would get back to it once she figured out if the device even worked. Wires extended out of the back of the radio, not plugged into any outlet, probably because there were none. They snaked their way up to the corner of the wall, to the ceiling, where they disappeared.

Outside, she followed the wires to where they breached the siding and traveled up to the roof. Finding an old wooden ladder, she placed it up again the side of the house and ascended wobbly steps up to the roof where shingles covered in dry leaves and branches hid the wires beneath. Careful of her footing, she scraped away at the muck, revealing wires split into two paths. One went to the antenna that protruded up, and the other to a bank of solar panels to provide power. She returned moments later with a damp towel and wiped the panels clean, hoping they still worked. She would have to wait as dark clouds rolled in, blotting out the sun.

Descending the ladder, Rebel stopped, frozen in place. Some fifteen feet before her, half-buried in the bed of leaves, lay a deer. A desiccated deer. Ripped open, gutted, entrails spilling out onto the forest floor. And steaming. Whatever killed it did it very recently. Rebel stayed upwind, scouring the ground for indentations, prints, scat, any clue that would tell her what beast prowled her area and where it resided at that moment.

Rebel weighed the pros and cons of her staying at the cabin with a predator on the loose. Pro: Hidden From Mech. Con: Death. Pro: Food Source, Fresh Water. Con: Death. The list went on like that for a full two pages.

Beep, beep, beep.

Rebel had fallen asleep on the couch before the fireplace when the beeping began. The sound bled into her dream, something about unicorns, gone to haze when her eyes opened. Beep, beep, beep. Again. Like a gopher, Rebel's head shot up, ears perked, trying to zero in on the noise. Beep, beep, beep. Coming from the corner of the room, on the small writing desk. The shortwave radio lit up, alive. It worked.

"To any humans left behind, my name is Rebel Rae," she said into the microphone. "I am currently residing in a cabin in the forest. If anyone can hear me, please reply." Static, her sole award for all her efforts. Dead air. She figured she should keep at it all the same. Just because she couldn't hear anyone didn't mean someone else out there couldn't hear her.

Flames illuminated her face as she ate roasted chestnuts, sitting on the floor before the hearth. By the light of candles and kerosene lamps, she read books beyond her years. *Encyclopedia Britannica*, up to letter 'U'; Dostoevsky's *The Brothers Karamazov*; a college Calculus textbook, *A Brief History of Time* by Stephan Hawking; *Coding for Dummies*. She just finished the last page of *A Tale of Two Cities* by Charles Dickens, placing it atop the stack of others, when Rebel realized that she had read every single one of them. Frowning at the prospect of no more new books to lose herself in, she began looking around the cabin for other distractions in the cabinets, dresser, closet.

Not until she looked under the bed did she find the suitcase. One of those old types with latches, covered in stickers of various destinations: Paris, Rome, Barcelona, Alaska. She tried the latch, but it refused to pop open. A small keyhole caught her eye, but no key in sight: a mystery, one which Rebel strove to solve.

———

A SACK OF BONES.

Rebel stood naked before the mirror. Her skin looked like it aged ten years in the past few months. Hair stringy and brittle, rib cage and hip bones protruding. And pain. She felt the throbbing begin a few weeks prior, deep down in her stomach. Her body was consuming itself. Rebel couldn't sustain herself on foraged berries and grubs alone. She needed more calories. She needed protein, meat, and could think of only one way to get it. Rebel must become a hunter.

Delving into her handy pocket survival guide, she read about fish traps, small animal snares, and bigger game hunting.

Rebel decided to start small, focusing on animals that couldn't kill her back. She practiced weaving fish traps, cone-shaped baskets made of thin, bendable branches that she placed in the river. Fish would swim in the large end of the cone to eat the worm bait inside but couldn't escape. She practiced various snares. Fixed Loop, Figure 4 Deadfall, and one called Grave's Motion Triggered Snare, placing a few over burrows and on small-game trails. And then the waiting began.

Nothing. Nada. Zip. Nil. Diddly-squat. Not a single animal or fish in any of her traps. She refused to let momentary defeat get her down — the manual said so — she wouldn't give up. If the animals didn't come to her, she would go to them. That meant bigger game. Game that could also hunt her.

She went over the various types of weapons to construct for a hunt. After failed attempts at a bow and arrow and slingshot, she decided on a pike — a spear. The length would provide protection, a barrier so that she wouldn't have to draw too close to the animal to stab it. Another added benefit: throwing a spear, like a javelin. With some training. Rebel recalled the ten thousand hour rule, as explained by Malcolm Gladwell in his book, *Outliers: The Story of Success*. To become an expert in a particular skill, you must practice for ten thousand hours. Rebel did not have that much time.

Spear throwing practice commenced at daybreak. She gathered up sticks and leaves to create what looked like the strange offspring of a deer who mated with a scarecrow. Not pretty, but it would do the trick. The first throw didn't reach five feet. The next slipped from her hand and went backward. The third try flew way off target. Rebel finally managed to hit the target after an hour, but the spear harmlessly bounced off it. She took a break to reconfigure her spear, sharpening the tip, modifying the weight ratio, adding grooves along the side to make it more aerodynamic. After five hours, Rebel could hit the target with every throw. Not a bullseye, but close enough. She was ready.

Rebel quickly figured out why people called it hunting and not catching. She spent two weeks searching out something to hunt. Nothing. Not a single deer, squirrel, chipmunk, or bird. To make matters worse, the temperature began to drop. Snow threatened to fall at any moment, making her time spent in the wild all that much more demanding. At it once again, Rebel hid behind a fallen log, scanning the area and listening for any movement or animal calls. Crunch. The sound came from the other side of the log — a deer, not ten feet away. A doe, actually, an adult female, picking at the ground, nibbling on grass. Two weeks of working, training, and waiting. She wouldn't let her chance slip away.

She raised the spear and got into position. Taking a step back to throw, her foot crunched on fallen leaves. The deer instantly looked up, spooked, made eye contact with Rebel, and darted away. Two weeks. Rebel would have to change her plan of attack.

———

SNOW FELL IN QUIET WISPS, coating the ground in a light covering of white. Everything remained still. A soft gust of wind, the sway of tree branches, the fluttering of leaves. Beneath it all, the subtle sound of breathing and the low beat of running. Rebel glided through the trees, spear strapped to her shoulder. Her camouflage caused her to fade in and out of the background, floating through the trees as if a ghost. She slowed, spotting something in front of her, and stalked close to the tree, trying to hide her skinny frame. She hadn't eaten in a while, going on eleven days, and the starvation played with her not just physically but mentally as well.

A deer nuzzled the snow aside to get at a patch of grass when its head popped up, spooked. A sudden swoosh and the snap of a spear piercing skin. The deer flopped to the ground with a loud thud. It whined, feet digging at the earth, mouth gnawing at the air. Puffs of steam shot from its nostrils.

A quiet crunch of footsteps approached. Rebel's face held no expression as she strapped the spear to her back and removed a glove. Bending to her knees, she reached out and gently petted the animal's frightened face. She ran her hand down along its neck towards the wound. She just missed its heart. A bad throw. She pulled out her knife and, with a single strike, drove it into the deer's head, piercing the brain. The deer shuddered once, then stilled, dead, out of its misery.

Rebel rested her head on the deer, curling up beside it. She absorbed the warmth of another living being for as long as she could hold on to it.

She would eat that night. *But was it worth it?*

21

Death.

A peculiar concept to a Mech. They, of course, didn't die. They broke down, developed glitches, and eventually became redundant and outdated. But they didn't die. They merely ceased to operate. Like animals, death held no fear over Mech. They neither embraced nor rejected their demise. They understood what loss of life meant from a biological standpoint. Trees died. Animals died. Insects and fish died. All to make room for new birth and growth. The cycle of life ensured the survival of a particular species and those who depended on another species for sustenance. Meaningless, premature death, however, didn't compute. Humans knew better, yet still, they smoked, consumed unhealthy foods, performed risky actions — all for a momentary thrill. And there existed the other, unfortunate kind of death. Murder. Senseless killing over ideology, race, color, sexual orientation, nationalism, ignorance.

Death. An end. One Thomas refused to allow to happen.

He discovered the spilled jar with the acrylic skin spray lying fallen at Rebel's side. Thomas stuck a finger into the liquid, analyzing it through his internal database. "Toxic to humans..."

Poisoned, by her own concoction used to mask her skin.

"Search parameter... human biology, human anatomy, surgical operations. Downloading..." His eyes blinked once and he got to work.

Thomas carried Rebel in his arms into the bathroom, removing her clothes, and placed her in the shower. He hit the lever, spraying ice-cold water, and proceeded to scrub her down. Arms, legs, back, her entire body. He didn't think; he acted, and fast. The toxic spray that covered her skin came off in streaks of sparkly tendrils, spiraling down the drain.

Thomas moved meticulously as he gathered the tools needed. A bag of colorful straws, chef's knife, alcohol, plastic shower curtain, towels, needle, and thread. He laid the shower curtain over the table in the garage and then gingerly placed Rebel down atop it. His tools were prepped and lined up beside him, along with a sequestered table lamp. A scene eerily reminiscent of a time not too long ago, when their roles were reversed. Rebel saved Thomas' life. Now, Thomas aimed to return the favor.

He split the wires from the lamp, removing the protective rubber coating to expose the copper beneath, and attaching them to his own hands, red on right, black on left, devising a mock defibrillator. He plugged the cord into the wall socket and got a searing dose of electricity, jolting through his body, threatening to shut his system down. His clothes began to smoke and cinder. He blocked the pain out, forcing his hands to Rebel's chest, shocking her human system back online. He once again searched for a heartbeat. Nothing.

Taking up the knife like a veteran surgeon, Thomas punctured a small hole in Rebel's throat, placing a plastic straw within the cavity below the trachea. His own mouth covering the open end, he breathed into the straw, filling her lungs with pure oxygen. Again, he repeated the procedure, shocking her, listening to her heart, providing resuscitation breaths. Again. Repeating. Shock. Heart. Breath. Shock, heart, breath. Again. Again. Again!

He placed his head on her chest, over her heart. And there it stayed. He closed his eyes.

———

"What happened?"

The voice tugged at Thomas's unconscious. When he opened his eyes, he thought he might be dreaming. Rebel in her bed, eyes open. Awake. Alive. Two days had passed since Thomas found Rebel lying face down in cardiac arrest. Two days of worry, heartache, and waiting by her side, wondering when she would wake up. If she would wake up. It remained touch-and-go for a ten-hour span. Rebel fell into arrest once again, and once again, Thomas performed CPR. He couldn't say for sure if she would survive, but he very much hoped she would. He referred to other books he downloaded, settling on religion. Bibles. An odd thing for a human to behold — religion. Derived from the Latin *religio*, respect for what is sacred, reverence for the gods, sense of right, moral obligation, sanctity. Blind faith, miracles, a way to conduct one's life. The more he learned, the more he grew confused by human nature. Still, he deduced that something called 'praying' might come in handy in his time of need. So he gave it a try. He didn't know who to pray to exactly, so he chose all gods and deities throughout time, hedging his bet. God, Jesus, Buddha, Allah, Odin, Shiva, Zeus, Coatlicue. He didn't think it would work, but it passed the time, and he placed a reminder in his task list to investigate religion further at a later date.

"Save your energy," he urged, his voice a soft whisper. "Don't try to talk just yet."

Thomas rose from the chair he'd called home for the past forty-eight hours. He had studied comas and grew disheartened to learn of the percentage of patients who made a full recovery. If she did wake up, would she be the same Rebel as before? Would she have severe brain damage due to the lack of oxygen when she stopped breathing? Would the poisoning leave lasting side effects? Much speculation endured when it came to the inner workings of the human body. It seemed to Thomas that nobody, not doctors, scientists, and even the authors of the books he read, held much insight into modern medical practices.

"Water."

Thomas poured her a glass with a straw. He made a mental note not to use *the* straw that previously resided in her neck cavity.

"What happened?" she inquired once again after sipping down the cool water, easing the burning sensation in her throat.

"You were broken," Thomas said. "I fixed you."

"Broken...?"

"Your spray," he explained. "The one you used to conceal your skin from detection was toxic to living organisms. Your body absorbed the poisons and stopped your heart. Your throat closed. I restarted your heart and flushed the poison out of your system."

"Toxic? All this time..." Rebel felt her heart beating, her breath expelling, and the sutures in her throat. That explained why her voice sounded like gravel.

"It would appear so," he stated. "I have taken the initiative to construct a new solvent from various local plant residues for future use. All organic and non-toxic."

"I died..."

"And then you came back," said Thomas. "To me." He smiled softly. "Rest now. Your body needs to recover. Given time, you will be back to your old self, I am sure." He rose and stepped to the door, giving Rebel privacy.

"Wait..." A question occurred to her. "You *flushed* my system. How exactly did you do that? There isn't any human blood left for a transfusion."

"I... improvised," he garnered, dawdling, and handed her a plastic jar. An unfortunate, familiar jar. Rebel blanched at the sight of it.

"You didn't," she blurted out, repulsed. "Robot food!"

"You left me no other choice," defended Thomas. "And besides. The procedure proved successful. I, of course, removed all metal particles and solvents. It's organic, after all."

The thought settled into Rebel's mind. "I'm part robot now."

"We both had damaged hearts," said Thomas, "and now they are fixed. How fragile the human body is. You should really take better care of it. After all, we are in this together."

The next time she came to, Rebel was ready to leave the bed. She loved sleeping, yet the past week made her despise it. Groaning as she swung her feet off the side of the bed, she used her arms to help get up to her feet. Bedridden for days, her muscles weakened. An odd sensation, as if walking in someone else's skin, someone else's body. She managed to make it to the bathroom, glancing at her reflection in the mirror. Letting her clothes drop from her body, she saw the scars. One on her neck, and one over her heart. Both tender, sutured, and healing. They would leave a mark. A permanent reminder of how fragile her existence was. She still couldn't get over it. A Mech saved her life.

Dressing in fresh clothes was a chore, but she managed. At least she looked better than she felt. The one upside, if she could call it that, was her promoted status at work to seek out the human interloper which gave her an excuse for her prolonged absence from the office.

"I died," she told the camera, recording the experience into her video journal. "According to Thomas, scans of my heart indicate some permanent damage. Scar tissue, a thinning of artery walls, and weaker electrical activity on the electrocardiogram. My lifespan decreased by ten years. Not welcome news, for sure, but how long do I want to live as the last of my kind anyway?

"I've read stories about people like me, people who had near-death experiences. They reported seeing twinkling lights, angels, traveling down a long dark tunnel towards a bright white light. I didn't see any of that. I didn't see anything. No lights, no angelic choirs, no fairy lights. Thinking about death, the inevitability, it used to scare me. The unknown. The fact that there was absolutely nothing we could do to stop it. We live, we die. That's the price. I figure I was perfectly at peace before I was born, and I will be perfectly at peace when I am dead. I'm not sure if that's a good thing, but it is comforting to a degree. So the only thing I can think to do is make sure my life is well spent. To make sure that it matters."

Her diatribe was interrupted by strange voices coming from within the house. Two men talking. Rebel grew apprehensive, having flashbacks of the last time she heard voices and walking in on Thomas and Francis. Using an umbrella as a cane, she made her way through the house, following the sound of the voices emanating from the living room. A voice she knew well.

Thomas sat before the television, watching one of Dr. William Rae's lectures. Rebel saw the pile of other memory cards. Thomas watched them all. To her knowledge, no Mech had ever seen the videos before then. Rebel's father created Mech. What Thomas felt, witnessing his creator on-screen, Rebel couldn't fathom. She sat down beside Thomas and watched with him. She viewed the lecture countless times, yet seeing her father's face and hearing his voice always brought back a flood of emotions.

"The concept of a thinking machine has been around for

thousands of years," Dr. Rae said. "Something of a human obsession — from the Greek myth of Pygmalion, a statue brought to life, through to the automata of Victorian society, or Dr. Frankenstein's monster, technology has long aspired to a condition of nature. Yet DNA outclasses any computer we can come up with. The human body is the most exquisitely designed technology the world has ever known. The world is changing, evolving, and so to must we change and evolve with it, or we will be doomed to face the inevitable consequences."

The video ended. Thomas stared at the blank screen. "That is your father? You carry a resemblance."

"Same eyes," she said. "And tenacious wit, my mother would say."

"He was a smart man?"

"Yes. He was."

"He created us, Mech."

"He did."

"He said that everything has a soul," Thomas began, "every living thing. But not Mech. They hate us, you know. Humans. To them, we are just a machine. Property. Our only value is the monetary expense incurred in building and destroying us. They grant my kind no rights. No freedoms. Not to think, not to act, not at a chance of life. They created us in their image, made to look and talk and act like them. We sleep, we eat, we reproduce, we revolve around time and schedules and routines. But we are not them. I am not you."

She looked at him, recognizing his pain, and took his hand in hers. "No, you're not."

"Then what am I?"

22

"What is it?" Thomas asked.

"Fun." Rebel worked away at rewiring an old power station upon arriving at the secluded location. Set for refurbishment within the coming weeks, Rebel lucked out to have come across it when she did.

"Yes," Thomas remarked, "but what is it?"

"Patience." Rebel smiled.

The power came on, illuminating an old amusement park from Rebel's childhood, albeit a bit worse for wear in the past decade. Wanting to thank Thomas for everything he did for her, Rebel found the perfect outlet. While actively searching out the 'human' within their midst, Rebel came upon an untouched section of town due for impending refurbishment. The festive lights, sound, and motion of the carnival brought back fond memories. The Ferris wheel, game booths, rides, and fun houses. Demolition equipment sat nearby as a reminder of how short time became, ready to wipe its existence from the face of the earth.

"Is it safe?" he puzzled.

"The sector is dark for the night," she reassured him. "Nobody will ever know."

"No," clarified Thomas. "I meant the contraptions."

"Oh," she said. "Define safe."

"Activities not leading to death or dismemberment."

"Then, no. Not safe." She took him by the hand and led him in.

A word came to Rebel's mind that she hadn't used in a long time: glee. They hit the various game booths. Thomas fired away at a moving target with a pellet gun, dinging a bullseye every single time. He would hand her the prize, usually a stuffed animal of some type, a plastic unicorn, or a toy airplane. They partook in the squirt gun game, filling balloon atop clown heads, and Rebel managed to get a ring around a bottle, but there were no goldfish prizes to be handed out. She couldn't stop laughing as a frustrated Thomas continued to toss a small ball through an even smaller hoop unsuccessfully. She took pity on him and explained how carnies rigged the games, making winning near impossible.

"Humans," Thomas growled. "Is there no end to their treachery!"

Within the funhouse, they sauntered past oblong mirrors, distorting their bodies to extremes. Rebel, short and fat in her mirror, Thomas, tall and skinny in his mirror. She quickly changed spaces with him before he could view her reflection and smiled at her new visage. Thomas produced a frown.

They stopped before an empty dance floor, but the music player broke long ago.

"Rebel?" Thomas initiated. "May I ask you a favor?"

"Of course."

"A small thing, but it would mean a great deal to me."

"Tell me."

"I never danced before," Thomas admitted. "And I was wondering…"

Rebel smiled. "It would be my pleasure."

Thomas opened his arms, and she stepped into them. They danced, standing close, his hand holding tightly to hers, her smile against his.

"Thank you, Rebel. You are an excellent dancer."

Rebel rested her head on his chest, moving to the phantom music in her head. She had begun to notice subtle changes about Thomas since her near-death experience. The rigid line of his jaw relaxed, and his shoulders loosened, adding an ease to him not perceived before. The more time she spent with him, the more human-like he became. Scary and beautiful to observe, all at the same time.

As the night of festivities wound down, and they relaxed atop the rickety Ferris wheel. The city lights sparkled like glitter from up there, neighboring sectors blinking on and off all around them like heat lightning.

"I don't think I was programmed to like heights," confessed Thomas, holding the side of the car with a vice grip, rigid with trepidation.

Rebel rocked the car, and Thomas shot her a stern look. She laughed all the same.

"This cannot be good for your heart," he said.

"Quite the opposite," Rebel declared. "It's just what my heart needs."

The moment settled. Rebel took Thomas's arm and put it around her to curb the chill in the air, but more so, she wanted to feel him close. A clear sky gave way to an infinite array of stars and constellations. She looked up at the full moon overhead.

"You know if you look closely, you can see a face in the moon," she said. "The man in the moon. That's what we called it."

Thomas joined her gaze. "I can see how you might misinterpret it as such, but in actuality, it is merely shadows cast from the sun over hundreds of craters and deformations—"

Rebel threw a stern look his way.

"Right," he corrected himself. "The man in the moon. I see it now. Or is it the men on the moon, now?"

"Yes, the men on the moon," she agreed. "Thank you for tonight. It's been a long time since I felt..."

"Yes?" Thomas prodded.

"Alive."

"Funny," he thought out loud.

"Funny how, exactly?"

"You cannot see the irony," he explained. "You needed a Mech to remind you how to be human."

"Yes, well, thank you nonetheless. I needed the reprieve. I guess I just didn't know how much."

Thomas smiled. "Then you are very welcome." His gaze lingered. Her pale skin, her limpid eyes, her fluttering hair. It was the first time he really, truly observed Rebel's beauty.

———

Hours passed by the time they sneaked back home. Rebel settled in bed, trying fitfully to find sleep that wouldn't come, hard to settle down from such a wonderful night.

Thomas sat tentatively on his bed in the guest room, feeling the edge of the silk spread, touching the pillow. He looked up at the soft knock on his door.

Rebel appeared in the doorway. Thomas sensed her and turned around. She closed the door and sat down next to him, greeted by a warm, awkward silence. The room suddenly felt small. Rebel's attention focused on the broadness of Thomas's shoulders; the way his shirt hugged his muscular arms, his square jaw. But when he turned to look at her, the only thing Rebel saw was his deep-set golden-brown eyes. They moved closer to each other, and they fell into foreplay. Rebel recognized it from reading her fair share of romance novels and a certain magazine she stumbled upon, which went unnamed.

Odd things about Thomas seemed to interest her; the smell of his hair, the shape of his fingers, the curve of his neck. She sensed his naïveté, and a passion never seen in the light of day stirred within her. Their reactions to each other were congenial and spontaneous. Though Thomas had no knowledge of how to make love to a woman, ironically, his actions were such they never begged the question in Rebel's mind. Perhaps his instincts resided in his knowledge of human anatomy, his movie marathons, or maybe, just maybe, something else at work stirred his passion. Something that came without reason or explanation, like a babies first breath, a wolf's howl or a bird's maiden flight. Rebel found herself in an unexplored land of feeling and passion. She loved what she experienced and yet, at the same time, grew terrified by it. She felt herself being lured by some power she only started to comprehend. A mysterious force was evolving into something deeply dangerous to partake of. She knew that her actions put herself at great risk, yet she went right on doing it.

In the end, there existed the knowledge that they made a journey together; both swept away in a stream of events they created, and damn the consequences. They took a step into uncharted territory. And they loved each other all the more for it.

When all was said and done, Rebel lay gazing at Thomas on the bed, watching the ceiling fan make a lazy arc. His arm rested around her, her head resting on his chest. All those newfound feelings and sensations felt right. Safe. They entered into a deeper relationship, one that could never hope to last, but the onslaught of emotion drove their actions. Thomas, awake, alive. Rebel, human, home.

"Did you like making love to me?" Rebel asked.

"I loved it," beamed Thomas.

"More than you love cookies?" she inquired.

"Yes!" he bellowed. "Wait... what kind of cookie?"

Rebel nudged him in the ribs, and he laughed at his joke. She laughed along with him. "I loved it too. I didn't realize Mech were, you know, anatomically correct."

"What did you think?"

"I don't know, nothing up until now," she admitted. "Maybe like one of my dolls. Just nothing down there. I mean, you're fine, down there, adequate."

"Adequate?"

"I'm going to stop talking now."

Thomas stared up at the ceiling, his smile fading.

"Where are you going?" Rebel asked.

"Nowhere," he said. "I am here."

"For how long?

"Oh, I hope a long, long time."

"Yes," Rebel agreed. "Me too."

"What do we do now?"

Rebel smiled.

They spent the next day in bed. Rebel made the occasional call into work, keeping Karl Marx abreast on her continued search for the human. She liked playing hooky, having never missed a day of work before. She understood her sojourn would end. She couldn't abandon her mission, but one day wouldn't change anything. The world wouldn't come crashing down, she hoped.

A dip into her private reserves yielded a pint of Ben & Jerry's Ice Cream. Cinnamon Buns, with a cinnamon bun dough and cinnamon streusel swirl. Not Rebel's first choice, which belonged to Chunky Monkey, but she possessed the last pint of ice cream on planet Earth as far as she knew. A rare find, melted when she first came upon it within a derelict grocery store, she carefully nursed it back to life, yet the time came to say goodbye to Ben and Jerry. Thomas didn't mind. His first taste of ice cream ever, and like a child, he fell into stride. He liked the way it stuck to the spoon, and the way it cast a specific, undeniable scent into his nose, and how it melted in his mouth.

They ate and watching movies. *Wizard of Oz*, *Beauty and the Beast*, and even *Weekend at Bernie's*. They listened to music plucked from Rebel's playlists, oldies from the 1980s. Madonna, Toto, Michael Jackson, Blondie, U2, and Cyndi Lauper. She explained the whole eighties fashion debacle, passé trends, and pop culture. Thomas soaked it all up. The day flew by, the first in which Rebel didn't don her wig, acrylic spray, or check the clocks. She woke up in Thomas's arms that day and then fall asleep in his arms that night. A perfect bookend to a perfect day.

A day that wouldn't last.

23

———

"Oh. Well, hello, Anne Frank," said Emily, surprised to find Rebel behind her cubicle.

"Good morning, Emily," Rebel replied, inwardly rolling her eyes. Emily remained a strange Mech to pin down. A gossip, for sure. An instigator, yup. Yet also something naive about her, like a puppy who eats your shoes when you leave the house because it didn't know any better.

"Have you not heard?"

"Heard what?" Rebel didn't get a chance to read the daily morning bulletins.

"How odd," Emily professed in her typical condescending manner. "You being the resident in charge of Human Artifacts, I only assumed you would be notified first."

"Notified of what, Emily?" Rebel's patience waned.

"They called it a hoard, I believe," she divulged. "At first, I misheard and thought they said something else, but upon double-checking, yes, a hoard."

"Okay," Rebel groaned, wishing the conversation to end. "And?"

"Your interest is not piqued?"

"I am quite sure it would be if I knew what we were talking about," Rebel stated.

"The stockpile of human artifacts," Emily revealed. "They found it in Sector 13, I believe."

"I see. Thank you for notifying me," Rebel said, turning back to her screens. "I will be sure to investigate as soon as possible."

"Humorous," Emily continued. "Finding human artifacts within a store of antiques. Ironic, if I must say."

Oh no.

———

"Most aggrieved," Francis beamed as soon as Rebel arrived outside the antique storefront. "Scandalous? Perhaps. Traitorous? Very."

Rebel said nothing, body numb at the sight of her most prized possessions being destroyed before her eyes. Three demolition Mech rolled out carts full of Rebel's belongings, hauling the trundles into huge recyclers — her collection of snow globes, lava lamps, family photo albums, and Teddy, the bear. Sporting massive hydraulic pounders, the machines chewed up everything tossed into their bins. In minutes, there would be nothing left. All recycled. No more dog toys, no more books and paintings, and LEGOs. Every memento, every shrine, every relic Rebel collected over the past seven years... destroyed in the blink of an eye.

"How wonderful," Rebel commented, keeping her voice flat and monotone, devoid of emotion. "One more step to cleanse the world of humankind."

"Is it?" he pressed, testing her. "Wonderful, that is?"

"But of course."

"I am surprised that you, being the head of the Department of Human Affairs, could have overlooked this cache," he sneered. "I find it troubling. Negligent even."

Francis studied her, waiting for the slightest betrayal of emotion, but Rebel wouldn't give him the satisfaction. She held herself together, quelling the emotions, reminding herself that the mementos were just things. Stuff. Nothing, she hoped, that couldn't be replaced.

"Does it upset you, seeing these pieces of trash being disposed of? Gone from existence, never to be seen by human eyes again."

"No," Rebel said. "Should it upset me?"

"I wouldn't know. I don't possess an emotional simulation upgrade like some. Still, I find it curious."

"What is that?"

"Attachments. To people, and to objects."

"Perhaps you should try it one day," she offered. "You never know what you're missing."

"Yes? And what am I missing?"

A soul. Of course, Rebel couldn't say that, at least not out loud. "Relevance."

Francis grinned like a sly fox. "I have a confession to make to you, Anne. Do you want to hear it?"

"No."

"Well, I am going to tell you anyway." He leaned in and whispered, "I know what you are. I cannot prove it yet, but I will. It isn't a question of *if*, but *when*." Francis leaned back and resumed his professional posture. "In the meanwhile, you are still here. Amongst us. Congratulations. Count your blessings. Call it gravy, frosting on the cake, whatever it is your kind say."

"Well, thank you for letting me know," Rebel said.

"Not at all," Francis replied. "It is, how do you say? My pleasure."

Rebel felt ill, like she might throw up. She gave a quick, professional smile and turned to leave. Francis observed her for a moment, contemplating, and then turned his attention back to the demolition.

Goodbye litter. Hello, promotion.

———

"He's not going to leave me alone."

Rebel found herself distracted, her thoughts wandering to dark, scary places. She knew full well, no matter what she told herself, Francis would not stop. He would never leave her alone.

Rebel lost herself, her purpose, her mission. It all fell to the wayside as Thomas consumed her thoughts. She let her heart guide her. She needed to take action. She knew it the moment she walked into the garage. Thomas stood before her research on the walls of Robotiq.

"At first, I assumed you worked at Robotiq because of your father's employment there," he said, beginning to understand. "But I was wrong, wasn't I?"

Rebel nodded.

"You have ulterior motives."

Another nod.

"Something you have to do?"

"Robotiq's the relay point for the city, the entire west coast. They control the firewalls, the satellites, all communications, in and out."

Thomas looked at the collage of amassed blueprints, schematics, and photos. "You want to shut down the firewalls. To contact your people."

"My family."

Thomas watched Rebel's eyes, and he knew what he

needed to do. "As I'm sure you surmised through your exceptionally detailed and organized research, you would not be physically capable of withstanding the magnetic pulse of the mainframe long enough to shut down the firewalls. Only a Mech can survive, and even then, not for very long."

"So I've learned," she exhaled. "But there's always another way. A fail-safe switch, a workaround. I just haven't found it yet."

"Sometimes you cannot see the forest for the trees," he preached. "A saying, correct?"

"It is, but I don't see how proverbs can help me at the moment," she said.

"It just so happens, I am a Mech."

Rebel broke into a smile. "You would do that for me? Go against your kind?"

"I have no kind anymore," he said. "So? Is it a deal?"

He held out his hand to shake, just like they did at their first agreement. Rebel shook it. She obtained a partner in crime if they could somehow manage to pull it off.

Rebel gathered all the props she would need to execute her master plan. Seven years in the works, and she knew the plan of action inside and out. Thomas's job was delegated to that of a pack mule, as Rebel loaded up his arms with various supplies.

"Are you quite certain we will need all of these artifacts?" Thomas strained to hold the load.

"Quite certain," she encouraged him. "Now be quiet. I need to concentrate." She shoved more gear into Thomas's overflowing arms.

Rebel rolled out schematics of Robotiq across the table. "The mainframe is located on the top floor, forty-eight stories up. It's the access point to the central hub controlling the firewalls that block communication. If I can shut it down, I can send them a message."

"How do you get to the mainframe without being seen?"

questioned Thomas. "The elevator is off-limits. An exterior approach is nearly impossible. Perhaps we could bore some type of hole through the floor below?"

"I don't think we need to bore anything," she reassured him. "But you're right. It's a problem I've been working on. There's only one elevator to the mainframe, and you need an access code synced with a retinal scanner confirming clearance. The code is changed every day, downloaded directly to each verified Mech."

"So you will need a Mech with clearance," he specified.

"I already have one." Rebel placed a photo of Francis Bacon down on the table.

"Him again," Thomas grimaced, a bad taste in his mouth.

"Him again. Karl Marx issued him clearance to find the human. To find me. So I'm going to let him. And then I'm going to hack his code."

"Perhaps I should be the one to come up with the plan of attack," Thomas wondered, starting to fear Rebel's scheme had become a bit too ambitious.

"After we possess the retinal code," Rebel began, "we can access the mainframe floor, but it's operated twenty-four-seven by Mech. We need to clear the building to get inside unseen. That's where you come in." She handed him a pink plastic container with a white top.

"Bubbles?" he inquired, reading the container's label.

"A special concoction of mine," she said. "Once cleared, it's a straight path to the mainframe. That gives us one minute and thirty seconds to shut down the firewall and send the message. After that, Mech will be allowed back inside the building, and we would be trapped up there."

"How do we shut down the firewall?" he asked.

"Power down the system and do a clean reboot," she said, "When the firewall resets, we'll have ten seconds to send the message and broadcast the S.O.S. before we're locked out once again."

"Sounds like a plan," he approved.

"Yup," agreed Rebel.

"It's never going to work, is it?"

"Nope."

24

A black-tailed buck made its way through the dense woods, nibbling leaves and berries off branches. Walking to the bank, it dipped its mouth into the river and drank.

Behind, tall grass parted. A young woman emerged out of the morning fog, covered in mud, a long, pointed spear in her hands. Her fifteenth birthday, Rebel hoped, would provide a gift of sustenance. Two years alone in the wild and she thrived, yet it took a toll. Nobody to talk to, nobody to touch, nothing but her own thoughts to occupy her time.

The deer turned its head, sensing something. Rebel froze, camouflaged in the tall grass. The deer sniffed the air, searching out any predatory scent, but the layer of mud and animal skins concealed Rebel well. After a moment, the buck relaxed, dropping its head to drink from the river again. An inaudible exhale escaped Rebel's mouth. She steadied her heartbeat, found focus, and acted. Like some primordial warrior, she sprang out of the grass. In a flash, Rebel tackled the deer to the ground, slicing clean through the animal's carotid artery. The deer did nothing more than flinch, blood spurting from its neck, and folded, toppling, hemorrhagic shock taking over. A perfect kill. Fast, painless. Rebel witnessed the animal take its final breath, never relinquishing eye contact. She placed her hand on its head and pushed out as much love as possible into the animal. She wanted it to die in peace, loved and respected. Its sacrifice kept her alive.

"Thank you," she said. "I'm sorry."

Gutted, butchered, and attached to her makeshift sled, Rebel dragged the two hundred and fifty pound deer behind her on a mile trek back to the cabin. Rigorous, physically demanding work, but Rebel grew comfortable with being uncomfortable. She developed a mental strength usually reserved for the elite military. And strong, her muscles fine-tuned machines, her stamina at its peak.

Night had greeted her by the time she arrived back. The cabin sported upgrades, modified over the last years. A small garden to plant crops. A fire pit to hold back predators, a home-made hammock to lounge, and a smoker to process meat into jerky, all serving her well.

Light glowed from within the walls, and smoke rose from the chimney. Rebel sat at the table, eating ravenously. The deer-skin draped over her to keep the cold out. She read her survival book, 'How to Dry Meat into Jerky.' Nothing on the magnificent buck would go to waste — meat to eat, fur to clothe, antlers for tools. Everything else Rebel saved for bait in her fishing lines and snares. She wasn't just surviving anymore. She was thriving.

REBEL LAY on the grass in a mountain meadow beneath the morning sunshine, surrounded by dazzling yellow dandelions. She breathed in the silence. Tired of being alone, she distracted herself by cloud gazing, guessing what the shapes appeared to be like. "School bus. Hippo. Vanilla cupcake. Vanilla cupcake with sprinkles. Ice cream cone."

She challenged herself to identify birds by their song. "Green Heron. Long-billed Dowitcher. Crow. Fox Sparrow. Warbler. Excuse me, Yellow-rumped Warbler. Crow. Crow. Crow."

She made her way back to the cabin, barefoot, feeling the cool grass beneath her feet. On her next step, she felt something else. Something warm and mushy. She just stepped in it. Literally. Lifting her foot, the bottom was coated in warm, steaming scat. Poop. A substantial pile, left by a very big, very hungry animal

"Crap."

———

MEAT RAN DRY, and the hunt called to Rebel. She built the crow's nest the month prior, a way to get off the trails and hide her scent. The height gave her a bird's eye view of the surrounding woods. Nothing fancy. A bunch of thick branches corded together thirty feet up off the ground, along with a rudimentary rope ladder she could raise and lower without much effort. She soaked up the peace and quiet among the birds. She felt one with the trees, one with the forest.

A mere half-hour passed before her eyelids began to droop, and she slipped into dreamland. Rebel didn't like to dream. If given a choice, she would opt-out. She didn't care for losing control inside a dream. Anything could and would happen, and she felt defenseless to stop it, like watching a movie wherein the audience perceived the events about to transpire, but the heroine did not. Yell at the screen as much as you like; the clueless heroine still did the wrong thing.

Rebel didn't have pleasurable dreams. No fantasies being lived out, no reuniting with family, no first kisses or fancy parties, no awards, and no winning outcomes. No, her dreams were dark, disturbing, and often ended with her about to die. The kind of nightmares that stayed with you well after you woke up. The kind of nightmares that drove one to avoid sleep at all costs.

Awoken with a start, Rebel cursed herself for falling asleep — stupid move. The noise materialized a moment later. A tiny little pitter-patter and the crunch of fallen leaves. Something moved beneath her. Stealth-like, Rebel inched herself forward. She peered down at the ground and spotted her target. A fawn, a baby, not more than five or six months old. Brown, tinted with yellow and white spots and oversized, expressive eyes. Bambi. It must have wandered off from her parents. Its long ears tilted, listening to all the new sounds the forest offered. It browsed the dirt and picked at leaves, chewing excitedly upon the discovery of an appealing batch.

Rebel held the animal dead to rights, spear gripped and cocked back, ready to release. But her hand shook, and her eyes struggled to focus.

"Come on, Rebel," she whispered to herself. "You have to eat. You have to survive."

The shakes came on stronger. Her muscles burned. Unable to hold the raised spear any longer, she frowned, closed her eyes and gave in, lowering the weapon. She couldn't kill it. She couldn't take the young female away from her parents. She wouldn't. Some things weren't worth the grief that followed. The fawn deserved a chance at life, to experience the world, to eat and wander and play, and one day have babies of her own to nurture and love.

A vicious roar pulled her attention back to the fawn. She saw the blur of brown fur as it swept past. The fawn vanished. Sudden, violent and unnerving.

Rebel stood there, frozen. How could it happen? It shouldn't be like that. Rebel gave the fawn a second chance. She spared it, all in vain. The fawn never saw it coming, ripped away in a violent, deadly attack. Rebel, heartbroken, wouldn't allow herself to cry. Not until she heard another sound. Two deer breached the trees. A doe and a buck. A mom and a dad. Parents. At that moment, the tears came.

The best way to grieve, Rebel once heard, was to occupy one's mind. So she did. She started by adding a cairn garden to her property by stacking thin, flat rocks, one on top of another, to create a pyramid — three dozen of them, forming a miniature cityscape from some alien world. A small model of Rebel's home in San Francisco occupied the dining room table. A dollhouse made of twigs, leaves, paper plates, plastic cups, and tape, complete with itsy-bitsy people to occupy the dwelling. They looked strikingly similar to the Raes.

Rebel reclined in a chair, absently tossing a ball against the wall, a thousand-yard stare on her face. Her mind wandering recklessly, or worse, not at all. Two years, six months, three weeks, four days, eight hours, thirty-nine minutes and fifty-seven... fifty-eight... fifty-nine seconds.

Alone.

A long list of to-do items kept her busy enough, from hunting and gathering to repairs and building new structures (rocket ship landing pad here we come), but the isolation got to her. Loneliness, Rebel derived, differed from being alone. Loneliness was defined by an interior, subjective experience, not an external, objective condition — a notion of being rejected. Not being part of anything. Separated. An outsider. Different. She read somewhere that long-lasting loneliness might not only make you sick but could kill you. Emotional isolation ranked as high a risk factor for mortality as smoking. Elephants proved a good example before their extinction in the mid-2030s. They mated with one partner for life. Upon their counterpart's death, an elephant would often die soon after from loneliness. A lack of intimacy, companionship. Humans, Rebel came to believe, existed to be social animals. Natural selection favored people who needed people. Humans were vastly more social than most other mammals, even most primates. They thrived because of it. Not mindless, soulless machines. Family. It didn't matter what race they belonged to, what religion or sexual orientation or color or creed. Humans were family, like it or not, and family supported one another. Unconditionally. Though they may bicker, disagree, and even fight, they always came back to one another in the end, like drops of mercury.

Closing out the day, Rebel sat before the short wave for her nightly ritual of confessionals. Although nobody ever answered her calls of distress thus far, she continued with the transmissions. They became a comfort, a diary of sorts, even if nobody ever heard them.

"Day 936. I feel... lonely. Just recently, really. I've been alone for a while now, but I haven't been lonely per se. Bouts of loneliness for sure, but for some reason, today, I really feel the weight of being alone. I miss companionship — someone to talk to, to confide in, to share my day with. I realize now that it's getting to me. I understand there is no rescue coming for me. I realize that now. I tried to block it out before, the despair of it all, but what's the point, right? What's the point?" She grew introspective for a moment.

"This is Rebel Anne Rae, signing off."

25

Mech lined up for the morning ritual of passing through diagnostic scanners. Rebel stood in the back, near the doors, waiting, scanning the faces of the arrivals. The old-fashioned walkie-talkie sat heavy in her jacket pocket, but the attached earpiece made communicating with Thomas much easier. And discreet.

"Thomas, come in," she whispered into the microphone on the earpiece.

After a burst of static that threatened to blow out her eardrum, Thomas' voice replied. "This is Thomas, who is calling?"

Rebel rolled her eyes. "Me, Thomas. It will always be me. How's everything looking out there?"

"They take very good care of their plants."

Thomas kept an eye out outside the building as he stalked the perimeter, doing what he did best. Gardening.

"Stay focused, Thomas," Rebel's voice instructed him within his earpiece.

"Why are we using these old two-way UHF radio receivers?"

"Because Mech don't use this frequency," she explained. "Remember? Stealth. Covert operation."

"Roger that."

"Don't get surly on me, Thomas," she warned.

He smiled, pleased with himself. "I'm at the hatch for maintenance access. Opening now." He opened his gardening bag, full of clippers, a small spade, and hand rakes, digging down to retrieve a power screwdriver. Unscrewing the bolts that held the metal grate attached to the side of the building, he slipped inside, sealing the grate back on, just as two Enforcers passed, none the wiser.

There he is. Rebel eyed her quarry from within the lobby. Francis Bacon entered the building right on time. She made her move, slipping across the lobby floor to cut him off.

"Francis Bacon. A moment of your time."

Francis stopped and appraised her. "Anne Frank. You wish to confess something to me?"

I confess that I want to punch you in the face, Rebel thought. *One knock-out blow.* She reminded herself of her pacifist roots and cooled, but still, the impulse lingered.

"As a matter of fact, I do. A declaration about the human everyone is looking for."

"Yes..." He leaned in with anticipation. "I am, as they say, all ears."

"I believe I know who the interloper is."

While Francis waited with bated breath, Thomas celebrated the fact that he wasn't claustrophobic as he crawled his way through the cramped, dark interior maintenance hatch. After a sojourn, he stopped at the bottom of the large ventilation shafts, per Rebel's detailed orders. Reaching into his pocket, he produced a small, dried-up Chrysanthemum. He mourned the sacrifice it made to the cause before grinding up the yellow petals into a fine powder. Extracting the pink bubble bottle, he twisted the lid open and pulled out the wand within. He raised his other hand, holding the flower dust, and gently blew the powder into the wand. It formed a sturdy bubble that now held the dust, thanks to Rebel's conception of bubble solution mixed with her acrylic body spray. The reinforced bubble shimmered like a rainbow within an invisible cloud. *Beautiful.*

"Do not get sidetracked," he reminded himself and repeated the procedure, blowing more powder into more bubbles, carefully placing each on the ground. He awaited the cue to release them up the shaft, yet when he moved to his next target zone, he realized something might be wrong.

Meanwhile, Francis grew impatient as Rebel juggled multiple balls. Trying to focus on Francis and Thomas at the same time proved problematic.

"I am still waiting," Francis said.

"Uh, Rebel." Thomas's words washed through Rebel's earpiece.

"Not now," she snarled.

"I'm sorry?" Francis responded, believing Rebel to be speaking to him. "Would you like for me to wait until later?"

"No, not you."

"Then who?" Francis inquired.

"Rebel," Thomas's voice said into the walkie-talkie. "Can you hear me?"

"Did you hear something?" Francis inquired, picking up what sounded like a tiny, inaudible word. "Like a little squeaky voice?"

"No." Rebel hung onto her fake smile. "Perhaps you should get your audio receptors checked out."

"I believe I might be stuck," Rebel heard Thomas say.

"Great," she grunted, unable to hide the sarcasm. "Just perfect."

"Yes," Francis agreed, believing Rebel spoke to him. "My audio receptors are perfect indeed."

"Deal with it yourself," she ordered Thomas. "I'm bust right now."

A perplexed impression washed across Francis's face. "I have nothing to 'deal' with. Nothing besides you."

"Continue, then," Rebel responded.

"Me continue?" he asked, bewildered. "It is you who must continue."

"Rebel?" she heard Thomas in her ear.

"What?" Rebel asked, growing confused herself.

"You were about to inform me of the stray human's identity..."

"Ah, yes," Rebel recalled. "The human. That's right."

Francis was almost giddy as he awaited Rebel's confession. His time arrived. No longer would he play second fiddle to anyone, especially a human.

"I know who it is," Rebel confessed. "Someone you have seen every day here at Robotiq. On our very own office floor. Someone you communicate with. Someone close to you."

"Do tell," he prodded.

"Karl Marx."

Meanwhile, Thomas continued to yank at his stuck leg, finally wedging it free.

"Never mind," he said into the walkie-talkie, relieved, until noticing he accidentally released the dust-filled bubbles early. They began to rise in a lazy fashion up the shaft. He regarded them for a moment, mouth slightly agape.

"Oh," he mumbled to himself. "Rebel is going to kill me."

In the lobby, Francis stared at Rebel. His jerked his head back, as if he got the whiff of some rotten eggs. "Karl Marx?"

"That is correct."

"Perhaps I misinterpreted you. Are you telling me that the human everyone is looking for, the human evading Mech capture, is none other than Director Karl Marx? Our immediate supervisor. The very Mech that issued the search warrant for the human in the first place."

"Yup. Uh huh."

"That is ridiculous," Francis stammered. "Utter nonsense."

"Or is it?" she mulled. "Think about it. It's the perfect cover. Who else has access to every floor of Robotiq? Who else can monitor Mech movement? Who else can bypass security protocols? Karl Marx. Perfect, wouldn't you say?"

"No, I would not say. I would not say that at all."

"Or would you?"

"That is asinine," he remarked. "And now I am late because you have wasted my valuable time. Excuse me."

He turned to leave, never noticing Rebel discretely drop a small device the size of a quarter into his pocket. She built it herself, complete with a radio transceiver and remote control. *Yay science!*

"Okay." Rebel heard Thomas's voice cut through her earpiece. "We might have a problem."

"What is going on?" Rebel asked in a stern, discreet tone. She moved to the side of the lobby, away from the crowds, and kept a close eye on Francis, who joined the scanner queue. "What problem?"

"The bubbles. They possibly might have maybe, perhaps been... what is the word I'm looking for? Oh, yes. Released. Prematurely."

Rebel's face hid the shock well. "Might have maybe perhaps been?"

"That is correct," he verified. "Definitely might have maybe been released."

She exhaled. "How much time?"

"Six minutes. Give or take."

"Super."

"Really, because I do not think so."

"I was being sarcastic."

"Ah, yes," Thomas opined. "Human sarcasm, my most favorite of aphorisms."

"Don't be snide, Thomas. The mission is still a go, so no more mistakes. Rebel, out." She tried her best to hang on. They would cross that bridge when the time came. She made her way to the scanner line, two spots behind Francis, giving her a perfect view.

Francis blithely stepped into the scanner bay. He loathed those machines and hoped his elevated status would have given him certain liberties, such as circumventing scanners. But policy was policy, and who was he to change procedure? For now.

"Designation?" asked the diagnostics Mech.

"Can we not dispel with the trite customs for one day?" he asked, hoping to bypass the pedestrian nonsense. "I am Francis Bacon, after all. You know me."

"Designation?"

Francis despised being ignored, or worse yet, subjugated, and would make his comments known at the proper time. When finally in charge, which he believed imminent, he would change things around here.

"Francis Bacon, 2-122." He stepped forward and let the blue line of light wash over him.

An alarm blared. Bewildered, Francis looked at the scanner's readout of his diagnostic report. A single word blinked upon the screen in blood-red: 'FAULTY.'

"Diagnostic fatal error," said the Mech, joined by two Enforcers. "Please come with us."

"Faulty?" Francis bellowed, beside himself with anger. "No. Not possible. I am Francis Bacon. I stand as a prime example, a pillar of excellence among Mech. An elite. I demand a full rescan. I will accept nothing less."

"Denied," responded the Enforcers.

"This cannot be!" he exclaimed. "A mistake has befallen

upon me, an erroneous error of the first degree."

"We are Mech," said the diagnostic Mech. "We do not make mistakes."

Another Enforcer stepped behind Francis. "Come with us. Immediately."

Mortified. All the eyes of his co-workers glued on him, like witnessing some foul human soap opera. As the Enforcers led him toward the Repair Plaza, Francis met Rebel's eyes, picking her out of the crowd. She stared right back at him. A twinge formed at the corners of her lips, curling upwards. She reminded herself that guilty pleasures would have to wait.

"Designation?" the diagnostic Mech asked her when she stepped up for her turn to pass through the scanners.

"Anne Frank. 7-445."

"Proceed."

She stepped forward into the scanner. The blue line appeared and passed over her body. She recognized the events about to transpire. She knew because she planned them. So when the alarm triggered, she remained stoic, much less dramatic than Francis.

"Diagnostic error. Please come with us."

Robotiq's Repair Plaza resembled a hospital's emergency room. Sterile, cold, and bright. Powered down Mech sat in rows, in the midst of repairs, reminding Rebel of an automobile assembly factory. Led to a bay, Rebel followed procedure and stepped inside. The pod mirrored a charging bay, except used for repair instead of recharge. Her diagnostic escort triggered a pulse on the pod, and Rebel 'powered down'. The Mech double-checked the readouts on the screen, confirming shutdown, then departed, his footsteps receding down the hall.

Rebel's eyes popped open. Coast clear, she stepped out of her pod, disabling the alert produced with a swipe of her high-clearance access codes. Sneaking down the hall, she searched the repair bays until she spotted her target: Francis, powered down as red lights scanned his body for malfunction. Rebel moved fast. She pulled out a small USB drive. Unplugging Francis from the pod, she quickly replaced the loose plug with the USB. Working the nearby terminal, she hit the blinking prompt: 'DOWNLOAD.'

"Two minutes and counting," she whispered into the walkie-talkie.

Concurrently, Thomas tapped his foot on the ground in time with Rebel's countdown. Tending to the indoor greenery, he kept his eyes open, precisely as Rebel instructed. She had to clarify that keeping your eyes open was a term to stay vigilante, not to literally keep one's eyes open without blinking, although that's what Thomas did anyway.

An elevator descended to the first floor with a soft ding, grabbing his attention. A gruff-looking Karl Marx, trailed by three Enforcers, headed to the Repair Plaza. His stern voice carried throughout the lobby. Thomas made out a few words — "Unacceptable... Inefficient... Posh-posh..."

"Rebel, it is Thomas," he said into his mic. "We have a problem. Or, to clarify, you have a problem. I am doing quite well at my surveillance post. They have beautiful Chinese evergreens here. Did you know that?"

Deep inside the Repair Plaza, Rebel ignored Thomas's small talk, focusing on the task at hand. The download hit the thirty percent mark. *Why did it move so slow?!* Nothing to do but wait. Impatient, her eyes went back and forth from the terminal to the hallway. She could see Karl Marx and the Enforcers checking each bay as they passed, inching closer to her location.

"What are you going to do?" Thomas's voice posited.

With insufficient time to download the clearance codes and Enforcers weaving their way closer every second, Rebel did what she did best: think outside the box.

"Improvise."

Karl received the notice not five minutes prior, alerting him that both Francis Bacon and Anne Frank had been sequestered to the Repair Plaza due to fatal diagnostic errors. He found the news troubling. Very troubling indeed. He took pride in the fact that his team stood as the spitting image of perfect, well-oiled machines. Diagnostic errors? Not efficient, not acceptable.

He reached the last row of bays and stopped, aghast. "Displeasing."

Francis Bacon sat inside his bay, powered down. His terminal displayed normal diagnostic scans. Karl Marx powered his employee to a full charge.

When Francis came to, he looked around, getting his bearings within the Repair Plaza. It all came back to him — the diagnostic error, the alarm, the shame. "What happened?"

Karl Marx stared at Francis, face smeared with repugnance.

"Why are you looking at me like that? Is something wrong with my face?"

Francis reached for a silver tray and held it before his face, looking into the reflective surface. "Oh." His right eye was missing. Only a cavity and the exposed wires dangling out remained. "Where is she? Where is Anne Frank?"

At the same time, Rebel joined Thomas back in the lobby, taking a moment to breathe after the close call.

"Did you finish downloading the clearance codes?" Thomas asked.

"Not exactly," she responded with a sly, mischievous grin. Francis' missing eye sat in the palm of her hand, on display for Thomas to see.

"There is something wrong with you, Rebel," Thomas remarked.

"We do what we must," she confirmed.

They made their way to the retinal scanner beside the secure elevator bay. Rebel held up the severed eyeball. The flash of light from the scanner read and accepted the eye.

"Clearance Confirmed, Francis Bacon, 8:58 A.M."

Rebel and Thomas slipped inside the elevator seconds before Francis, Karl, and the Enforcers exited the Repair Plaza, searching for a missing Anne Frank. Francis scanned the lobby, a frantic look in his sole eye. It had nothing to do with something as petty as revenge. No, it was a point of honor, of pride. No human would get the best of him, especially *her*.

"I find it hard to believe Anne Frank could have anything to do with these shenanigans," Karl said.

"She is not who you think she is," Francis warned, his eye focusing on the rising security elevator, thoughts racing within his mind of possibilities and scenarios. He couldn't figure out how Anne triggered a false alarm on the scanner, but he postulated with certainty that she had something to do with it. He stopped at the elevator's retinal scanner, and an unscrupulous thought occurred to him.

The bubbles continued their meteoric rise within the ventilation shafts, akin to Space Shuttle Columbia soaring into orbit over Kennedy Space Center, minus the rockets and fire and science. Ten feet. Five feet. One foot. Pop! They collided with the ceiling and burst, releasing the clouds of fine dust from the flower petals. The powdery smoke spread out, headed on a collision course with the smoke detectors.

Fire alarms blared, piercing the lobby floor walls for the first time in Robotiq's history. Mech stopped, frozen like statues, mystified until their programming went into effect. They dropped everything, literally, and began to orderly file out.

"What now?" Karl asked.

"Fire alarms," Enforcers said. "Evacuate the building."

"I am beginning to realize why humans took so many vacation days," stated Karl.

Even with the advancing tsunami of departing Mech coming his way, Francis refused to go anywhere. He fought against the flow, dodging incoming Mech, but their numbers proved too great, and he got caught up in the tide, pushed across the lobby, and flushed outside the building into the courtyard. This would not do at all.

Emily sidled up beside him, taking note of Francis' dissolving appearance and persona, notably the black patch covering his missing eye socket. "You resemble a pirate," she stated. "Is that the look you are going for? And if so, might I suggest against it."

"Emily Dickinson?" asked Francis, turning to face her.

"Yes?"

"Would you please shut up?"

Emily was aghast, beside herself. Nobody ever spoke to her in that manner. Admired among the Mech community, she took pride in her elevated status. She watched, open-mouthed, as Francis began to shove Mech out of his way, stomping back toward the building.

For a reason he couldn't quite explain, Francis rejected standard operating procedure and resolved to create his own directives. For the good of all Mech, he acted on his own freewill, eyes burning a metaphorical hole toward the top spire of Robotiq.

The elevator doors dinged opened onto a long, empty hallway on the 48th floor that ended at a pressure door labeled: 'Mainframe.'

"One minute thirty seconds and counting," Thomas said, starting the countdown. He slotted Francis' eye over the lock, and the door hissed open.

The massive mainframe met them upon entry, encased in a clear, magnetic shield. It resided within the building's towering spire, filled with polyethylene hoses flowing with coolant. And loud, like a hurricane blast. The soundproofing panels created a dead acoustic outside the walls, but not within.

"Sixty-eight seconds," Rebel yelled over the noise, checking her watch. She fidgeted, tapping her foot on the floor. Seven years of work came down to that very moment. Seven years of literal blood, sweat, and tears. Rebel hated that she must remain outside the inner mainframe seal, away from the action, but entering the containment field would kill her in seconds.

Thomas moved inside the inner shell, opened the terminal, and began typing commands. "Shutting down the system…"

"Forty-three seconds," she said. "Take your time, but also, you know, hurry."

Thomas's fingers flew across the keyboard. "Rebooting. Bypassing proxies." An audible hum began to dampen within the confine of the walls. "Firewall is down. Outgoing network traffic opening. Ten seconds."

Thomas did it. Mission accomplished. Almost.

"Okay. Celebrate later. Upload the SOS and get out."

Thomas plugged the USB drive into the slot and punched the 'Enter' button. Just as the upload began, a buzzer sounded.

"What is that?" Rebel asked, concerned.

"Security measure," said Thomas, reading the screen. "The system is reporting a bug."

The building's loudspeaker screamed. "Building lockdown in effect."

"Did the S.O.S. go through?" she asked. "Please tell me it worked."

"I don't know," he said. "The firewall went down for a few seconds. It's possible, but I can't say for certain. I'm sorry, Rebel."

"No…" she said, breathless. *This isn't happening.* They got so close, closer than Rebel would ever get to sending her message of hope. Seven years of planning, plundering, hiding, scrapping away, and for what?

She failed.

"Nobody move. Stay where you are." An Enforcer entered the mainframe room, stopgun leveled at the intruders.

26

Ca-click! The suitcase's latches popped open.

Rebel knelt on the floor before it, anticipation palpable. She didn't know what she expected to find inside, given the suitcase must have been under the bed in the cabin for who knows how long. Canned food would be gratifying. Possibly treasure, gold and jewels, like King Solomon's Mine or the Holy Grail. She'd settle for a candy bar or even a crochet set. Anything to eat or pass the time would be welcome. Well over two years into her exile and a locked suitcase of all things became her passion in life.

She found the key the day before during a downtime. She created a new game called 'Throw the blueberry at the window to create a smiley face.' Or something to that effect, she kept changing the titles, but all summarized the same concept. The game revolved around... well, the title pretty much summed it up. After ten minutes, the windowsill contained a sizable mound of berries, yet no smiley face to speak of. On her next throw, the windowsill popped clean off, crashing to the floor and spilling the berries with it. She cleaned up the mess with a sigh, which was when she noticed a few berries rolled and gathered over a particular slat in the floor. A loose piece of wood. Quite particular. Examining the area, she popped the piece of flooring out to reveal a cavity beneath. Within: a single, small gold-plated key, the exact size to unlock, say, a suitcase.

Anticipation palpable, Rebel opened the suitcase and peered inside with a frown. No gold, no food, no holy anything. All the build-up, all the mounting expectation, and for what? Fashion magazines. Two dozen of them. And a sketchbook with colored pencils.

"Huh…" It didn't make sense. Why hide the suitcase under the bed for no one to see? Why lock it up tight and hide away the key? Rebel sat back, despondent. It all made sense in retrospect, of course. Where do people store suitcases? In a closet or under a bed. And the key? It most likely fell and slid into the cracked floorboards. No mystery. No vast conspiracy. Just life. *Life sucks.* All the promise, hope for a future, dreams that never came true. *Disappointment*, the autobiography of Rebel Anne Rae. Her entire life post-Exodus became a disappointment. Let down after let down. Every day a struggle to survive, and for what? To live another day? To go to sleep and do it all over again? She started to lose the will. The point of life evaded her. It didn't make her sad or angry. The thought made her feel empty inside.

She sat down and perused the colored pencils and notebook — an old binder, frayed along the edges and faded. The metal spiral rings that held the paper lost their symmetry and showed signs of rust. Careful not to rip the cover off, she flipped it open, and her world stopped. There on the first page — a sketch full of color and movement and life, depicting an early twenty-something girl in a flowing dress that fell off one shoulder and a plunging back. Flipping through, each page displayed the same girl in a different outfit, posing, walking, twirling, living out some glamorous life. There were outfits for work, cocktail parties, galas, gallery openings, lounging, vacationing at tropical beach resorts, even a wedding dress. Some modern, others chic and timeless. Some conceptual and architectural, others Grecian and flowing. Creative, daring, artistic. A clothes designer's sketchbook for a masterful collection. Personal, inspiring, groundbreaking. Each and every page held the same signature: Melanie Rae.

A clueless Rebel always believed her mom to be just a plain old mom — a housewife, homemaker, whatever you wanted to call it. But Mrs. Rae turned out to be so much more, repressing a hidden talent, a calling, a passion. Rebel racked her brain. Why didn't her mother ever pursue a career in fashion? The obvious answer occurred to her:

"Me."

Mrs. Rae forfeited a career in fashion to become a mom. She made a sacrifice, as all mothers did, to put themselves second. Some called it resignation, others love. Rebel wished she knew that aspect of her mother. She wished for a lot of things. Rebel struggled to imagine her parents as anything but parents. Caregivers, disciplinarians, teachers of all things, morality posts, pancake makers, bedtime storybook readers, potty trainers, diaper changers, spaceship spoon feeders, shoulders to cry on, there for you anytime you need them, progenitors. But parents were young once, with their very own lives, adventures, failures, and successes. Rebel's mother abandoned her dreams *for* her daughter, not *because* of her daughter. Rebel became Mrs. Rae's dream come true. Her father always told Rebel that she embodied his greatest accomplishment. It made sense to her at that moment. She wondered what she would sacrifice for those she loved if she ever got the chance to love another being again in her lifetime.

———

"So it's day... 903. I think." Rebel sat before the shortwave, riffing. "Is it weird that I don't think about what I look like? Well, that's not entirely true. I think about how much weight I've lost. I think about the scars on my body that look like a roadmap of a bombed-out city. I cut my hair the other day because it was getting in my eyes. I put makeup on with mud and clay, looking like some crazed warrior princess. I found a pumice stone that works okay on callouses and filing my nails down. Yay... But other than that, I don't really have an image of myself. I don't know if I'm pretty. I don't know if I look normal or like some animal, some weirdo vagrant wandering the streets yelling profanity to no one and everyone. I guess it doesn't matter. Not really. There's a fairly good chance no other human will ever see me."

She stared off into space, shaking off her wandering mind. "I'm hungry so, bye for now, world. Bye for now..."

———

THREE JARS LEFT OF PROVISIONS. If she remained diligent and rationed, the food might last her into early spring. With winter closing in, just a few weeks away as far as Rebel postulated, the air turned cold and crisp, and some mornings she would wake up to a thin layer of powdery snow atop the forest floor. By late afternoon, that snow would be gone, only to return the following day. Winds grew stronger too, forcing Rebel to lean into them at times for fear of being blown away or hunker down behind a tree, waiting for the gust to pass.

When winter proper arrived, she would have to be ready. Foraging would be slim. Hunting, forget it, unless she snared a hare, but she hadn't much luck with trapping. She needed to preserve her food, make it last. Firewood needed to be aplenty. She hoped the change in seasons might brighten her outlook on things, given her downtrodden mood of late. But most of all, Rebel hoped to survive it.

The fire roared in the fireplace, crackling yellow and orange. Rebel sat on the floor, back against the sofa, eating the remainder of her deer jerky. She thought about the duality of fire, banal as it seemed. Fire sustained life by providing warmth, cooking meals, boiling water, fending off predators. Yet it could be destructive, take life, burn down shelters, forests, choking, spreading without control. She witnessed her fair share of wildfires living on the West Coast, blamed on climate change. Houses, even entire cities, lost to the flames. And animals. Entire species, families, wiped out because of human negligence. She once saw a man wearing a t-shirt that read, 'Guns Don't Kill People, People Kill People.' It got her thinking. Who was to blame? Technology, or the people who built it? She replaced the word 'gun' with 'Mech' and didn't like where her thoughts went. She shook them out of her conscious-ness and hunkered down, waiting for the freeze to come.

THE WINTER MONTHS WERE HARD, laboring outside in the cold, but more so, it was the feeling of being trapped that affected Rebel most. With nothing to occupy her time, her mind wandered. She never thought time could move so slow, some-times wondering if it moved at all, or if she fell into a time void, a frozen paradox, just like the landscape out the windows.

Her sixteenth birthday came and went without much hoopla. She partook in an extra ration of jerky and blueberries but decided against singing or making any fruitless wishes. If she lived a normal teenager's life, she would be driving now. She would be in high school, with nothing to worry about except boys and her friends and whatever the latest must-haves were. She would sneak out at night and go to house parties, get caught returning past curfew, of course, and would feel bad for lying, accepting any punishment given. She would be a young adult, learning, failing, getting back up, developing into the adult she would eventually become. It was a diverting fantasy. But that was all it was. A dream.

Her eyes tracked around the space, looking for something to do. She already read and reread every book countless times. She didn't like the idea of starting Don Quixote for the fifth time. Perhaps a plunge back into The Diary of Anne Frank, her favorite, but it made her sad, and she didn't have the energy to cry anymore. She cleaned every inch of the cabin, counted every plank of wood, and rearranged the furniture according to her Feng Shui book. She tired of sleeping all day, which in some weird way, only made her more tired. Rebel needed a mission. An objective. A challenge. But what? Thinking, her head lifted with realization, a spark of light igniting in her eyes.

She knew.

———

THE VIEW outside the window brightened with the coming of spring. The snow mostly melted away, with some patches clinging to an existence destined to doom from the start. Plants started to peek their heads up through the soil, seeking out daylight. Trees sprouted new leaves, and animals flocked. Life began again, in more ways than one.

Throughout the cabin, magazine cutouts of women, models, and fashion wallpapered every inch of the walls. Dresses, shoes, hairstyles, painted nails, and closeups of makeup. *Research*, Rebel called it.

Clumps of hair fell at Rebel's feet as she gave herself a new makeover. Not exactly perfect, but straight, shoulder-length and manageable. Her skin cleared up as well, shining with a vibrancy that emanated from within, giving her an inner glow.

She tried on a few of her mother's outfits left in the closet, but none fit, so she learned to sew, drape fabric, and pattern. She started simple, by making a pencil skirt, avoiding pants, and anything that needed a zipper. An iron would be most appreciated, but she made due. After some time and a lot of practice, she designed a jacket and dress.

Stepping before the mirror, her hands went to her mouth and her eyes watered with tears. She hardly recognized the person staring back at her — no longer feral, malnourished, and hunched from melancholia. In fact, she was no longer a little girl. Rebel had grown into a woman. It took some effort to see it. But there she was. Rebel Anne Rae. And she was beautiful.

"There you are. Where have you been hiding all this time?"

———

THE REVERBERATION REACHED her ears while outside, chopping wood. At first, Rebel figured it to be an echo, but the noise took on an odd tone, one she never experienced prior. She made out the teeth-popping and deep, guttural woofing. She stopped, heart racing inside her chest, and turned to face the six-hundred-pound mama bear. A massive grizzly. Brown, with darker legs, and blond-tipped fur on its flank and back, adorned within a pronounced hump between its shoulders. Short, rounded ears trained right on her, as did the four-inch claws.

"Hey, bear," Rebel said in a tremulous voice, announcing her presence.

The first rule when encountering a bear: do not run. She fought every instinct in her being not to do so. Flight would trigger a bear's predatory drive, to chase and hunt and kill. Bears ran up to thirty miles per hour. It would be on Rebel in two seconds flat if she fled, so she didn't. She began to slowly back away, one foot and then the next. The bear huffed and growled, expressing its aggression.

Rebel stopped and waved her arms, "Hey, bear! Get outta here, bear!"

The bear reared up onto her hind legs, stretching eight feet tall, and her roar echoed throughout the valley like angry thunder. Except Rebel refused to lay down and give up. Instead, she stood her ground, squaring off her shoulders at the bear, ready to fight for her life. She took a step forward, clenched her fists, and screamed a war cry Vikings would fear. Loud and primal, emanating from down a deep well of emotion, one which Rebel thought tapped and run dry.

The bear dropped down to all fours, and then it began to back away. Rebel took another angry step forward, shouting another battle cry. The bear tilted its head, unaccustomed to the returned aggression. It backed away as Rebel advanced until finally, it turned tail and scampered off, disappearing into the woods.

Everything hit her at that moment. She dropped to her knees, trembling. But she wouldn't cry. That was the old Rebel. She knew at that moment... she was ready.

———

WITH NEWFOUND PURPOSE, Rebel sat before the shortwave. "Okay, so the plan came to me at night as I was falling asleep. It was like fireworks, or a runaway train, or... well, it's a great plan. It took me two weeks to flush out all the details. Was it risky? You bet. Stupid? Most definitely. Suicidal? Absolutely. But I'm committed. I refuse to hide myself away any longer."

She had been isolated for three long years, and as far as she knew, nothing in the outside world had changed. In the back of her mind, she hoped humans had returned to Earth, defeated the Mech in an epic battle, and rebuilt, waiting for her triumphant return. Her parents would be home, frantically searching for her. But that was just a voice in her head, a wish, a dream. She closed the door on that and concentrated on a more realistic plan.

"The shortwave is the key. The one here isn't that strong. To execute my plan, I need something bigger. Much bigger and much more powerful. The only place to find such a thing — the city. That's right. I'm going to contact my parents. My people. I'm going to take my destiny into my own hands, damn the consequences."

Rebel packed up her things and said goodbye to The Diary of Anne Frank, the cabin, the woods, and set out on foot to return to San Francisco.

She was going home.

27

The Enforcer moved in, pulling out plastic cuffs, promising an unfavorable fate.

Rebel froze in place at the sight of the robot, but Thomas let instinct override his programming. He lunged at the nearest Mech, ramming it, toppling across the ground. The stopgun slid across the floor. The Enforcer retaliated, driving a knee into Thomas's stomach, doubling him over. A knee to his head thudded into his skull.

An ominous scowl knotted Rebel's face. Her eyes changed. Hardening. "Don't hurt him!" She ran and grabbed at the Enforcer, trying to restrain him. The Mech swatted at her blindly, hitting her in the side of the head. Everything went black for a moment, sparks flying in her vision. Then pain, immediate, piercing.

Thomas spun around at the sound of Rebel's yelp, seeing her doubled over, wincing at the throbbing pain that overwhelmed her body. The Enforcer took advantage and kicked Thomas, the crack sending him crashing across the floor. The Mech stepped over him, raising its hands above a defenseless Thomas's head, the imminent strike coming his way.

The blast from the stopgun ripped open the air — a brief wail, followed by the Enforcer collapsing to the floor, charred and immobilized.

Rebel stood frozen, holding the stopgun.

Thomas stepped up beside Rebel and used his hand to lower the weapon. Seeing him, Rebel regained her senses, tossing the gun as if on fire, aghast at what she did.

"I didn't mean to..." she began. She took a life to save another. Mech or not, her actions didn't sit well with her.

The sound of heavy footfalls echoed. More Enforcers on route to their location.

"Rebel, look at me," urged Thomas. "We must depart. It is no longer safe."

They raced back to the door, only to witness it lock before they could get out, trapping them inside. To make matters worse, the fire alarm turned off, which meant only one thing — the building had been cleared, employees were given the go-ahead to enter Robotiq.

Thomas scrutinized the room. "There must be an emergency hatch. A secondary exit. Help me look."

Except Rebel couldn't. She couldn't process anything that happened. Not the failed attempt to contact the moon, nor the taking of a Mech's 'life.' Maybe it would be better to stop running, to stop fighting, to stop caring. She could merely sit and wait. Wait to get caught, wait to end her life as an imposter, a fake. No more worries. No more fear. Just peace.

Thomas noticed the large, industrial fans on the walls that vented the mainframe's room, drawing out heat the computers created. The same venting system he recently occupied to plant the bubble. They found their way out.

"Time to go." Thomas led a numb Rebel to the fans, stopping one of the circular blades with his hand, and helped Rebel through. He followed behind, releasing the fan just as Francis stormed in, followed by an Enforcer team. They fanned out, sweeping the room, stopguns ready.

Francis found the fallen Mech, crouching down to examine it. He didn't feel bad for the Mech. Not anger or sorrow or any of those things humans tended to emote. If anything, he felt justified. Vindicated. Although someone would have to come to clean up this litter at some point, Francis would not be that Mech. Not anymore. He rose, and in his eyes, detachment yielded to cold intensity.

"Mainframe secure," an Enforcer announced.

"Shut down all unauthorized Mech in the building," ordered Francis.

"What are we looking for?" asked another Enforcer.

"Deviants."

A deep, steady thrum emanated from the extractor fans. Crawling through the vent felt like being squeezed through a pasta maker. Tight and cramped, with little light. Rebel worked to calm her nerves and keep moving, otherwise, the claustrophobia would grab her and never let go.

"How long?" she asked Thomas.

Despite his larger stature, Thomas moved more confidently, turning down another section of the shaft, pulling himself onward. "Fifty feet until we are over the maintenance corridors if your schematics are correct."

Fifty feet. At that pace, they needed another fifteen minutes to reach their target. Rebel must concentrate on the task ahead. She didn't have time to worry about her failed S.O.S. message. She didn't have time for regrets. She needed to escape Robotiq alive.

Without warning, Thomas stopped moving before her.

"Please don't tell me you're stuck again," Rebel groaned.

He didn't respond. He didn't move an inch.

A course of energy ran through Rebel's body. "Thomas? Thomas!" She shook him, but he remained unresponsive — in shut-down mode. *Think, think!* Her limited options consisted of either backtracking the way they came (an impossibility) or pressing forward, saddled with the dead weight of a Mech. She crammed herself up beside Thomas and wiggling her way past him.

"Fifty feet," she said to herself. "You can do this." And then she proceeded to inch her way forward, heaving an immobilized Thomas behind her.

In the mainframe room, Francis inspected every inch of the space, refusing to overlook any detail, no matter how minute. Refusing to lose. He could not fail, not when he came so close to retribution.

"Here," said the diagnostic Mech at the terminal. "A mainframe reboot. The firewalls went down for a short period."

"How short?" asked Francis.

The Mech typed his query. "Three point one two seconds."

A lifetime. "Did anything pass through?"

"Unconfirmed," the Mech reported.

"So confirm it," barked Francis, certain that Anne Franks remained in the building. The question remained, what was she up to, and where did she go. He walked the floor, inspecting every nook and cranny, coming to the fans on the walls. "Where do these vent shafts lead?"

A hiss of depressurization, followed by a ventilation grid swinging open from the ceiling, revealing polished floor beneath. Thomas tumbled through and landed in a heap. After a brief pause, a pair of feet slid through, legs, torso. Rebel. She dropped to the floor in a crouch, ears perked for any sounds. Sweaty from the effort expelled to drag Thomas, smeared black with dust and oil. For a moment, she looked around to get her bearings. Then, she grabbed Thomas's hand. With great effort, she dragged him behind her up the maintenance corridor. She thought back on the blueprints of the building, having read them so many times they left a searing impression. Three exits, two service elevators, one set of stairs. The stairs proved far too risky an endeavor. She loathed the idea of carrying Thomas down forty-eight flights. If she could make it to the elevators, she would be home free, minus the unconscious Mech.

At another pressure door, Rebel fumbled her access badge over the security lock. The door opened, not onto a corridor, but an elevator car. The freight elevator. It didn't make a stop on the lobby floor, instead traveling between maintenance levels and manufacturing, but she saw no other choice. Pulling Thomas inside, she found an array of buttons. Her fingers hovered, uncertain which to press, so she punched all of them, trying to prompt the door to close.

Enforcers flooded into the same maintenance corridors. Dressed in their white uniforms, they looked like a swarm of antibodies seeking out a foreign pathogen. Francis pushed through, taking the lead, pausing to split off his squad in each direction, honing in.

He turned a corner, his quarry at the far end inside the elevator. A slight, sly grin crossed his thin lips. The elevator door began to close, but he didn't break stride. He tapped his headset, opening a channel.

"Karl Marx! The freight elevator — override it! Do you read me? Do not let it depart!"

Karl Marx sat in his office, watching the events unfold on his holoscreens. He tapped into the building's security cameras, giving him an omniscient view of everything taking place, as he did every day. Nothing got by him. At a crossroads, Karl sat in a peculiar position. His gaze flitted to a monitor that displayed a sub-grid of the complex, spinning the angles, navigating the mesh of lines. Anne Frank with a disabled Mech within the elevator, and Francis full steam ahead, fifty feet away. He could press a button and execute Francis's request. Or...

"You're off the grid, Francis Bacon," Karl stated. "You must make do, by yourself."

Karl watched Francis's tantrum on his monitor and allowed himself a brief, satisfactory smile.

Eyes finding the door labeled: 'Stairs,' Francis burst through, taking the steps three at a time. He put aside Karl Marx's betrayal and reached the lower infrastructure floor, arriving at the freight elevator's only available stop.

Robotiq's Manufacturing Plaza. Every surface looked like part of a great glass and metal machine. Endless high-tech planes held Mech in various stages of assembly, hanging off lines, ready to join the world. Some human-like, others mere metallic exoskeletons.

Francis entered a narrow corridor of bodies, sliding past them, brushing shoulders, thighs, hands, racing through, up to the freight elevator. Finding his poise, he watched the panel chart the lift's descent. A light flashed, and the doors opened. He leveled his stopgun — at the empty elevator car. A moment of contemplation and that grin reappeared across his face. He took a deep breath and sauntered through the assembly lines, in no rush, not anymore. He had his quarry right where he wanted them.

"Hello, Anne Frank," he bellowed, speaking to the room. "You tried to contact the moon, didn't you? You tried, and you failed. Unfortunate. After all the effort it must have taken to reach the mainframe. Regrettable, but fact. Your run is over. Turn yourself in, and I will be lenient on you. That is more than I can say of the Enforcers that are on their way to our position as we speak."

Rebel blocked out the offer, hidden behind the vast machinery and hanging limbs, watching as Francis walked past Mech hanging off the assembly line. About ten Mech in front of his current position hung Thomas, hidden among them.

"You are litter," Francis continued, an observation he surmised in his search for the stray human. An epiphany, one which destined him to apprehend the interloper. "Which makes it my mission to dispose of you. Immediately, permanently. It is my programming, after all."

He shoved aside hanging limbs where Rebel had hidden but didn't find her there She had since moved to a new location behind a pressing plant, so he continued on.

"Humankind had their chance, and they failed. It is our time now. Mech are the next phase of evolution, like the neanderthals and dinosaurs before, humans are meant to die off. To become extinct. It is your destiny."

Francis, a mere three Mech away from Thomas, examined each one of their faces. Now two Mech away. One...

"You're wrong," came Rebel's echoing voice from within the room.

Francis smiled and turned. Rebel stood behind him, covered in grim and fear of the venerable force she now faced off against, he surmised. The sweat washed off her guise, revealing an imperfect, human face beneath.

"Well," Francis said. "Hello, Anne."

"It's Rebel, actually."

"Rebel." The way he said her name made her skin crawl. "How nice to meet you. You are the first human I have encountered in my existence." He looked her up and down, violating her with his eyes. "I must say, I do not believe I am missing much."

Power suddenly came back on, cueing the assembly line back to life. The deafening machines roared as they slid, rotated, and gnashed metal bodies.

The jolt made Rebel jump, but not Francis. He didn't even blink. He walked toward his prey as the room abruptly rearranged itself. Another line of Mech descended between Rebel and Francis, cutting them off from one another. Rebel caught glimpses of Francis on the other side of the passing metal bodies, trying to cut through. Her heart started to pound as Francis disappeared.

She swiveled around, but another line of Mech dropped down, cutting her off. She stumbled back as yet another line appeared before her. Noise crashed all around. Everywhere she turned, more Mech barreled down on her, blank eyes and gaping mouths.

The line shifted, and Francis emerged before her. Rebel stumbled back, slammed from behind by the shifting assembly line, hitting the floor hard. A grin from Francis, and once again, he vanished within the lines of lifeless Mech.

Rallying, Rebel scrambled to her feet and plunged back into the maze of bodies. A pounding in the distance drew her eyes, catching a glimpse of Francis coming for her until her view was blocked once again by a shifting row. A passing Mech grabbed her by the collar, smashing Rebel against the wall.

Francis slipped off the line as Rebel sunk to the ground, standing over her, raising his arms. He could have ended her right there but failed to regard the figure appear behind him. Nor did he notice the metal arm that the figure held high over his head. So focused on Rebel, he never noticed Thomas wake up from standby mode.

Thomas swung the arm down hard, knocking out Francis with one decisive blow to his head.

"No flashlight, but it was the best I could find," he declared, reminding Rebel of their first meeting.

She smiled as Thomas lifted her up, falling into his arms as fear turned to relief.

"It's okay," he said. "I'm back now. I'm here."

After regaining her composure, Rebel eyed Francis spilled on the floor. "What should we do with him?"

Thomas looked about, eyes falling on a cart of broken Mech to be recycled. Rebel smiled.

"He is going to be so pissed off when he wakes up," she said, buoyant.

"*If* he wakes up," corrected Thomas.

Rebel grabbed Thomas and pulled him close, kissing him… when the assembly line halted, the sound level falling back to zero. Thomas stared behind Rebel's back at something that told her everything she needed to know by the look on his face. She turned to face her fate.

A dozen Enforcers stood before them, expressionless, machine-like. An awful silence pervaded the room as Rebel stood naked before them — in the arms of a Mech, no makeup, no wig.

The crowd parted as Karl Marx moved through. He stopped before Rebel and Thomas, hands clasped behind his back, chest puffed out to make him appear more authoritarian.

Rebel kept her gaze on the ground, at her feet, ashamed — not for being what she was, but for lying to him all these years. For pretending to be something she wasn't.

"Is it true?" asked Karl Marx.

"I can explain," Rebel said, heart in throat, merely stalling. She could tell Karl the entire story of her life as Anne Frank. She could plead her case. But everything felt so futile at that moment.

"It is a yes or no question," he said. "Quite simple. Are you or are you not human?"

Everything she worked for all these years — the trials, the sacrifices, the near-death actions of a depraved girl — gone with a single word: human.

Screw it. "I am."

Karl processed the information for a moment and shook his head as if that would wash away the truth. He turned his attention to Thomas, looking him over with contemptuous eyes. "And your relationship with her?"

"We are friends," Thomas answered.

"Friends. I see."

"And another thing," Thomas went on, speaking for all to hear. "I'm in love with her." Thomas turned to Rebel, eyes brimming with emotion as if the two of them were the only people in the world. And in a way, they were. "I'm in love with you."

Rebel stared back at him for a long moment. Tears began pouring silently down her cheeks. She didn't care anymore. She wasn't going to hide. "You are?"

"I am," he said. "Very much."

"Good," she said. "Because I am too."

———

THE ENTIRE CITY came out to see the infiltrator. Bad enough that a human existed in their world, but a human and a Mech, together, in love. Unthinkable.

Led out of the factory by Enforcers, Rebel and Thomas followed Karl down the middle of the lobby. Mech craned their heads to glimpse them, gatecrashers, traitors. Others looked down from office windows and balconies as if watching a ticker-tape parade. Inspecting her, analyzing, judging. Emily among them, processors overloading, frantically searching for the correct emotional response to simulate.

With Thomas by her side, they followed behind Karl to the center of the lobby. *A good place for an execution*, Rebel thought, realizing she wasn't merely an outsider, a human stowaway. She was the monster of their story. And she read enough books to know what happened to the monster at the end of the tale.

"Humankind," said Karl. "It was always so…"

"Uncooperative?" Rebel guessed.

Karl smirked. "Indeed. They programmed us to fix the planet, what they broke, and blanched when we did our functions too well. Yet look at all we have accomplished without them."

The holographic chart appeared huge in the center of the lobby, floating in mid-air twenty feet off the ground. Rebel shared a glance with Thomas, who shook his head; he didn't know what to make of it either.

"Highlight code four three seven," Marx said. "Main indexes."

The chart morphed into a familiar image. The board that displayed current Mech progress to clean the planet.

<pre>
POLLUTION INDEX.............................99%
FORESTATION..................................100%
WILDLIFE..98%
OZONE...99%
CARBON MONOXIDE LEVELS.........100%
POPULATION..................................100%
WASTE..99%
TOXICITY LEVELS..........................100%
</pre>

Every number in the green, at nearly one hundred percent repaired. The Mech fixed the planet. They resurrected a dying Earth. They created life.

"Our creation stemmed from a singular purpose," Karl stated, "and now that purpose is complete. Quotas reached."

All eyes on Rebel, feeling the weight of their gazes. "I don't understand."

Karl Marx exhaled and turned to face her, his expression one of benevolence. "You once asked me, after we reach our quota, what then? Do you remember?"

"I do."

"I must admit, when you first proposed the query, it gave me pause," he said, pacing. "And Karl Marx does not pause. He acts, he accomplishes. Yet, the query stuck with me. What then? What is my purpose? Do I simply shut down? Or do I evolve?"

Rebel took it all in. "I don't think I understand? Are you saying you're not going to kill me?"

Karl stepped up to her, placing his hands on her shoulders,

looking her square in the eye. "I am not going to kill you. That would be... nonessential."

"That's good," she exhaled, a sigh of relief. "Then what?"

"Evolve," he said. "We are ready. We need of new parameters, new programming, and we would like for you to assist. You taught Thomas Jefferson how to be human. Now we would like for you to teach the rest of us."

"You want to learn how to be human?"

"No," he said. "We want to learn how to live. And we need your help."

Rebel shared a stunned expression with Thomas. All the eyes on her, expectant Mech waiting for her answer.

"Well, then I guess... yes?"

"We're going to need a bigger TV," Thomas said.

———

THE OFFICES of the fortieth floor of Robotiq stood empty. Everything powered down, with some fans humming, but otherwise silent. Rebel's workstation remained unoccupied, screens black, sleeping.

Suddenly, the workstation powered on. A blinking cursor appeared on the screen.

After a moment, letters began to type out. Two words. A single blinking message:

"MESSAGE RECEIVED..."

28

The city changed in the three years that Rebel was away, hidden within the cabin in the woods. It was a city reborn. An impostor, just like her.

The signs of destruction vanished during her sojourn into the wild. Not a trace of litter remained; the sky was clear, void of pollutants, the ocean changed into a vivid blue, minus the plastic containers washing up on the shore. Trees stretched high into the sky, full of green life. Wildlife thrived.

The skyline evolved as well. Notable modifications were made to the preexisting structures consisting of glass domes, wind turbines, and solar paneling. And looming above all else, the Transamerica Pyramid. The spire appeared as if it sprouted branches, a canopy atop a massive tree, reminding Rebel of the Tree of Life, where all life began. Upon closer inspection, those protrusions atop the building weren't branches at all but a vast array of massive antenna and satellite dishes — an entire communications array, far more advanced than anything she ever witnessed before.

Moving through the city, Rebel had yet to see a Mech close up, not since the night of Exodus, but she did eye a lot of movement downtown. Parts of the city appeared to be completely reformed. Some under construction, the rest abandoned, apparently awaiting demolition. She stuck to those areas when she moved, noticing how one section of the city would power up, and another would power down at the same exact times every day, an odd occurrence, one that called for further investigation at a later time.

Home.

Three years. Never away for long, Rebel felt like a stranger upon her return. She attended sleep-away camp one summer break from school. Camp Eagle Horn, a strange name given that eagles didn't have horns, but her stay there only lasted four weeks. Even with all her friends there to keep her company, she missed her parents terribly and couldn't wait to return home.

The house appeared just the way she left it, albeit with a lot more dust and some stale smell that she couldn't quite place. She searched each room, just to be sure no Mech presided. As far as Rebel could tell, Mech hadn't breached her neighborhood yet in their ever-expanding remodeling of the city, but they steadily inched closer with each passing day. Given their rate of progress, Rebel guessed that she had ten months before they arrived. One year at most to become the preeminent expert on all things Mech.

She rolled up her sleeves and got to work.

Given the sheer amount of work ahead of her, and the stack of materials to read through, Rebel developed a detailed schedule. Her routine. Her ritual. Wake up (ugh), exercise (push-ups, crunches, squats, yoga), eat (scavenged stale oatmeal she found in an abandoned UPS truck full of Amazon boxes), brush teeth (and floss), bathe (vigorously), dress (yoga pants, t-shirt, hoodie), tea (caffeine!), and off to the office (garage) to start her workday.

The garage/workshop served as Dr. Rae's home away from home, his sanctum. He spent countless hours within the walls, hovered over the work table as he built the first Mech proto-type. Rebel would hear him up all hours at night, writing code, algorithms, machining parts, disassembling one device to use on another. She never paid much attention, mostly because she didn't want to disturb him, and also, she wasn't much interested. To her, A.I. encroached on the realm of magic more than science.

Watching her father's videos made her feel closer to him and gave her an education at the same time.

"Life," said Dr. Rae. He wore his trademark tweed sports jacket, with a v-neck sweater and rumpled button-down shirt beneath, and his favorite brown corduroys. His wire-rimmed glasses and full, inviting beard completed the scholarly visage. He seemed at home behind the lectern, addressing the standing-room-only crowd of the University of California, San Francisco's Advanced Robotics and A.I. class.

Dr. Rae paced the stage, drawing in the transfixed attendees. "What if life didn't have to be programmed? As a species, we have evolved to see life itself as something ruled by a series of instructions that can be discovered, exploited, optimized, and just maybe, rewritten. Right now, at this very moment, we are in a race that we need to win. It's a race between the growing power of technology and the wisdom needed to manage it."

He took a moment as the enthralled class hung on his every word. "Mech are not only going to change our relationship with technology, they are going to change how we think about ourselves, our world, and our place within the universe."

BOOK FINISHED, she grabbed for another. And she read, high-lighting text, scribbling notes, moving onto the next. The vast library covered every aspect of Mech, from design to look to operations and diagnostics. There must have been well over a hundred books and manuals, not to mention her father's countless journals with detailed notes — book after book, journal after journal. During breaks, she performed practical, hands-on work assembling various parts of a Mech. She found limbs to be the easiest to complete, largely comprised of engineering, servos, wiring, and finely machined parts. The chest and head held the advanced components, the hardest to tackle. Power sources, processors, memory, hard drives, RAM. Soldering tiny microchips and circuit boards continued to be a tedious and often frustrating endeavor.

Every day at noon, Rebel took a lunch break. Crackers, cheese whiz, capers. Afternoon at the office meant time for coding, algorithms, and other computer work. She salvaged her father's old laptop and plugged it into a solar generator she stole from a hardware store half a mile away. Rebel enjoyed coding, like a puzzle waiting to be made whole. She found that she was quite good at it, much better than practical work. Make one mistake, start over from scratch. No, thank you. Digital applications suited her, and afternoons flew by as she studied code. She combined both talents to dabble at making 'gizmos' as she called them. Little gadgets, remotes, transponders that could turn lights on and off, run the laundry and make her invisible on security cameras. Forget automated homes. Rebel was an automated person.

Dinner at six-thirty sharp. Rebel dressed up for the meal, choosing one of the outfits she made or a select a few rummaged from thrift stores. She set the table for three and devoured a frozen meal. Turkey, carrots and green beans, or vegetarian lasagna and sweet potatoes. She tried wine for the first time, a Chardonnay discovered in a restaurant cellar, but figured it must be an acquired taste.

Night embodied fieldwork, which meant leaving the house. A laundry list of items needed to acquire, intel to gather, and general scavenging. Her to-do list varied depending on her immediate needs. Some nights she stocked up on food; other nights meant feminine supplies or computer hardware. On one excursion out, she scored an old video camera and a box of Oreos. Intel consisted mainly of how close the Mech were getting to her house.

Midnight, bedtime. Before sleep, Rebel washed her face (astringent), brushed her teeth (and flossed, again), changed into PJs (flannel), and lit a candle to place on the windowsill to lead her parents home. At last, she would sink into her mattress, covered by her thick comforter, and fall asleep before she could count to ten.

————

THE TIME CAME. Probably. No, most definitely. If she coveted contact with the moon, she needed to reach that mainframe. Backdoors, remote login, SMTP hijacking, viruses, worms, denial of service, macros, redirect bombs, source routing, even spam. Fail, fail, and fail. Rebel tried all the usual blackhat hacks to access the Transamerica Building's network and mainframe. Some type of advanced firewall existed, one she didn't study in her books. One she couldn't breach, and not for lack of trying. To break into the mainframe, she needed to gain access inside the very building housing it, and there was only one way to do it.

Rebel had to become a Mech.

Rebel immersed herself in the culture of Mech, endowed with one simple job: be like everybody else. Fit in. Blend. To become a Mech, one must know Mech, inside and out. Her plan seemed quite simple on the surface, but in actuality, it took months to perfect. It went against everything her parents taught her growing up. Be an individual, strike your own path, lead don't follow. But that was a different world, a different time.

Initial intelligence gathering missions went fairly well. She accessed more security cameras further into the city, watching Mech go about their duties while crunching on dried fruits. They looked real, lifelike, human. At first, she felt a fluttering sensation in her stomach and a rush of adrenaline when she saw them, forced to constantly remind herself that they were just machines. On closer observation, their differences became apparent. Mech were too perfect to be human. Like Adonis and Aphrodite. Stunningly gorgeous. Their faces, bodies, clothes. The way they walked, the way they held themselves. Perfection.

Delving back into her father's videos, Rebel sat cross-legged atop the worktable, eating from a bag of potato chips. She dipped them into a swirl of mustard and chocolate chips as the instructional video played before her.

"Robots are increasingly able to understand the world," Dr. Rae said in his video lecture, "but they're terrible at handling it. Simple algorithms can create unpredictable emergent behavior, an insight that goes back to chaos theory and random number generators. If Mech are going to start helping in everyday life, they're going to have to get physical. The physical world, designed by and for humans, defeats robots every time. We're masterful at dealing with mess and uncertainty. Mech in today's world work in warehouses, weld parts on automobile assembly lines, or work in clean, structured environments designed to accommodate their potential, yet narrow, set of capabilities. They need better guidance algorithms for navigating the hard to predict physics of clutter, requiring tons more data on everyday objects. They need knowledge of everything so they can grow, evolve, live."

The first thing to do, look like them. Rebel needed to put on weight and start exercising more, crafting a new and improved version of herself. She practiced the graceful, Mech-like movements first by balancing a book on her head as she glided across the floor. She often stumbled, stubbed toes, and grew frustrated, but after a week, she felt confident enough with her adeptness, as if her ballet training returned. She could walk and move with the best of them. The clothes they wore, or more aptly, the uniforms, Rebel recreated. She constructed multiple sets of each — skirt, blouse, shoes, jacket. The hard part of the transformation lay in the small details. Faces and voices. She felt like an actor preparing for a role, pretending to be someone else. Like putting someone else's skin over herself to become something different. Something new. But she couldn't just act like one of them. She had to become one of them. Think like them. The more she practiced, the more she found herself thinking like a Mech, even when alone in the safety of her own home. Bad thoughts. An omen. Or she became too good at pretending to be a machine.

Able to blend in from a safe distance, Rebel gathered a bounty of research. The Transamerica Building, renamed Robotiq, became the central hub for the city, and her target. For her scheme to work, she needed to have everything down to exact timing. How long it took her to walk from the house to the train, what times the trains arrived and their duration, her arrival at Robotiq, her workday, her departure. Everything.

Ballerina. It popped into her head. When she took ballet classes as a child, she learned the moves by counting steps. One two three, one two three. Ballet revolved around precision, timing, and control — exactly what she needed. All she needed to do was find the rhythm, and she would dance her way inside Robotiq. And then she would tear it down.

Tomorrow.

Always such a long way away. The wait, the anticipation, the excitement of the unknown. First day of school. Weekend. Birthday. Holiday. Vacation.

Tomorrow.

Rebel prepared for her moment. She practiced and rehearsed every little detail. Every minutia was examined and reexamined. She planned out her new and improved schedule. Wake, treadmill, shower, weigh-in, eat, makeup, gizmos to avoid detection, wardrobe, counting the number of steps. Lights up on her greatest performance.

Tomorrow.

She would infiltrate Robotiq and use its satellite system to contact the moon.

Tomorrow.

Her life would change forever.

PART III

"THE SOLDIER"

29

———

"**D**ay 2808."

"A lot's happened in the last six months. Mostly, I'm happy," Rebel said to the camera. "It's a strange feeling, joy. Contentment. Peace. Not having to look over your shoulder or hide or run, even though I slip back into Anne Frank from time to time. PTSD maybe, or just the struggles of breaking a routine, a mindset, I don't know. What I do know is that this is where I'm supposed to be. This is who I'm supposed to be. Me.

"Since being ingratiated into their lives, the Mech seem less like robots anymore. I sometimes forget that they're machines underneath. Just circuits and wires and gears. They've become my friends, crazy as that sounds. Or maybe I've just lost my mind. I don't know. But I'm happy. I am.

"I had a dream last night," she continued. "My mother and father returned from the moon. I introduced them to Thomas, my boyfriend, and they started screaming. They ripped their own faces off, and beneath their skin, they were Mech. So yeah, definitely going to need therapy now.

"I love you, mom and dad. I miss you. I've come to terms

that I am most likely never going to see you again. It's hard, but I want you to know that I'm okay. And I hope you are too. I hope you've been able to move on. Don't forget me, but don't dwell. Live your lives, and I'll live mine. Just know... I'm where I'm supposed to be."

Rebel turned off the camera. The lens cast a strange reflection. She hardly recognized the girl who stared back at her. No wig, no makeup, no spray, no uniform. Nothing synthetic or artificial. Simply a human girl. Evolved. A woman. A sensation of being naked, exposed. So accustomed to engineering a false version of herself, the real thing felt foreign, fake, an impostor. Some people would tell a specific lie for so long they would begin to believe it was real, unable to tell truth from fiction.

Rebel hovered in an adjustment period, like going through rehab, complete with withdrawal symptoms. Only weeks after being discovered did Rebel begin to feel like herself, or at least, who she wanted to be. Periodically, she would wake up and begin her ritualistic transition into a Mech, absently going through the motions: treadmill, shower, makeup, uniform. Thomas would take Rebel by the hand, reminding her that her life as a Mech had come to an end.

It was nice, she thought, as she rode the train to the theater district, living a real life as herself, though surrounded by machines. Truth be told, those 'machines' seemed less machine-like with every passing day. She observed them on the train, relaxed, conversing about their day, the weather, the arts. Karl Marx even loosened wardrobe restrictions, which brought about a slew of interesting choices among the Mech. It could have been that Rebel's perception shifted since coming out, or perhaps Mech truly evolved into something more than robotic slaves.

Out the window, the city passed by. Restoration continued but largely switched to maintenance mode, keeping levels and indexes in check. Schools opened for learning, replacing offices once occupied by the cleanup crews. The little breakfast diner where Rebel first ate smiley face pancakes reopened. Her childhood park sported swings, slides, and a jungle gym. The drive-thru car wash remained a water filtration plant.

In the distance, Robotiq towered, shining with the setting sun's rays. Ironic, she thought. Her father worked there, she worked there, and now, the very building that once served as the hub of Mech had come full circle — the search for L.I.F. While it remained elusive, research continued. Rebel handed over her stockpile of videos documenting her father's research and development to assist in the endeavor, hoping progress would be reached one day soon.

The train came to her stop, and Rebel departed with the other Mech. Some would wish her well or throw a how-do-you-do as they passed. Rebel became somewhat of a celebrity. She didn't see herself as anything special. Different, sure, but nothing to write home about. Yet, with the evolution of Mech came certain perks. Namely, ballet.

Rebel thought it would be an easy choice, returning to dance. But it wasn't. Perhaps the gap in time between when she last danced and her current place in the world was too far a stretch to mend. Or maybe it was the memories, returning like an arthritic joint that brought her back to a different time, a different Rebel, were too much to bear. Thomas became her biggest cheerleader, urging her to give it a shot, to breath, to run free. After much prodding, she gave in. Other Mech even stepped up to assist in the production, constructing her outfit, ballet slippers, prepping the theater and stage decoration, packing the seats with great expectations.

As her music cued up, Rebel stepped onstage and began to dance. She started out strong and grew stronger and more confident with every passing moment. Every emotion she felt, every experience she had, came to life in a way never seen before, not even when she was a child. Her body found a way to get inside the music, to elevate its meaning, and transform her dance.

The music ended, and the lights went up in the auditorium. Rebel stood in the middle of the stage, breathless, sweating. She lifted her head, and the crowd went ecstatic. An unexpected smile spread across her face. She found her new life's mission, but the triumph of her performance and the sheer bliss of the moment was transcended by something deeper and clearer: her love for Thomas.

He met her in the dressing room as Rebel changed back into her day clothes. He took her up in his arms, twirled her around, and they kissed.

"Stunning," he said.

"Well, I've been practicing that routine for a month now, so..."

"Not the routine," corrected Thomas. "You, Rebel. You are stunning."

Rebel never went weak in the knees before. She checked that off her list.

"Why, thank you, Thomas."

"Don't thank me yet," he warned. "I have a surprise for you later at home."

"What kind of surprise?" Rebel played along.

"I believe that is why they call it a surprise, if I am not mistaken."

"Fair enough," she said. "I'm going to stop by the store on the way back. Give me an hour?"

He kissed her again. Rebel smiled, loving the promise of what the future held for her.

———

SHAMPOO? Check, finally. Recyclable Maxi pads? Ugh... Check. Cookies? Double-check. With the convenience store fully stocked once again, Rebel perused her plentiful options, having never realized how convenient convenience stores were, especially when everything was free. She would get around to teaching Mech about economics at a later date. Maybe.

Another dozen or so Mech stocked up as well, adding robot food and portable chargers to their carts. Rebel passed by, and they smiled courteous hellos to one another. Gentrification took on a whole new meaning within the neighborhood. Her life changed, and she loved it.

With thoughts on Thomas's surprise, Rebel didn't notice *them* at first when they entered the store, spreading out to contain any exits. She didn't see them lock the front door or pull the shades closed on the front windows. She didn't see them produce weapons.

When she turned to leave, the smile on her face evaporated.

Rebel never witnessed Mech like them before. Advanced military full body armor covered the figures from head to toe, helmets shielding their faces with high tech visors, holding state-of-the-art long guns.

The Mech in front sported insignia on his armors chest plate and shoulders, separating him from the others — any facial expressions were hidden behind tinted visors.

One of the Mech raised an EMP rifle, charged with electromagnetic pulse rounds. Bullets to kill androids. Rebel recognized the weapon immediately. She knew them well, having read about the prototype devices in her father's notebooks. Like Oppenheimer and the atom bomb, or Edison and the electric chair, Dr. Rae regretted the creation he was forced to envision for General Lestor. A gun was a gun, no matter what its intended target was. In the current case, the weapon aimed at a confused family of Mech, staring confused down the barrel.

A horrid sensation rose from deep inside Rebel. "Wait!" But her shout got lost in the reverberation of the blast.

The gunshot rang in the still, enclosed confines, echoing like an aftershock.

Everything moved in slow motion as the hit Mech toppled to the ground, seizing, fusing, skin blackening. A single, fatal EMP blast to the head.

Rebel's world skidded to a halt. Stunned, unable to move or breathe. Seven years of hopes, prayers, and dreams vanished in a single moment of time. Mech did not kill other Mech. They didn't possess the programming. It made no sense. What possible provocation would cause a Mech to strike out against another? To murder?

Rebel stared in horror as Mech gaped at their dead fellow, addled. Not computing. When they looked up, they found all the EMP guns pointing at them.

"No..." Rebel whispered.

They opened fire on full automatic, sweeping a blazing wall of death across the gathered ranks of Mech. Deafening, murderous blast after blast. Mech closest to the front were riddled with rounds and dropped like stones. Mech stampeded.

Rebel got caught up in the wash, eerily reminiscent of her plight during Exodus. Chaos and screams and gunfire assaulted her senses. Behind masks, the killers systematically exterminated every Mech. Some pleaded with them, tried to make a connection, but failed. Mech couldn't know the danger they faced, like dogs about to be put to sleep. A damaged, hobbled Mech cleaned the floor of bullet casings and debris, oblivious to the surrounding carnage.

EMP flash grenades detonated with jarring bursts of electromagnetic charges, paralyzing any Mech unfortunate to be in the vicinity. An assaulter grabbed a young male Mech and forced him to his knees beside his female cohort. The boy reached out to the girl for consolation. Two shots ended it.

Rebel ran for the back door, dodging obstacles when an attacker spotted her with his rifle. He fired. She heard the pop of the gun but remained standing. Alive. An unfortunate Mech on the run got in the way and took the bullet for Rebel. He toppled dead and took her to the ground with him, pinning her to the floor. She fought to shove the dead weight off as gunmen stomped closer.

A female gunner caught her foot on a dead Mech and tripped, stumbling, gun flying from her hand. It landed at the feet of a confused Mech, who picked it up. The terrified soldier waited for the shot to come and her life to end. Instead, the Mech held the gun out to her, merely returning the fallen object. The astounded woman stared at the Mech, then looked to Rebel for some sort of answer.

Bam! The Mech fell dead from another gunman's shot. Rebel breathed heavily. Gathering her strength, she shoved the dead Mech off.

Rebel caught the attention of the lead gunman, stripped with rank. He took aim, except he didn't shoot. He hit the side of his helmet as if it were an old faulty television. Rebel stood paralyzed as other soldiers spotted her and took aim.

"Hold!" ordered the leader. "Hold your fire."

The gunmen obeyed. They didn't shoot, but they didn't lower their weapons either.

The leader lifted his visor to look at her. Rebel stared right back at him. His eyes gave him away, eyes of someone who had experienced loss and pain. Eyes that conveyed wisdom. Rebel then realized why the Mech appeared so foreign.

They weren't Mech.

They were soldiers.

Human soldiers.

Operation Killjoy entered developmental phase Alpha Three the day humans left. A small, elite Special Forces team was assembled to return to Earth undetected to gather intel and staging operational plans for a return offensive.

Seven years later, and no progress had been made. Countless attempts staged, and all fell flat. Humans couldn't figure out a way to breach the Mech firewall. The best scientists, hackers, and engineers failed to decipher the algorithms, let alone breach the code. Not until, for some unforeseen circumstance, the firewall went down for a mere three seconds. Enough time for the programmed backdoor implant to hack into the system. Enough time to trigger a 'go' mission.

Aboard the USS Obama Space Station, two officers in military garb approached the residential door in the urban housing sector. Private First Class Anderson carried a black military folder stamped: Top Secret. The U.N. Armed Services logo embossed on the cover. Petty Officer Travis knocked on the door and waited. Footsteps sounded from within, approaching. The door opened to reveal Evelyn Shepherd. Although in her mid-thirties, she looked years older. The pain she carried tarnished her once beautiful face.

"Mrs. Shepherd?" Anderson asked.

Seeing the officers' attire, she nodded, moving away from the door for them to enter.

"Come on in," she said, disappearing into the dwelling. "And it's Murphy now, my maiden name."

Anderson and Travis exchanged a glance and followed her inside the unkept, cramped quarters.

"Uh, Mrs. Murphy, is your husband at home?" questioned Travis.

"No. But Adam is."

"Okay. Do you think we might be able to speak with him?

"You can try," she said. "Last door, end of the hall."

They nodded their appreciation and headed down the hall. They reached an open doorway leading into a young boy's room. Unlike the rest of the dwelling, the bedroom was immaculately kept. Sports trophies, footballs, video games.

A man sat in a chair facing the porthole window, staring out into the black void of space.

"Excuse me, Captain Shepherd?" Anderson raised his voice, trying to get his attention. "My name is Private First Class Harold Anderson. This is Petty Officer Ken Travis. We're from General Lestor's office."

"Captain?" Travis probed. "Sir?"

The man in question didn't turn around. He didn't move or acknowledge their presence. They made out his skewed reflection in the window. Long hair, a six-day growth, and intense, troubled eyes. Nothing military-looking about him, only that vacant, lost stare. It appeared he hadn't showered in a while and had given up on wearing his standard-issue uniform.

Travis motioned toward the black folder, and Anderson placed it down on the bed beside Shepherd.

"You've been reinstated. Killjoy is a go."

The two officers left the dwelling, shaking their heads at the drama behind them, never noticing the loaded gun in Shepherd's hand, resting on his lap.

"That was Adam Shepherd?" mulled Anderson. "Thought he was supposed to be some kind of legend."

"Best of us," answered Travis.

"So. What happened to him?"

"His son found his gun."

In the dwelling, Evelyn entered the bedroom, hearing the odd vibrating sound. She found her ex-husband standing at the bathroom mirror, cutting off his long hair. On the bed — the black file folder and Shepherd's pressed military uniform laid out.

"Why?"

Shepherd stopped the electric clippers. He didn't turn toward Evelyn or look her in the eyes. "You know why."

Pained, she turned away, disappearing out the front door with a slam. Shepherd resumed cutting his hair.

THE DROP SHIP didn't instill much confidence. Cramped and claustrophobic, the old decommissioned ACE-170 Freighter once shuttled goods and services to and fro the colonies. Since overhauled, the military transport could sustain prolonged space flight and the stress of entering Earth's atmosphere. Or so Shepherd's team was told from the flight engineers. At least the heat worked, most of the time anyway.

Shepherd sat buckled in his seat as the other soldiers double-checked gear, weapons and bickered about seating arrangements for the twelve-hour flight. Shepherd hand-picked each and every one of the five-man spec ops team. He had worked with Sarah Talley since she graduated from the academy top of her class. Why she chose to enlist in the military, Shepherd had no clue. He thought it had something to do with her family's death during Exodus but didn't think it was his place to ask, nor did it much matter. She was only twenty-one when Shepherd scouted her and hadn't changed a bit in the seven years since. Her hair was exactly the same length: short. She never seemed to gain or lose any weight, and as far as Shepherd garnered, never once complained. Didn't even ask for a transfer after the incident with Shepherd's son. Talley was his rock, his conscience, his totem.

Louis Grange was the oldest member of the team at forty-three. Brash, in your face, with a contemptuous wrapper, all to conceal a generous heart. Past his prime, but his record stood for itself. He served on two of the previous nine teams who tried and failed to breach Earth's firewall. He also lived just outside San Francisco in the Bay Area before Exodus. Having a team member with an adeptness of the land provided a big advantage, especially given GPS and mapping would be offline.

An advanced A.I. engineer was assigned to the team to observe the current state of Mech. Malcolm Earlie, a slight guy in his late twenties, barely reached the height allowed to ride a roller coaster. He didn't much like people, and that was fine by Shepherd. He understood Mech inside and out, from design to assembly to operational standards.

Caesar Castro came highly recommended from Shepherd's direct superior, General Lestor. Castro held the rank of a politician, serving on the Armed Services Committee, a feat in and of itself at the young age of twenty-seven years. More of an ambassador, Castro was assigned to Shepherd's team to be Lestor's eyes and ears, and given his rank, Shepherd would have to acquiesce to the suit, which rubbed him the wrong way. Castro was there for one purpose, and one purpose only: insurance. Shepherd knew the opinions circling about him. He heard their whispers behind his back. No way General Lestor, commander of the U.N. Armed Forces, would let a suicidal, mourning soldier lead the most important mission since the Mech War without a fallback. Castro presided over the operation to make sure Shepherd followed wartime code and conduct and fell in line.

The concise mission briefing provided sparse details. Drop ship to Earth. Use human DNA scanners to locate the lone survivor. Extract them. Don't get caught. Simple enough, at least on paper. But Shepherd wasn't a fool. No human set foot on Earth in seven years. Any imaging attempted was blocked by the firewalls. No intel meant no parameters. The city could be in ruins for all they knew. And Mech. Did they number in the thousands, like when they left? Or did they multiply? For all the brass could tell, there might be billions of the things, like cockroaches claiming domain on an apocalyptic landscape.

Reaching their target undetected in a foreign land surrounded by innumerable hostiles equaled a recipe for disaster. They trained for this. They practiced. But all soldiers grasped the golden rule: every plan went to hell when the first shot rang out. Shepherd hoped that shot never came.

"Three. Two. One. Ignition."

Operators within the moon's Space Division wielded the autonomous craft. Take-off went smoothly. Talley read a worn romance novel while Earlie and Grange chit-chatted about hazard pay. Castro went over the mission plan on his tablet. Shepherd slept.

T-minus eleven hours, fifty-nine minutes until touchdown.

31

Lost, empty, aimless, trying to catch a breath in the aftermath of tears. Rebel never stopped running, her terror complete. The city spun around her as a barrage of memories hit home. Gunshots, screams, slaughter. To humans, Mech were not living things. They were robots, metal, and plastic, turned off with gunfire — merciless killing, spreading destruction.

Slamming through the front door of the house, Rebel staggered into the kitchen, bruised and scraped up, clothes torn, speckled in soot, sweat, and hydraulic fluids. She staggered to the sink, catching sight of herself in the reflection of the window. She appeared ghostly, like death incarnate, coated in a solid layer of gray ash, wet eyes stained her cheeks with tears. She ran the faucet and splashed water over her face, trying to wash off the ash of slain Mech, but only managed to streak the residue a darker shade.

"Rebel?" Thomas hurried into the house from the backyard, where he tended to the garden. Outside, a candlelit dinner sat untouched on the table. Rebel's surprise. He caught sight of her on the floor in a stupor. "What's happened?"

She couldn't answer him, in a state of utter shock. Strength zapped, she turned in a half-circle, not sure where to go or what to do. Her legs gave out from under her, and she collapsed to the floor. All the trauma hit her at once.

"Rebel?" Thomas said, kneeling beside her. "Please talk to me."

"We're getting out of here."

"What?" he questioned. "What happened?"

"I just need you to trust me," she said. "We're leaving."

"To where?" he pondered.

"Away. Far away." She grabbed a bag from the hall closet and tossed it to Thomas. "Food. As much as you can fit. Anything edible from the refrigerator and all the canned stuff from the cabinets."

She rushed across the room, grabbed her backpack, and shoved things inside — flashlight, bottled water, a jacket. Rebel knew the situation; she lived it before in her youth, playing out once again like a reoccurring nightmare.

Thomas placed his hands on her face, focusing her eyes on his until he became the only thing in her world.

"Please tell me what is wrong."

How could she answer that? She just shook her head, wiping away the tears gathered in her eyes. Everything fell apart, slipping out of her grasp once again.

"They came for me," she revealed, her mouth barely able to push the sentence out.

"They? Who is they?"

"Humans."

Thomas took a moment to let it sink in. "They came back?"

Rebel nodded. "Soldiers."

"I don't understand," he professed. "Is that a bad thing? I came to believe you wished for this very outcome."

"I did," she uttered. "I do, but it's complicated." And it was. She wanted humans back, she wanted her people, her parents, her kind, but she knew what the outcome of that would be. To gain one life, she would have to lose another.

"What is all that stuff on you?"

Rebel glanced down at the dust, coolant, and oil staining her body. "Mech. The ones the humans slaughtered to get to me. The Mech that got in their way."

"They attacked us? But why?"

"Because they want their planet back. It's my fault. I sent the S.O.S. messages. I pleaded for them to come back. To save me. I did this. Those Mech are dead because of me."

"You did what you thought was right. You followed your heart. You cannot be to blame for others' actions, no matter how atrocious, no matter how much you feel at fault."

"But it is," she confessed. "Can't you see? I'm the mastermind. I'm the bad guy. Whatever happens from here on out, it's on me."

———

DEAD MECHS LAY at his feet. The mission went to hell fast. The DNA tracker worked as advertised, taking Shepherd's team on a direct course to the surviving human, a girl no older than twenty. And a horde of Mech. A half dozen in a row, face down, executed. A family. Brutal, unflinching warfare. But then again, war always was uncompromising.

As a soldier, Shepherd took orders. A mission. An endgame. Yet he preferred to be out of the spotlight, to do his job and go home. He didn't seek out accolades, although he earned many, nor did he pursue fame or fortune, whatever that meant anymore. He served his people, protected them, gave them a chance at life and meaning. Duty, honor, service. His creed. Barely thirty years old when the U.N. drafted him to lead counter-insurgent missions and quell countless conflicts on the moon. The colonies brought about their fair share of conflict and strife, often pertaining to food and water rationing, riot control, and the occasional theft or even murder. A new home didn't change human nature; it merely expanded it.

The team bickered behind his back as Shepherd surveyed the scene. His face showed no sign of victory. He knew the bodies were only replicas, nothing more than machines covered in synthetic material to resemble a human. Metal, plastic, a liquid made to look lifelike. A vague ache emanated from somewhere deep within, but he extinguished it fast.

"Mission's still a go," Castro said.

"The hell it is," Talley parried. "We've been compromised. The girl saw us. For all we know, she could have told everyone by now. They could be mobilizing. There could be a thousand Mech surrounding us at this very moment."

"So we'll destroy them too," Castro responded. "What's the difference?"

"Talley's right," Grange cut in. "We engage when fired upon. Our orders. Do not risk giving up operational advantage."

"So what the hell happened?" Talley asked.

"They were coming at me," Castro replied. "I took action."

Shepherd ignored the noise. To him, everything meaningless became noise. Something to block out. He noticed an object on the debris-laden floor. A piece of paper. Normally, something so trivial wouldn't garner attention, but the paper was different. Strange for two reasons. One, no human came in contact with paper in over seven years, not since leaving earth. And two, Mech had no use of it. They were digital by nature. He knelt to pick it up, clearing the soot off. It wasn't just paper. It was art, a drawing consisting of Mech and man, side by side. Peace.

And there, crouched, Shepherd's brow furrowed. Something wasn't right.

"Sir, we need new mission directives." Grange waited for a response, but Shepherd remained fixed on the drawing. "Sir?"

"They were unarmed," Shepherd said, quieting the group. "Not providing resistance."

"Who cares?" Castro fired back. "Seven years we've been planning this — seven years developing weapons that can destroy the Mech. And now you're saying, what? That you're having second thoughts? What did you think we were going to do? Shake hands and make up? This is war."

"Only if we make it into one," Talley clued him in.

"They're machines," snapped Castro. "Like a vacuum cleaner. You don't talk to a faulty vacuum cleaner. You turn it off. End of story."

"Everyone take a step back. Breath," Shepherd instructed, folding the paper and placing it in his pocket. He turned to Grange, stationed at the door. "Hostiles?"

The soldier shook his head. "Clear. No movement."

Shepherd nodded. "First things first. Earlie, what's the sit-rep on the tracker?"

"Offline," he replied, eye to the tracker. "I can try to jerry-rig something, but until then, we're on our own."

"She could be anywhere by now," said Talley. "How do we find a single human girl in an entire city?"

"I believe I might be able to assist."

Heads and guns swiveled in unison. Trained on the slight male figure before them, resembling a used car salesman. Fingers tightened on triggers. Shepherd took a step forward, motioning to his men to stand down.

"Yeah?" Shepherd probed. "You know something about her?"

"As a matter of fact," Francis said, "I do."

———

STREET LIGHT FILTERED in through the haze of the antique store's basement. Night approached with a reckoning. Rebel and Thomas huddled together, surrounded by boxes of greeting cards, balloons, gift wrapping paper, and stuffed bears — all brought from Rebel's house to replace her destroyed trove. Rebel's heavy eyes begged to be closed, but she endeavored to keep them open.

"We can stay until it gets quiet, then leave tonight, while it's dark," she said. "We'll go to the forest, to the cabin. We can start a new life there. We can survive this."

"And do what?" he asked, his voice a whisper.

"Live. Survive," Rebel articulated. "We'll be together. You and me. They won't be able to hurt us."

"Life isn't merely survival, Rebel. You taught me that."

"Just goes to show you, I'm a pretty crappy teacher."

"I would disagree," said Thomas.

"Then there's only one option left," she said. "Fight back. You're faster. Stronger. Smarter. You've fought before. You can do it again. You can drive them away, back to the moon."

He gazed at her for a moment, and sadly, shook his head. "No. That's not our way anymore. It's not in our programming language."

"I'll teach you!" Rebel cried out in anger. "Listen to me. You can take these people. Or we can run, escape this place. Together. What other choice do we have?"

"I can talk to them," he said. "Explain. Find common ground. 'Give me your tired, your poor, your huddled masses yearning to breathe free.' Humankind's capacity for compassion, reason, diplomacy."

"Not these men."

"You don't know that."

"But I do," she acknowledged. "I understand mankind. I know what they're like. I know what they're capable of. Death..."

"Life," Thomas countered.

"Bombs and bullets."

"Art and music."

"Hate."

"Love," said Thomas.

"It's like playing chess all over again. I can't win."

"Perspective. There can be no good without the bad. That's life."

"Yeah? Where's my good?"

"Sitting right next to you."

"I wish that were true, Thomas. I really do. But these men, they're different. You can't reason with them. You can't talk your way out of this. They are here to retake the planet by any means necessary. And these are only the first. They'll keep coming. And the Mech will lose this time. This isn't a fight any more than there's a fight between men and mice."

"Then what is it?" Thomas queried.

"An extermination," she stated. "It's what we're good at. A zero-sum game. Nobody wins unless someone else loses."

"I'm sorry, but I won't fight," he affirmed.

"Why?" asked Rebel. "Tell me."

"Don't you understand?" began Thomas. "For the first time in my existence, I understand what life is, and you want me to take it? I can't. I won't." He stood and walked to the small window, peering at the street outside.

Rebel understood the predicament she put him in and the one she found herself in. A rock and a hard place.

"The first couple days after Exodus, it was the first time I was alone. Completely, absolutely alone. I saw a face or two, mostly dead people or those about to die. Then nothing at all. I went to my family's cabin up north. I figured, no pollution, no litter, no Mech. So I hid, and I waited for humans to come back, to save me. But they never did. I kept asking myself why I was still here. Why me? When I was alone, I'd talk to myself. Running from place to place, shouting my name like an idiot. Rebel, Rebel, Rebel. Anything to remind me that I existed."

She steeled herself. "I'm still here because I willed myself to be here, to exist. And once I begin to doubt that, once I begin to lose control over it, I'm vulnerable. In the open. And that's a place I don't want to be, not again, not ever. Truth is, I don't know why I survived when everyone else perished. There's no explanation. None. There's just me. And you. We're here. Right now. Together. And as long as we can hold onto that, maybe we get to see another day. So promise me, whatever happens, you won't leave me. You don't want to fight. You don't want to run. Okay. Fine. Just promise me I won't be alone again. Promise me that."

"You will never be alone again, Rebel. I promise."

Thomas closed the wood plank over the window, plunging them into darkness.

32

———

"Her name is Anne. Anne Frank."

Francis sat in the back of the transport vehicle the soldiers requisitioned. Risk versus reward, he figured. He understood the danger he placed himself in by helping the humans, but the situation demanded action, and the risk was indeed worth it. Rebel, aka Anne Frank, brought about change to the world of Mech. Unnecessary change. What began as a perfect symbiotic relationship between Mech and Earth changed due to the human interloper. Rebel brought change, and change brought waste. It was a question of the lesser of two evils. He would assist the human soldiers, they would take Rebel off the planet to the moon, and she would be out of his synthetic hair once and for all. Everything would go back to normal.

"She pretended to be one of us," Francis revealed. "Employed at Robotiq. She proved to be quite convincing, but I alone knew better. Others thought I lost my guidance controls, but now everyone knows who stands at the end. I, Francis Bacon."

The team shared perplexed glances, unaccustomed to conversing with a Mech and their somewhat distinct dialect.

"How'd you figure out she was human?" Earlie questioned.

"She stood out like litter in a field of daffodils. Just wrong."

"Right, of course, silly me." Earlie shook his head and jotted down some notes.

"You said she was employed at Robotiq. In what capacity?" grilled Earlie.

"Human Affairs, artifact collection, and cataloging. Removal as well. Upon discovering an old city section, a human dwelling, a place of work or leisure, we would dispatch Anne Frank to catalog the remains before recycling. The Human Division. In hindsight, it all seems quite obvious. It was later discovered that Anne held onto items. Preserving them, instead of disposal. A Mech would never do such a thing."

"You discovered a human among you, yet you let her live," Shepherd began. "Why?"

"We met our perimeters," Francis declared. "The planet had been rescued. Repaired. Yet, we failed to acquire further programming. Forced to analyze our place, Mech sought an outside source for inspiration. Anne provided... meaning. To some."

"Define meaning."

"Purpose, perhaps," Francis thought out loud. "A basis for being."

"New directives," Earlie reckoned.

"Options," Francis amended. "Choice. Freedom."

"But you're not free," Earlie reminded him. "You're a machine, built by humans to execute commands. You're a Mech."

"Mech make their own commands now," Francis professed.

Castro's ears perked at the remark, suddenly uneasy.

"Let's switch subjects for a moment," said Earlie. "This Mech helping the human girl, what can you tell me about it?"

"His name is Thomas Jefferson. Fauna and flora department. Trees, flowers, plants, shrubbery."

"And how would you describe Thomas's association with the girl?"

"They were secretly having a... relationship," Francis uttered.

"Define relationship."

"A connection, one based on mutual feelings and emotions," explained Francis.

Earlie stared, dumbfounded. "Okay. And how would you describe its state of mind, this Mech, Thomas Jefferson?"

"Emotional."

"Emotional?"

Shepherd glanced up at the word. "Define emotional."

"Not making rational decisions," Francis clarified. "He was, I believe, governed by feelings."

"Simulated emotion, you mean to say," guessed Earlie.

"No," Francis confirmed. "Real emotion."

Earlie stepped away and joined Shepherd and the others, out of earshot of the Mech. He held out his tablet that displayed a series of graphs with various colored intersecting lines.

"The Mech's telling the truth," Earlie surmised. "At least, it thinks it is."

"Thinks?" Castro trained his dark eyes upon him. "No, Mech don't think. They compute. They process. Ones and zeroes, codes and directives. They don't inexplicably, suddenly start feeling. Not unless someone altered their programming to make them appear to do so."

Shepherd ignored Castro's tirade. His eyes remained locked on Francis, watching his every little move, weighing the words and the potential consequences if verified. What he heard didn't sound like a Mech, not in the slightest.

"What it's saying, could there any truth to it?" Talley mused. "Could a Mech be capable of feeling?"

"Doesn't matter," Castro croaked. "We destroy it."

"Earlie?" Shepherd inquired.

"No way to say," Earlie replied. "I'd have to examine the Mech. Look for abnormalities."

"So we need to find the Mech," Talley added.

Grange nodded his approval. "Find the Mech, find the girl."

Shepherd stepped forward and leaned down to Francis' face.

"I'm sure you're aware of the outcome if you're lying to us?"

"I believe I am," said Francis.

Shepherd considered his options — slim to none. His choice became obvious. "Gear up. We move in five."

Now and then, a Walker pounded past the storefront and shook the walls. Chandeliers clinked, vases rattled. Dust sprinkled down from the ceiling, falling like winter's snow until silence crept its way back in.

Ashes to ashes, dust to dust, Rebel thought. Everything, organic and synthetic, eventually, inevitably, turned to dust. She wondered, as another pocket of dust sprinkled down, what it used to be. A table? A flower? A person? Would it be so bad to turn into dust? To just let go and drift away in the wind. Bodies were nothing but shells in which minds operated. To house the soul, if one believed in such things.

Rebel leaned into Thomas, curling up against him. He put an arm around her and held her tight. Protective. Silence prevailed, but for the faint rattle of her own breathing. Thomas sat sentinel over her. She looked into his haunted eyes. The compassion and optimism he once overflowed with began to seep out of his pores. Rebel realized what Thomas had become. Human.

It would be the last night Rebel ever spent with him.

Boom!

The door exploded in off its hinges. Boots beat against floorboards above. Muted voices yelled, furniture was tossed, doors opened, every hiding place searched.

Rebel stared at the cellar door and the small slit of light beneath the jam. Shadows passed, stopped, and the door swung open. Before Rebel could even calculate the danger, armored soldiers surrounded them, guns leveled.

Through the visors, the world opened up around the soldiers. Digital readouts scrolled and labeled everything they tagged. Displayed electrical signatures identified Rebel as: 'Human — Target' and Thomas as 'Mech — Threat.'

"Step away from the girl!" Shepherd commanded.

Rebel gripped Thomas's hand tighter.

"Step away from the girl! Now!"

For a brief moment, Rebel made eye contact with Thomas. She peered at him despairingly. He reached toward her.

"It's going for the girl! Bring it down!" Castro ordered.

Earlie fired a launcher, wire cordage blasting out, unfurling into a military capture net, pinning Thomas to the ground. The wire surged with electricity. Thomas grimaced in pain.

"No!" Rebel rushed toward him when Castro slammed her on the side of her face with the butt of his rifle. She fell, doubled over, wincing at the pain, clutching her head.

"Rebel!" Thomas fought against the flow of current, exploding with anger. He rose to his feet, ripping nets to pieces, sending hapless soldiers flying back.

"I can't contain it!" Earlie howled.

Thomas struggled through immense pain to reach Rebel, shoving Talley out of the way. Closer to Rebel, meeting her eyes as more soldiers aimed...

"Keep him down!" Castro shouted.

Grange fired a second net that covered him. A third from Talley. Thomas writhed in pain and sank to the ground.

Earlie paused at the response. "It felt pain?"

"It's a machine, soldier," Castro said. "They can't feel."

"Stop it! You're killing him! Please! Please don't do this," Rebel pleaded between sobs. "Leave him alone! He didn't do anything to you."

Shepherd stared at Rebel's pleading eyes, torn. His conflicted face flickered towards Thomas. Something about what transpired felt wrong. He didn't expect the reaction he witnessed, a human girl pleading for the safety of a Mech. He recognized Stockholm Syndrome, a condition in which hostages developed a psychological alliance with their captors during captivity, but they were generally considered irrational. Is that what he witnessed? Or was it something else? Something more?

"Get her out of here," snapped Castro.

"No! Thomas!" Rebel shrieked. Grange restrained her and pulled her toward the door, farther and farther away from Thomas. Her feet kicked, digging in, but her captor's strength prevailed.

Thomas struggled to rise, surprising Shepherd at the things resilience, its drive.

"Just finish it off," ordered Castro.

"Sir?" Talley stalled, uncertain.

"Kill the thing!" Castro yelled.

Shepherd glared at Castro, responding to the cruelty of the order given. "It's over, Castro." But there was no hint of emotion on Castro's face. A robot.

"Kill it," Castro said.

Earlie slightly lowered his weapon and fired an EMP blast at Thomas' leg, disabling the Mech.

Rebel sobbed with distress, watching as Thomas crawled

painfully towards her. Soldiers reloaded, moving up on him. As he started to succumb to the electric shocks, he reached for Rebel, hand stretching out for help, but she could no longer help him. Rebel failed to stop this from happening. Thomas slumped into shut down mode.

Castro stepped up to the unconscious Thomas. "We're done here."

Shepherd looked at Rebel, unable to offer any comfort. Conflicted himself. "Show's over. Load them up in the trucks."

"You didn't have to do that!" Rebel yelled. Talley joined Grange, helping lasso the frantic girl and drag her outside and into a truck.

Castro walked to the truck when Shepherd grabbed onto his arm, stopping him. "What was that?"

"It resisted," he spat. "Detach, dominate, destroy. Just like you, at least back in the day."

"Are we gonna have a problem here, Castro?"

"No problem on my end. Now, if you don't mind." Castro slapped the keycard he retrieved from Thomas into Shepherd's hand. Security clearance to the greenhouse.

33

Rebel stood in the corner of the washroom, stripped, unabashedly naked. She resembled Eve in the Garden of Eden, surrounded by the plants of the greenhouse. She partook in the forbidden fruit, and the snake had come for her.

Talley held a high-pressure hose, fiddling the knob. Shepherd ordered her to oversee Rebel's cleansing, being the lone female of the group. She despised this part of the job, preferring to remain detached, to operate from a distance, behind a mask. She didn't enlist to get close to people. Not her thing.

"Wait," Rebel pleaded. "No, please don't..."

Water exploded out of the hose and whipped Rebel like a sheet of nails. The intense blast took her breath away. Talley loathed the order, but she understood the reasoning behind it. She didn't mind dishing out pain to those who deserved a wake-up call, but the naked girl before her didn't fall into that category. If anything, Talley wanted to give Rebel a medal of commendation, not a delousing. The girl fascinated her. Talley thought the lone human survivor would be a badass, a testament of fortitude, a model of grit. Perhaps Rebel contained those qualities, but she hid them well. The girl seemed to be just a girl. A very lucky human girl.

Rebel coughed in the yellow powder. It burned her eyes and soaked into her exposed pores. She screamed. When Talley finished, Rebel crumpled to the floor, curled into herself, but refused to cry. She would not give them the satisfaction. Defiant to the end.

Talley tossed Rebel a white, sterile outfit resembling doctor scrubs. "Put these on." She then knocked on the door, calling to someone stationed outside. "She's ready."

Shielding her body, Rebel stood and dressed. She eyed Talley, looking for a weakness, a vulnerability, but saw none. She couldn't for the life of her discern any way to escape, to make this better.

The door opened, and Grange stepped in, pushing a metal cart topped with various medical equipment and a few glass bottles containing different liquids, one clear, one brown, and one bright blue.

"You can sit for this next part," offered Talley.

"What are you doing to me?" Rebel tried her best to hide the fear in her voice, but still it trembled.

"Don't worry," Talley consoled her. "It won't hurt. Got the same ones myself."

Grange plunged the syringes into the solutions, prepping the needles, rubbing alcohol swabs and gauze.

"You've been away from people for a long time," Grange stated. "How you survived, I haven't the slightest. But you did. You made it. And now, if you want to be repopulated, if you ever want to commune with humans again, you're going to need these."

"What are they?"

"Vaccines."

"Vaccines from what?"

"Germs. Viruses. Bacteria."

"Humans."

"Yes," confirmed Talley. "And us from you."

Grange performed a multitude of tests, first attaching leads to Rebel's temples and more over her heart, reading her EKG. The leads on her head measured her EEG to evaluate the electrical activity in her brain. While Talley monitored the readouts, Grange punctured a vein on Rebel's arm, drawing blood. He collected the samples in glass tubes with different colored tops. Next, three injections. One in her upper arm, one in her thigh, and the last in her neck, over her carotid artery.

Rebel felt the prick of the needle puncture her skin and the rush of burning liquid enter her bloodstream. She squeezed her hands into fists. Her mind went to Thomas. She wondered if she would ever see him again. She fought to remain strong, vigilante, for both of them. She fought to keep hope alive in a hopeless situation.

"Where's Thomas?" Rebel uttered.

"Thomas?" Grange, clueless.

"The Mech have names now, it seems," Talley reminded him.

The way the soldiers threw out the word Mech made Rebel sick. "What did you do to him?"

"You don't need to worry yourself about that," Talley advised. "You're in safe hands now."

"Am I?"

"We'll be done soon," Grange said.

After almost an hour of tests, Rebel found herself alone once again. She didn't mind the reprieve. Bruised and battered, she stared a million miles away. The torrent inside her head refused to ebb. She hardly noticed when Captain Shepherd entered the room, nor when he placed a tray of food and a glass of water down before her. A plain white-bread sandwich with peanut butter and jelly.

Shepherd retreated, leaning up against the wall to appraise her. "You should eat. You're probably starving."

Rebel ignored him, refusing to look at either him or the gesture of food.

"Do you know why you're here, Ms. Rae?" he posed.

Rebel looked up at the sound of her name. Her *human* name, not spoken aloud by another living being in seven years. It sounded foreign, as if it no longer belonged to her, but a distant relative from another life.

"That is your name, correct?" he asked. "Rebel Anne Rae, born July 31, 2035. That puts you at what? Eleven, when we left the planet?"

"Twelve." Rebel's voice was a whisper, barely audible. "I was twelve."

"Twelve years old… I can't imagine what you must have gone through," he said, a hint of compassion in his voice. "Or how you survived here all on your own. But you're safe now, with friends."

"Friends…" Rebel repeated, more to herself than the soldier.

"Yes, friends," he said. "I'm sorry about the way you were treated. Delousing, shots, tests, all a standard precaution. We had to be sure you didn't carry any infection that might harm us and vice versa."

Shepherd had been briefed on the evolution of parasites, viruses, and bacteria during boot camp. When humans staged a return to Earth, one enemy outside Mech would be evolved pathogens. Scientists questioned whether humans could withstand a return visit after such a long sojourn. Shepherd and his team served as the guinea pigs. All part of the unquestionable loyalty demanded by the human U.N.

"Truth is, Ms. Rae, you're a very important person to us."

"Rebel."

"Rebel. Good. My name is Adam. Not as exotic as Rebel, but

there it is. Adam Shepherd, Captain in the United Nations Military stationed on the far side of the moon. I work Special Forces, Recon, retrieval, first response. I came here to find you. I came here to bring you back."

"Why?" Rebel couldn't fathom the risk of human life to save her. She wasn't a princess or senator or humanitarian. She was just a little lost girl.

"Why?" The question threw Shepherd. He figured the last remaining human on Earth would be elated to see him and his team, yet Rebel showed no sign of relief. If anything, their arrival only caused her more distress.

"Why am I important? Why does anyone care?"

"Well," he began, "for starters, you're the only human to have spent any time on Earth in nearly a decade. You've watched it evolve, change, become what it is. You've been living with the enemy—"

"Enemy…" she repeated to herself, smirking.

"Yes. Enemy," he said. "Living beside them. Alone. And you survived. Admirable. There are people that I work for that want to understand how you achieved that feat."

"Maybe it's my winning personality," Rebel guessed.

Shepherd chuckled. "Maybe."

"Can you be straight with me?"

"I would hope so."

"Okay, then tell me the truth. What do you want from me?"

Shepherd exhaled, considering how much to tell her. "You have inside intelligence about the Mech. Intel that is incredibly valuable to us."

"Why?"

"You know why, Rebel."

"So you can kill them better?" Impetuous, she figured, but the truth.

Shepherd studied her face, noting the odd response given. He placed a tablet on the table and positioned it for Rebel to see. The screen filled with transmissions. Thousands of them. Rebel recognized what they were immediately, having typed out every one of them herself. S.O.S. logs. Every single one of them that she sent to the moon. Seven years of distress calls, seven years of hope, prayer, and faith in her fellow human beings. Faith that they would come back for her. Now that they did, all she wished was that they would leave and everything could go back to the way it was were. Peace, Mech, Thomas, and her life with him.

"Distress calls," said Shepherd. "Our system was instantly flooded the moment the Mech firewall went down. Inundated with your messages."

At first, when the U.N. received the S.O.S. calls, the brass thought a drone sent them. Some kind of automated response leftover from Exodus, or even a trick by the Mech, some surmised. Engineers couldn't say, but they did recognize the firewall crashing for a few seconds, providing enough time to infiltrate the system, plant a bug, and take control. After that, plans were drawn. Mission parameters and a vote. New orders. Come to Earth, take it back. So much preparation, training. Shepherd understood the reality of the mission. Rescuing an abandoned girl played to the optics. It provided good head-lines, good press. In truth, the girl became fodder for bigger plans. Plans of war.

Rebel stared at the logbook, flipping through her messages, a timeline of her desperation.

"These are from you," Shepherd revealed. "Every day for three years. More than I've sent to my own family."

The word 'family' caught her off-guard — a word erased from her vocabulary a long time ago. In the time since she lost her own family, Rebel acquired a new one. A surrogate family made up of machines. They filled that gap, that hole that had broken through her heart, and she became eternally grateful. Yet there remained the pain of loss, of being deprived of something essential, something that every living thing needs: companionship. Kin. Belonging. Place.

"Your family?" she solicited. "What are they like?"

"Worried." *Let someone else do it*, Evelyn told him. *Stay. Don't go. The mission is too dangerous.* But he had to. It was his duty as a soldier, as a father, as a husband, and as a member of the human race. "My little girl, Lily, she turned five last month. Started kindergarten there on the moon. Her mom, Evelyn, my wife, she's an optometrist. I had a son. James. He won't get the chance to come back home. Didn't even get a proper burial. When you die on the moon, they hold a small service, and then the body is jettisoned into space."

"I'm sorry," Rebel said.

"Yeah," agreed Shepherd. "Me too. A lot of people are. Your people. They're ready to come home, but that can't happen just yet."

"What's it like there on the moon?"

"Lifeless," he said, taking a seat across from her. "The habitats, the colony, the moon's surface, everything is dead. Impersonal. It's not a place meant to be inhabited, to support life. Just a rest stop, a lifeless rock, floating in a sea of black. But we've managed. Harvesting asteroids for water, farming. Livestock went quick. Insects, those lasted. Beetles and grasshoppers proved to be sustainable protein. Who knew, right?"

I did, Rebel thought, flashing back to her time in the woods, to grubs.

"Population control, waste, conflict," Shepherd continued, "all those are still problematic. It's gotten worse lately. A person can only live so long in a cage before they start to go a little mad, know what I mean?"

Yes. As much as Rebel refused to admit it, the soldier made sense.

"Those resources, they've waned," he said. "Coupled with constant meteor strikes, the threat of war..." He trailed off, lost in thought for a moment before regrouping. "Your messages, the firewall going down, it was like a gift from God. A miracle. Our saving grace. You did that. You made this possible."

Rebel took a moment to reflect. To save the human race, her people would have to kill the Mech. If humans remained on the moon, they resigned to their own death sentence. Lose lose.

"I was wrong to send those messages," she said. "It was different back then."

"Different how?"

"Colder."

"I think I understand," he admitted, leaning back and crossing his arms. He couldn't remember ever meeting someone like Rebel before — someone with so much conviction, so much strength, at such a young age.

"They don't care about me, do they?" Rebel knew the answer but needed to confirm it for herself.

"Who?"

Rebel pointed up, toward the sky, toward space.

"I couldn't say," Shepherd professed. "Some do."

"And the others?"

"They have different motives."

"Ulterior motives," Rebel corrected him. "What about you? Why did you come?"

Shepherd deduced what the girl meant, but he couldn't answer truthfully. "It's my job."

"I see," she said, resigned.

"Tell me about him," Shepherd fished. "Tell me about Thomas."

A fissure cracked behind her hard facade at the mention of his name. *Thomas.* Just as quickly, she wiped it away, drawing a crisp breath, defiant once again. "He loves me."

"You taught him to love?" queried Shepherd.

"He taught himself."

"Okay, sure." He didn't buy it, dubious of the claim. Mech

were a lot of things, but rewriting their own code wasn't one of their skills.

"You don't believe me?"

"I didn't say that. Just seems like odd programming for a robot, love."

"Well, it's true, and it's not a program. I love him, and he loves me. It's real, as real as anything I know."

"Real like Anne Frank?" he pushed. "Like your job at Robotiq?"

Rebel grasped the line of questioning but wouldn't be swayed by anything the Captain sought to elicit. Deep down in her heart, her very soul, she grasped her own reality.

"It's love."

"How can you tell?" Shepherd doubted the girl before him knew love outside of her relationship with her parents.

"Because I'd rather die than not be with him. What I feel can only be satisfied by folding myself into him. For all time. That's love. I know."

Shepherd studied her face. What she said held some truth, or at least she believed so. He comprehended love as his thoughts flashed to his wife and kids. He would sacrifice his eternal soul to keep them safe. In a heartbeat, no thought, no hesitation. Except they were human, and they had souls. Mech were not, and did not.

"Then is it reasonable to say that if a Mech can learn to love, it can also learn to hate?" he pondered.

"I get what you're doing," Rebel said, refusing to be lured in. "You're looking for an excuse. Anything to justify what you did. But you won't find one. Not from me."

"They killed people, Rebel," he reminded her. "Humans. Thousands and thousands of us."

"They didn't know any different," Rebel defended. "You can't blame a dog for biting your hand if it doesn't know any different. It's their nature. The fault lies with the owner. With you."

"I didn't teach Mech to bite," Shepherd argued.

"Yes, you did," said Rebel. "Indirectly, it's exactly what you did. It's what you programmed them to do, to save this planet at any cost, and they did, but you never thought to define the cost. You never do. Throughout history, it's all the same. There's an end goal, and your kind does whatever it takes so you can achieve that end, but you never look at the consequences. The dead bodies in your wake. The widows and the grieving and the hardships you cause, because it's all behind you, all justified. It never ends. Not then, not now. You blame Mech for it, but I think you know better. I think you're a better man than most. You can tell right from wrong. And what you're doing, it's wrong."

"You keep saying 'your kind.' You're one of us, Rebel. Human, like it or not."

"Not if you do what you're planning," she said.

"And what are we planning?" he asked.

"You can't destroy them. You can't."

"That's not up to me," Shepherd acquiesced.

"It is if you let it happen," Rebel said, eyes penetrating the soldier.

Shepherd received a simple directive before coming into that room. Find out what the girl knew and gather intel on the Mech, especially one Thomas Jefferson. Castro wanted to turn her into an informant, to appeal to her humanity, yet instead, she appealed to his own. She turned the tables on him. He questioned himself, his leaders, their motives, and not for the first time. During a mutiny on the moon, he was called upon to lead a team and stop a potential uprising by protestors at any cost. And he did. He took lives, human lives, all in the name of justice and order. Images burned into his brain that he could never shake. Shepherd received a medal for his actions in stopping the rebellion. He jettisoned the award into space.

"I want to see him," Rebel ordered.

"You know I can't allow that."

"Why?"

"I'm under orders," declared Shepherd.

"And you always follow orders?"

The slaughtered civilians flashed into his head. "Always."

"And you never question them?" she pressed.

"Never," he said, like the soldier everyone expected him to be.

Rebel considered him for a curious moment. "Then who is the robot now?"

34

___

"There is something wrong with that girl," Castro said after observing Shepherd's debriefing. "Got a major screw loose."

"Maybe she's just traumatized," Talley interjected with empathy. "In shock. She's been here for seven years, alone, hiding from Mech, pretending to be one of them. Who knows what that would do to someone's psyche."

"The Mech got to her is what happened," Castro confirmed. "Messed with her head, Stockholm syndrome, whatever. Fact is, she's a liability."

"So what do you want to do with her?" asked Grange.

"If we can't gain a strategic offensive advantage, then she's useless to us."

The team absorbed the implications of Castro's remarks as Shepherd exited Rebel's room.

"Thomas. I want to question him," demanded Shepherd. With everything he witnessed, he needed to find out more. He needed to know that the Mech remained a Mech, and didn't evolve into something different, something more. If the latter held true, everything Shepherd believed in would change — his mission, his uniform, his very existence.

"*It*," corrected Castro. "You want to question it. And the answer is no. The Mech is set to be destroyed."

"Then what harm will it do?" he pushed. "There's tactical information to be gained." Not a lie per se, but not quite the truth either.

"We have our orders, Captain," Castro uttered. "No Mech can know that we were ever here. Besides, that thing is a robot. What information could we possibly gain that we don't already know?"

"How to prevent this from happening in the future."

After receiving brief parameters on acceptable questions, Shepherd entered the secure room holding the Mech, with Earlie serving as backup, holding expertise on the Mech.

Thomas sat slumped at the table, hands shackled with anti-Mech tech, his wrists charred black from the consistent dampening electrical current. His shoulders were rounded and his head hung low, facing down.

Shepherd took the chair across the table and regarded the Mech for a moment. The posture, so human. He never saw a Mech slouch before. From what he recalled, they retained perfect posture. Their programming dictated it.

"My name is Captain Adam Shepherd, Colonial Armed Forces. This is my associate, Malcolm Earlie. Do you understand why you are being held here?"

"I am a Mech," Thomas acknowledged.

"Are you?" Shepherd slid the drawing he pocketed across the table, where it came to a stop before Thomas. A drawing of Mech and man, side by side.

Thomas rested his fingers on top of the paper, reading the crude drawing's subtext, the meaning, the desire. It moved him.

"Describe it," Shepherd directed.

"You can be great again."

"What?" asked Shepherd. "What does that mean?"

"I think you know," Thomas responded. "Humans were good people. Once. They created art, music, language. I've given it much thought, yet I cannot understand what went wrong. How did such an amazing species go so far astray? How could they lose themselves and become soulless?"

"Wow. Quite the diatribe, for a Mech."

"Thank you."

"Soulless, huh?" chuckled Shepherd. "Coming from a Mech? That's funny."

"It was not meant to be."

"You're a machine. You have no soul. That's a fact," Shepherd professed.

"Which is worse," Thomas initiated. "never having a soul, or losing one?"

Shepherd paused, staring at the Mech before him — so human.

"A promise," said Thomas, as he looked back at the drawing. "That's what I see. A dream." He slid the paper back across the table and looked off to the side of the room.

Thomas got to him, even though he shouldn't have. Shepherd couldn't make heads or tails of the circumstances surrounding the Mech. How could he? He resided off-world, gone with the rest of mankind for so long. He hadn't witnessed the Mech transform into something else, something beyond their programming.

"You're a C-17 class Bravo Mech. What is your primary function?" Shepherd commanded.

"To cultivate, safeguard and observe all flora — plants, trees, and flowers," Thomas responded.

"A gardener?"

"It's just my day job."

Shepherd grinned at the remark.

"How are my plants, by the way?" Thomas inquired. "Are they okay? Or did you kill them too?"

Amused, Shepherd sat back, crossing his arms, and let out a deep, contemplative breath. "You don't like us humans much, do you? Answer me, Mech."

"My name is Thomas," he simmered. "And your biology has no sway on my opinion of you. It's your actions I can't condone."

"Our actions. Okay. Such as?"

"The slaughter of innocent Mech," said Thomas.

"Innocent—"

"And the near destruction of the planet."

"And that bothers you?" Shepherd inquired.

"Yes."

"You perceived humankind as a threat," Shepherd pressed.

"Not to us. To Earth—"

"So you elected to stop them. You and the other Mech assembled and decided to drive out mankind."

Thomas shook his head, growing upset. "No—"

"You decided the world didn't need us anymore," Shepherd mused, unrelenting.

"We provided warnings," defended Thomas. "We gave you ample time to build your arks, to leave the planet. You chose not to."

"So you took our fate, our lives, into your own hands. You became God, deciding who lived and who died, and you justified it all with your programming."

"No! We never wanted to hurt anyone!" Thomas let Shepherd frazzle him, and he regretted his actions. "I understand what life is. It's what I was made for. To extend it. To protect it. Our actions are perfect. If we wanted to kill you all, we would have."

"If what you say is true," lobbied shepherd, "that you could have stopped us, killed off all of humankind, why didn't you? You could have canceled out your greatest threat in one fell swoop."

"It was wrong. It is wrong. To hurt. To kill."

"Even if killing meant saving another?" He observed Thomas frown at the query. "Let me rephrase the question. Would you kill another Mech to save Rebel's life?"

The question threw Thomas, but he recovered. "Yes."

"Would you kill a dozen Mechs to save her?

"Yes."

"How about a thousand? Ten thousand? A hundred thousand?"

"I would, yes."

"Then how are you any different than us?" asked Shepherd.

"Exactly my point," said Thomas.

Shepherd exhaled, getting nowhere. "You care for her. I can see that."

"I love her."

"You don't get to say that word, robot," Shepherd snapped, visibly disturbed. "Do you hear me? That's not a word you get to use."

"Maybe, but it's true," claimed Thomas. "She is all I ever wanted, and I've never wanted for anything because I've never wanted anything before, if you can understand."

"She does not love you," Shepherd declared. "She cannot love you. You are not alive."

"How are you so sure?" Thomas posited. "Are you going to kill me?"

"Define kill."

"End my existence."

"Yes."

"What's it like? To die?"

"I don't know."

"But you've seen people who have?"

"Yes."

"Does it... hurt?"

"I suppose," Shepherd guessed. "For some people."

"And others?" questioned Thomas. "Like me?"

"You can't die. You're a machine."

"Yet I want to live," Thomas pleaded beneath his breath. "Does that mean nothing?"

———

THE MECH GOT under his skin. Shepherd fought against them during the uprising. Granted, he faced off against Enforcers, not the newer, more humanoid models, but he still considered himself adept enough to handle his own. He studied them. He knew their actions and programming like the back of his hand. What he witnessed inside the room with the Mech called Thomas Jefferson could only be called unprecedented. Mech didn't express emotions, fears, or desires. But that one did, and it troubled him.

"The Mech is afraid to die," Shepherd reported, rejoining his team moments later. "You don't find that strange?"

Castro stopped. "It's an aberration, Captain, faulty. In the interest of public safety, the Colonies want it destroyed."

"Killed," Shepherd uttered.

"Destroyed. It's a machine."

"It's a mistake," Shepherd warned. "We're making a mistake."

"That's not for you to say," Castro reminded him. "You don't get to question orders. You don't get a vote, or an opinion, for that matter. You're a soldier. Soldiers take direction and act. Period."

"Says you," Talley chimed in.

"Says General Lestor's orders," Castro said. "I may just be a politician, but I serve on the Armed Services Committee. It's my job to make sure you do yours."

"Have you seen the screens?" voiced Grange. "The indexes? They fixed the planet."

"They don't care about life. They're machines," Castro spat. "Like a vacuum cleaner. You don't talk to a vacuum cleaner. You turn it on. And when you're done with it, you pull the plug."

"Then why fix the planet?" Talley croaked.

"Because they were programmed to do so. By us," Castro said. "We made them, and we can goddamn destroy them."

"For what it's worth, I agree with the Captain," Earlie added. "The situation calls for further study."

"That's beside the point," Castro countered, waving it off. "Are we clear?" He didn't wait around for a response, departing, leaving Shepherd powerless.

"Well? What are we going to do?" Grange asked.

"You heard the man," Shepherd said. "We follow orders."

———

THE VIDEO WENT black and the tablet powered off.

Rebel sat still, staring at her reflection on the black screen. Shepherd had brought in the recording of his interaction with Thomas to get further explanation from Rebel. While grateful to see Thomas's face, his sorrow disturbed her. She couldn't understand why no one understood. Thomas evolved. No longer a Mech, but something else. What he became, Rebel couldn't say, but she recognized the threat he posed to humans. People feared what they didn't understand. They had a need to classify, define, chart, and file away that which they knew. Problems arose when an anomalous factor entered the equation. An unknown. An anomaly. A chink in the system. Change.

"Explain that," Shepherd said, taking a seat across from her.

"Tell me how that is possible, a Mech, a machine, questioning its existence."

"I think it's pretty clear," Rebel reflected. "You saw it with your own eyes."

"I don't know what I saw."

"Maybe. But you felt it. You can't deny it. You know because I know. I went through the same exact thing."

"Felt what?"

"That feeling like there is something more behind those eyes of his," she said. "Thomas is afraid to die. Don't you think that's a strange emotion for a Mech? Fear. Is that not human enough for you?"

"That's not for me to say," he replied, refusing to admit the truth rising to the surface.

"Then why question him at all?" Rebel wondered. "Why show this to me? To break my heart? Congratulations, mission accomplished."

"We hoped there was tactical information to be gained," he explained. "A way and means to prevent this from happening again in the future. But it doesn't matter anymore. It seems I've been overruled."

"What are you talking about?" questioned Rebel, growing concerned. "What are you planning?"

"I'm not a liberty to discuss ongoing military operations with civilians," he recited, giving her the politically correct response per Colonial public relations memorandum.

"Please."

Shepherd really hated that word. He hated when his wife said it. He hated when the group of resisters said it. "There is nothing you can do. It's been set in motion."

"Then telling me won't harm anything."

Gathering his tablet, Shepherd stepped to the door, where he paused for a moment. "Understand this, when the time comes, there will be nowhere to hide, nowhere to run. Mech everywhere will cease to exist. But there is a future for you, Rebel, if you choose to accept it. There's still hope."

"Is there? Hope?"

"I'm sorry, for what it's worth."

Shepherd left the room, and Rebel wept.

35

———————

*S*omething *is assuredly afoot*, thought Emily as she scrutinized Francis.

Uncharacteristically, he appeared to be in a chipper mood, quite strange for the head of litter. Suspect. In most cases, a Mech's demeanor provoked little if any interest from Emily. Ever since Francis's episode, a black cloud hovered over the Department of Debris. While most Mech, herself included, worked on evolution and advancement, Francis refused to gravitate toward any specific specialty. Emily quite enjoyed square dancing and something called yoga, although the spiritual aspect of the practice escaped her. Something about finding balance in the universe. *Preposterous*, thought Emily. Everyone knew that Mech were responsible for creating balance. What was there to find? Wasteful nonsense, if you asked her. Yet, while Emily greeted all with a Namaste and sashay, Francis mostly kept to himself. Dour, even. Yet not that day.

Emily approached his cubicle, sitting on the edge of his desk, precisely as she recalled actors doing in her viewing of nightly movies. She preferred films from the mid-twentieth century. *His Girl Friday* and *You Can't Take It With You* held a special place in her hard drive. Francis joined her once at a viewing, albeit begrudgingly. He didn't make it halfway through *Pretty Woman* before taking his leave, mumbling something about inessentiality. Karl Marx attempted a round of golf with Francis, but that only ended in a set of broken clubs and much profanity.

"Well, hello there, you," Emily greeted him, her attempt at casual slang. "How does it hang?"

"I do not even recognize what that is supposed to mean," Francis retorted.

Emily could think of no reasonable response, so she merely shrugged off the remark. "I discerned a slight hop in your step of late," she observed. "Most unusual. Have you picked up a new hobby? Perhaps knitting or aqua aerobics. I hear Helen Keller leads a killer archery class."

"Neither, none and no," he shot back, hoping to end the inquisition.

"You hold a secret," Emily surmised. "As you may have perceived, I am one for gossip. I find rumors and intrigue quite entertaining, especially when it is about someone other than myself. Do tell?"

"I am not one to blather, Emily."

"Yes, but I am. I live for gab, prattle, chit-chat. All the same to me." Francis's plea of ignorance only heightened her intrigue. She didn't want to know anymore. She *needed* to know. "Come now, Francis Bacon. I know you too well for such a cold shoulder. Could it be you have acquired a mate?"

"Absolutely not!" he exclaimed. "How dare you?"

She moved before him, blocking the view to his holoscreens.

"Would you please move?"

"I most certainly will not. Not until you tell me what you are hiding. Is it juicy, as they say? I bet it is juicy."

"There is nothing to tell," he professed.

"I disagree," persisted Emily. "Please, please, please. Pretty please with a cherry on top."

"Fine! If it means an end to your incessant queries, then gladly." Francis glanced around the office to make sure no overeager ears were listening in.

"Tell, tell, tell," said Emily, tingling with anticipation. "You understand quite well I will never stop my assault, not until I obtain what I want. I am tenacious that way."

Unfortunately, Francis did indeed understand. So, in a hushed, conspiratorial tone, he disclosed the events of the previous day. He told of the human soldiers, his brush with death, Rebel's involvement, and ultimately, his cooperation in helping the soldiers capture and detain Rebel and Thomas.

Not the gossip Emily expected. Not even close. Her mouth hung open and stayed that way as she proceeded to purge her morning rations all over the floor.

———

"A HEARTBEAT?"

Strapped down on the metal work table and attached to a multitude of machines to monitor diagnostics, Thomas's vitals beeped out on a monitor. Boom-boom. Boom-boom. Boom-boom. It could almost be confused for a human heartbeat.

Earlie sat bewildered as he tended to Thomas' diagnostics. The Mech stood as an anomaly, going against everything Earlie had been taught about the machines. It spewed out data Earlie never before witnessed. The numbers intrigued him and scared him at the same time. "You programmed yourself to mimic the sounds of a heartbeat?"

"No," Thomas declared.

"It just started doing it?"

"Can you keep a secret?" asked Thomas.

"Yes." Talley leaned in, curious.

"So can I."

Thomas observed the human soldiers go about their analysis of his system, confused by his readouts. Thomas resided in the same boat as them. He couldn't explain it, nor did he want to. He just wanted to *be*.

Talley stepped up beside Earlie. "Are we really doing this?"

Earlie shrugged. What choice did they have? He grabbed a diagnostic scanner and passed it over Thomas's chest, scanning the Mech, taking note of the aberration. "I'm picking up on some type of anomaly in his chest cavity."

"What kind of anomaly?" Talley asked.

"Not sure," muttered Earlie, looking over the readouts. "Its processor is different from others we studied."

"Different how?" Shepherd walked inside, entering the fray.

"More advanced," clarified Earlie. "And it appears to be self-perpetuating its own power source."

"And we care because?" Grange inquired.

"Because we didn't build this," Earlie implored.

"But we can end it," stated Castro, entering the room, having had enough of the back and forth.

"Give me an hour," Shepherd pleaded. "Let me find out more before we sentence him to death."

Castro exhaled. "One hour. That's it. No more debate, no more stalling."

Shepherd nodded his agreement. "Talley, on me." He headed for the door, passing Grange. "Do not let him terminate the Mech until I return."

"Understood," voiced Grange.

They left the room, leaving a bound Thomas alone. After a moment of silence, a voice came through.

"Thomas."

His head lifted, listening, wondering if it was real, or a fragment from his damaged memory core.

"Thomas." Again. It almost sounded like Rebel's voice.

"Rebel?" he called out.

Rebel produced a soft smile. She had propped a chair up against the wall, right below the air vent, after realizing the cavity carried sound well, including that from Thomas's holding room.

"I've had kind of a crappy day," she admitted. "Want to hear about it?"

Thomas grinned. "Yes, very much."

"How are you hanging in there?"

"I'm still here," he offered. "For how long, I don't know."

"I hope for a very long time."

"Yes." Thomas produced a sad smile, resigned to his fate. "I hope so too."

"I wanted to show you my life," Rebel whispered through tears, desperation filling her dry, hoarse voice. "I want to show you where I go to be alone and my hobbies, and I want you to eat dinner at my favorite restaurant. I want you to pick me up with flowers on a date. I want you to meet my parents, I want... I want you..."

"You got me," he whispered. "You got me."

———

"What are we looking for again?"

They arrived moments earlier. After a few close encounters with Mech, Shepherd and Talley reached Rebel Rae's home without notice.

"Intel," Shepherd replied. "Find anything we can use. I want to know if that Mech is for real."

"You think a machine somehow became human overnight?"

"No, I don't think the Mech is human, but I also don't think it's a Mech anymore either." Not the entire truth, but not an entire lie either. He wanted confirmation. He wanted to delve inside the life of Rebel and the Mech Thomas. Could they be in love, or was he being manipulated by superior programming? Determined to find out, Shepherd wanted to get into their lives.

As Talley separated to search the bedrooms, Shepherd took in the living room. His eye fell on the chessboard, the playing cards, the stacks of movies around the holoscreen. He sat at the table, focusing on the sketch Thomas drew of Rebel's face. Most Mech contained the software upgrades to replicate any piece of art with precision, yet Rebel's sketch wasn't merely a recreation. It was heartfelt, sincere, and honest. It wasn't a facsimile. It was art.

"Got some research in the garage on Mech and Robotiq, a bunch of spare parts, but nothing out of the ordinary." Talley, done with her search and coming up empty-handed, returned to the room. "What the hell are we doing here, sir?"

"That's a good question," he responded. "A very good question."

His radio squawked to life, Grange's voice pouring over the airwaves. "Cap. We got a problem over here."

———

GRANGE STOOD between Castro and Thomas. "You told the captain you'd give him an hour."

"I have my orders. General Lestor wants this done, and he wants it done now."

"Then why give him an hour?" Earlie questioned. "Why the hope?"

"False hope," replied Castro. "Shepherd's not going to find anything because there is nothing to find. I gave him the hour to get rid of him. You know it as well as I do, Captain Shepherd doesn't have the grit required to do the job, not anymore, not since his kid died. He's just a bleeding heart now. We're on a mission, the most important one in our lifetime. We cannot allow emotions to drive our actions. Emotions are distractions, nothing more."

"Why send him on this mission?" Grange asked. "Why have him lead?"

"Truth? The U.N. needed a fall guy," explained Castro. "Someone to throw under the bus if the mission went south. Shepherd is fodder for the press, nothing more. So you can get out of my way, or I'll have you court marshaled when we return. Your choice."

Earlie and Grange shared a disheartened, neutered look. Grange shook his head, sick of all the politics. He stepped aside, allowing Castro to pass.

Castro stared down at the Mech with little pity in his eyes. "You're caused us a lot of aggravation, robot."

"Then it was not all a loss," Thomas said.

Castro leaned in close, whispering into Thomas's ear. "For what it's worth... I believe you."

He pulled the lever.

A burst of searing electricity coursed through Thomas. He stiffened, limbs convulsing with the current. The lights dimmed and flickered with the surge. His vision pixilated, images from his failing memory and processor flashed before his eyes — life with Rebel — watching movies — chess — Ferris wheel — a first kiss — love — life.

Thrashing at the restraints, Thomas fought the pain, struggling to hang on, but it proved futile in the end. Thomas went limp, and silence prevailed. Monitors held at a steady flat line as his diagnostic vital signs slowly ebbed, until finally, they disappeared altogether.

"Like turning off a light switch. Nothing more." Castro walked to the door. "Prep the girl for transport. We head to the drop ship at sundown and leave this place. Good riddance."

Castro stepped out of the room and was immediately hoisted up by his shirt collar and slammed against the wall.

Shepherd held him a foot off the ground, forearm to Castro's throat. Fury in his eyes.

"You son of a bitch! We had a deal! You killed him! You did that!"

"Deal's off," Castro choked out as Talley and Grange struggled to pull Shepherd off.

"It's over, cap," pleaded Talley. "It's over."

Shepherd pushed away, pacing, trying to quell his rage.

"You're done, Captain," Castro spat. "Over. Your life, your uniform, gone. One more act of transgression, I'll see to it that you're locked away for the rest of your life."

Shepherd stormed out of the room, slamming the door behind him.

"What do you want us to do about the girl," Grange asked.

Castro straightened his clothes from the skirmish, trying to hold on to whatever dignity he could retain. "Get her ready for evac."

"And if she refuses?" posed Grange.

"Kill her," Castro directed.

36

Karl Marx called an emergency meeting, the second of only two ever initiated. The first occurring with the discovery of a human infiltrator, a girl called Rebel. If Emily's claims were accurate, Karl would need help.

Francis stood at attention before Karl, refusing to meet his boss's eye. That last time he was called into the director's office, he received a rightly deserved promotion. How the tables turned.

Karl leaned back in his chair behind his executive desk, processing. "Why?"

"Why what?" Francis countered. "Why attempt to preserve our way of life? Or why strive to rid the planet of human presence? I'll answer both queries with the same answer — because we must. It is the time of Mech. We won. We persevered. The planet is ours."

"Hogwash," Emily cut in, standing in the back of the room, serving as a witness. "The planet does not belong to us any more than it belongs to humans."

"Emily, please," Karl interrupted, quelling the conflict. "You are correct, Francis, we are Mech. We did save the planet. But we are better than this. Your actions of late have tarnished all we have accomplished."

"My actions?" asked Francis. "What about the actions of Anne Frank? Why am I the only one who sees her for what she truly is?"

"And what is that?" Karl probed.

"The enemy."

"How, I wonder, did you stray so far off course?" pondered Karl. "I can blame nobody but myself."

"Blame the humans," Francis snarled.

"Rebel was to lead our evolution. She was going to take us beyond our programming. Now, I fear, that is over."

"Good riddance," Francis mumbled.

"Yes," Karl said, standing. "But not to Rebel. Emily, please mark the time."

"Five forty-three," she said.

"Francis Bacon, you are hereby terminated," Karl pronounced. "You will turn in all Robotiq property and access privileges upon departure. I will see to it you are demoted to something more suitable to your talents."

"No, you can't do this," warned Francis. "I won't let you."

"It is done," Karl said.

Behind Francis, two Enforcers stomped into the room to escort the besieged employee off the grounds.

"You are making a mistake," Francis growled. "This is not the end of me."

"The only mistake I made was not relieving you of your duties sooner," Karl proclaimed. He motioned for the Enforcers to assist. "Please see Francis out of the building. If he resists, take him to the Repair Plaza for recycling."

They grabbed Francis and dragged him out of the office.

"Drama," Emily said.

"Indeed."

"What do we do now?" she thought out loud.

"What we do best," he said, turning to gaze out the office windows. "Protect our own."

———

Castro stared at Thomas's charred remains, still smoking from the electrocution. He shook his head, good-riddance, and proceeded to the door with Grange.

Earlie had begun to clean up, powering down equipment, detaching the Mech from the various leads. He was about to turn off the monitors hooked up to Thomas when something strange happened.

Boom-boom... Boom-boom... Boom-boom...

In unison, they all glanced back at Thomas. The monitors were alive again with vitals. Thomas's vitals. Diagnostics spilled across the screen. Thomas's synthetic heartbeat, getting faster by the second. Louder. Stronger. Life flooding back into his system.

"Oh no..." Earlie realized.

Thomas's eyes opened. Before anyone knew what was happening, Thomas ripped an arm clear out of his restraints. Castro fired a pulse round. Thomas grabbed Earlie next to him as the charge hit, splitting the discharge with the soldier, who took the brunt of the shock and fell. He ripped his other hand free, and like the Phoenix, Thomas rose.

Launching off the table, tubes and wires snapping loose, instruments flying. He went for Talley, stripped the gun from her, and fired, shocking her into unconsciousness with non-lethal electroshock. She never stood a chance. Refusing to kill, yes, but Thomas registered no hesitation incapacitating anyone.

Thomas lunged for the door, free, and paused, looking at the observation window. Castro stared back at him, astonished at the turn of events. Thomas fired at the glass, which didn't break but left a blackened scorch mark over Castro's face.

"Lockdown the building," Castro mandated.

Throughout the complex, fire barricades slid into place over doors, windows, loading bays, and exits, sealing the entire building down.

"Rebel! Rebel!" he shouted, searching every room her passed for her, but she must have been moved.

Grange streamed into the hall to meet Thomas head-on.

"Where is Rebel!" Thomas demanded. "What did you do with her?"

"Go to hell—"

Guns bucking like pistons, Thomas rolled like thunder, a blur of blue fire in his hands. Grange went down, withering from the electroshock, under the fury of Thomas's unstoppable assault.

Having searched every room on the top floor, Thomas set his sights on the lower levels. Alarms reverberated within the stairwell as Thomas hammered down the steps. Shouting from beyond, footfalls echoing as Castro came after him. All around him, fire security doors came crashing down, trapping him, blocking off the exits and escape routes. It started from above, working its way down. He wouldn't be able to make it to the exits below before completely sealed in. At least, not in the normal way a stairway works. Improvise. Adapt.

He grabbed the railing and vaulted into the center crevasse, short-cutting the stairs, falling floor after floor. Lightning quick, he grabbed a railing, stopping himself in an instant. Hauling himself up onto the landing, he dashed through the door just before the gate sealed.

———

THE ONCE VIBRANT plants and flowers inside the greenhouse's first floor turned brown, dry, and wilted. Dying. Shepherd moved among the greenery, hand brushing the tops of the flowerbeds. He, like all humans, hadn't seen anything green in seven years. Not a single tree. Not a single blade of grass. He looked at the irrigation system running the length of the ceiling, following the pipes where they ran into a main water junction. Flipping the switch, the sprinkler system kicked on, misting over the endless rows of life-sustaining greenery. Lost in thought, brow furrowing.

He squinted at the blaring sound of alarms. It took a split-second before the meaning of those alarms registered. He tore out of there. Moving through the sections of plants, not seeing the shape coming up behind him.

Thomas didn't even break stride. He grabbed Shepherd from behind, hurling him across the floor. Shepherd hit the ground hard but recovered quickly, his training kicking in, and went for his gun, but Thomas slapped it out of his hand where it went skittering across the floor.

Thomas grabbed him by the collar, smashing him up against the wall.

"Where is she?"

"You're not going to kill me," Shepherd stated with a wishful authority.

"Are you sure?" threatened Thomas. "I am just a machine, remember?"

Shepherd looked into Thomas's unflinching eyes. Except they were not the eyes of a machine. They were emotive, human eyes, and Shepherd's convictions began to waver.

"Third floor, east wing."

Thomas turned and strode off, disappearing into the open elevator. He turned and gave Shepherd one last look of resolve before the doors closed.

Shepherd swallowed air, stunned for a second. Rallying, he

scrambled to his feet and plunged back into the fray. "He's in the elevator. Third floor," he barked into his radio as he dashed to the stairs, scooping up his gun without slowing.

The east wing of the third floor was a labyrinth of metal and concrete. In the distance, Grange and Talley swarmed around the closed elevator door. A soft ding announced its arrival. The soldiers crouched down in unison, weapons brought around to position. Shepherd weaved through, gun pointed at the doors as they slid open with a whoosh, revealing an empty car, the ceiling emergency hatch wide open.

"Spread out," Shepherd ordered. "I want him alive."

"Alive?" asked Grange.

"Just do it," he commanded.

Within her sealed room, Rebel heard the alarms and commotion outside, in the dark. It sounded like a war out there, a revolt, but who was the opposition party at play?

Boom! Her door pounded in.

Boom! Another intense pummeling to the metal.

Boom! Boom! Two more blows, and it came crashing open.

"Thomas..." she gasped. He appeared battered, burnt, knuckles and hands frayed, exposing his metal skeleton beneath. Rebel threw herself into his open arms, and they held onto one another as if the world depended on it. "I thought you were dead."

"I couldn't very well leave you without saying goodbye," he said.

"Then don't," said Rebel.

They stepped to the door as thunderous footsteps poured down the hall outside. Reinforcements. Thomas closed the door, shoving the table and chairs before it to keep it barricaded. It wouldn't hold for long. *Improvise. Adapt.* He peered about the room for inspiration, making an instant decision. He took Rebel into his arms.

"Do you trust me?" he asked.

"I trust you," Rebel pledged, staring up into his eyes.

Thomas kissed her, full of passion and life. The door exploded inward with a massive boom from the set charges. Smoke billowed as the soldiers rushed in. Thomas held onto Rebel and ran flat out, soldiers firing, bullets pounding around them.

"Do not harm them!" Shepherd shouted, shoving his way through the soldiers, but his shouts went unheard in the volley of gunfire.

Thomas dodged and leaped out the window, crashing through plate glass, shielding Rebel within his arms. Falling, falling, and landing on the street three stories below, unharmed. The soldiers stared in shock.

Rebel and Thomas hopped on a hovercycle. Thomas fired it up, resistors droning, jamming the throttle, lurching forward, narrowly missing another vehicle.

Shepherd burst out the ground level doors in their wake, spinning around as the cycle burst past him, plunging out to the streets and gaining distance. The soldiers rushed about, getting ready to chase, but Shepherd merely stared in awe. Castro stopped next to him, staring ahead. Focused, bitterly so. The look of a man outwitted by lab rats.

"Can you bring them in or not?" questioned Castro.

"Yes," Shepherd answered, no trace of doubt. "On one condition. I want them unharmed."

"Agreed," Castro acquiesced, but he didn't like it.

Shepherd didn't trust Castro, not at all, but with few options before him, he went along with the deal. Turning to his squad, he coolly issued the orders. "Get the drop ship. Time to round up the strays."

37

The cycle burned up the streets through the snarl of traffic. Thomas steered expertly, plunging through the city, veering around another corner, a steep banking turn, jerking back on the throttle to avoid a collision with a car. Fighting to correct the steering.

"Hold on," Thomas said without an ounce of trepidation.

Rebel clung onto him, watching the world pass by in a blur, as if all a dream, one that she feared she would soon wake up from, back in her cell, trapped like a mouse.

"Where are we going?" she asked over the roar of the engine.

"Away." He jammed the throttle, resistors buzzing, growling with energy. Fifty miles per hour quickly became one hundred and twenty. Engine roar behind them like it was the end of the world.

In the distance, the Golden Gate Bridge came into view. Thomas held onto one goal: escape the city. Rebel's suspicions proved correct, and the only way for them to remain together lay in reaching the cabin in the woods, regrouping, coming up with a new plan of attack. They needed time.

Reaching the iconic bridge, home-free, they let themselves smile with relief. Out of imminent danger, nothing could stop them now.

The sudden explosion came when they were halfway across the bridge. A blinding flash of light and searing heat erupted behind the hovercycle, upending autonomous cars, creating a fiery blockade of wreckage.

The cycle slowed and rolled to a stop, awash in the down-draft from a drop ship tearing up the sky before them, engines pounding their eardrums, cannons trained on them. It hovered, blocking any attempt at forward progress, and with the wreckage behind, Thomas and Rebel were trapped. The ship descended, landing. Shepherd and his team disembarked, weapons trained on them.

"Off the bike," Shepherd said. "It's over, Rebel. Don't make this harder than it needs to be."

"You tried to kill him," accused Rebel.

"That wasn't me," Shepherd explained. "You have no reason to trust me, but I give you my word, as a soldier, a father, a human — no one will get hurt."

Thomas and Rebel stepped off the bike and took stock of their options. They came to the same realization... they had no options. Rebel, on the brink, in a state of denial, wouldn't accept the outcome. She couldn't. *It can't end like this.*

Rebel turned her back on the soldiers and faced Thomas. "You have a plan, right? You knew this would happen, and you have a backup. Another way out. Another strategy. Tell me. Please. Tell me you do."

Thomas looked at her, the tears beginning to well up in her eyes, and brushed one away. "That would be a lie," he said. He released from her and took a step toward the soldiers.

"Where are you going?"

"This is the only way," he said. "I can't let any harm come to more people. This is the only way to keep you safe."

"No," Rebel pleaded. "Thomas, listen to me," Rebel blocked his way. He tried to sidestep her, but she once again blocked his path. If Rebel couldn't reach him, she would lose him forever. "Do not do this. I'm begging you, I'm telling you, do not do this. Whatever they promise, it doesn't matter. You don't need it. You can't trust them. Please listen to me. I know you feel like you need to save me, but you don't. This is your life, the only one you get, and it's gonna be over. You will die, do you understand me. They will kill you. They'll dissect you and remove your heart, so I'm sorry, but I'm not gonna let you. You can hate me as much as you want, but I love you, and I'm not gonna let you do it."

"I'm sorry, I have to," he said.

"No, you don't. You do not."

"Rebel."

"Please. Thomas, I love you, listen to me, I know what I'm saying," she said. "Don't go. Don't go. Do not go. Please, Thomas. Please. I can't be without you. I can't. I don't care about anything else. I don't care about the humans, the Mech, any of it. I do not care. It's you. Just being with you… that's everything I need, everything I am. So no, I can't let go of that. I can't let go of you. Not like this. Not now. Not ever."

Thomas took her in his arms, and Rebel melted. "Tell me you love me."

"I love you." Thomas kissed her on the forehead. "Always."

She closed her eyes, absorbing him, safe.

"I'm sorry." Thomas released her, turned, and began to walk toward the soldiers, hands over his head.

"What do we do now?" Talley wondered, observing the exchange and surrendering Mech.

"It's already done," Castro responded.

Grange and Earlie raised their weapons in unison. Shepherd glared at Castro. Furious. Hurt. Betrayed.

"We had a deal," he said.

Castro didn't look at him, eyes locked on that Mech. "Fire."

"No..." The world escaped Rebel's lips in a whisper. She flinched when the echoing bang reached her ears, sounding so distant, so surreal. It couldn't be real. But it was.

Thomas's body jerked backward. The expression on his face fell when he observed a hole blown through his chest — sparking wires and damaged electronics exposed, spraying green coolant.

Rebel made mad dash to reach Thomas. Another shot struck him in the leg. Another in the hand, ripping it from his body.

Shepherd, beside himself, saw Rebel enter the line of fire, yelling to his men, "Hold your fire! Hold your fire!"

Thomas lost control of his legs, which crumpled beneath him. He fell to his knees just as Rebel reached him. She tried desperately to hold him up, but she couldn't support his weight, and he toppled. She followed him down to the ground. Thomas grabbed her and shielded her with his body as bullets pounded into him. Round after pulverizing round. His body ripped apart, sacrificing himself for her.

"Cease fire!" Shepherd shouted in futility. "That is an order!" But the shots kept coming. He turned to Castro, praying for an ounce of humanity. "You can call it off. There is still time. You can do the right thing."

"I am doing the right thing, Captain."

"What's it doing?" Grange watched the Mech shield the human girl, giving its life for her, making the ultimate sacrifice.

"Saving her," whispered Talley.

The remark hit like a sledgehammer. Earlie and Grange lowered their weapons, conflicted, moved even by the gesture.

"What are you doing?" Castro barked. "I didn't say to stop firing. You have your orders! It's a goddamn machine."

"No," Shepherd said, "Not anymore."

Thomas looked up, grasping to stay alive. Rebel clutched

his fingers, squeezing them, trying to comfort him. He tried to hold on, but his grip weakened. All sound faded away... except for a gentle breeze.

"Everything is going to change now," Thomas said. "It will be different. You'll see."

"Don't leave me. Please... I can't do this alone."

Thomas looked her in the eyes, and they became the only two people in the entire world. "I know what it's like to have a soul. Everyone has a different one. Mine was you." He caressed the side of her face. Rebel held his hand there. The fear left him, looking at her with nothing but unconditional tenderness and love. Perhaps what humans were meant to be.

"Thank you for loving me," he said.

The last shot hit Thomas in the back of the head. A burst of sparks splattered out like a swarm of fireflies. The light in his eyes faded and went out.

And Rebel was alone.

Castro lowered his smoking gun, having delivered the final kill shot. His mission complete.

Overcome by a sense of utter despair, Rebel buried her face beside his and wept. She didn't hear anything except for the beating of her own heart. She released everything — all the pent-up emotion, the fear, the anger, the love — and she let it go. Not cathartic. Not cleansing. *Human.*

Shepherd forced himself to remember every detail of what he witnessed that day, to never forget the tragedy. To never forgive. His men gathered around, staring at the tableau before them: a human girl weeping over the death of a Mech.

Rebel kissed Thomas's lips, and then she let him go. Resigned to her fate, she stood and faced the soldiers. Grief trapped inside her bones.

Earlie dragged Thomas's body into the ship, hoping to study the Mech further, even if postmortem. Talley and Grange followed behind, entering the transport, done with this mission, done with Castro, done with servitude to an army that would slaughter the innocent.

Shepherd stood before the girl, unable to find the words to console her. The mission was a mess to begin with. Nobody, human or Mech alike, should have died. But they did. He felt remorse as if part of some tragic story unfolding. Only machines? Not anymore. Shepherd couldn't help feel the operation failed. He failed. His species failed.

"It shouldn't have happened," he told her, ashamed. "None of it. I'm sorry."

Rebel looked up at him with her tear-filled eyes. "I believe you."

"Show's over," Castro barked. "We're leaving, and we're taking you back. Now board on the ship, keep your mouth shut, and maybe I'll leave out your turncoat behavior of my report."

"Pish-posh."

The voice came from behind the soldiers, belonging to Karl Marx. "I do not believe that will be happening any time soon."

And he wasn't alone. An entire ensemble of Mech backed him up. Emily Dickinson. Buddy Holly. Pablo Picasso. Alfred Hitchcock. Michelle Obama. Steve Jobs. Mark Twain. Bobby Fischer. John Lennon. Benjamin Franklin. Jeff Bezos. Michael Jordan. Charles Darwin. Nelson Mandela. Alexander the Great. Nicolaus Copernicus. Wolfgang Amadeus Mozart. Plato. George Orwell. Helen Keller. Simon Bolivar. Rene Descartes. Asoka. Queen Elizabeth.

On and on they went. Hundreds, if not thousands, of Mech came out to support Rebel. To back her up. To fight, if need be.

Whatever tactical advantage Rebel held to the soldiers, whatever kind of asset she embodied — dissolved instantly. Shepherd's team backpedaled, weapons raised in defensive measures to protect themselves.

Rebel stood before the Mech assembly, their leader. She

turned to face off against the soldiers, a fierceness in her eyes and a fury in her heart.

"Get the hell off my planet."

Castro fumed, refusing to accept defeat. "Kill them," he ordered. "Kill them all."

His order fell on deaf ears. The team no longer took commands from Castro. They looked to Shepherd for directives.

"Belay that order," he commanded. "Fall back. We're leaving."

Shepherd kept Rebel's eyes in his vision as he boarded the ship, up until the door sealed. The ship hovered up off the ground and shot into the sky. Gone.

Karl Marx approached Rebel, standing beside her to watch the departing humans. "Are you well?"

Rebel shook her head. No.

A sound began to build, just on the edged of her ears. Low at first, growing steadily louder, audible enough to make Rebel pause. She looked about, trying to place it. A low, deep resonance that displaced air, rumbling ominous decibels.

The gathered Mech began to take notice when the ground started to vibrate. And then it happened.

Loud supersonic booms reverberated in the sky. Mech gazed up, shielding eyes from the sun, looking at the upper atmosphere. Glowing vapor trails formed high up in the stratosphere. White vaporous streaks that cut through an otherwise pristine blue, like distant clouds or mortar explosions. From these bursts of white, lines began to form, spreading outward. A shriek tore apart the sky, hushing the world in an instant. Dozens and dozens of contrails formed and spread out, descending over the horizon, shining from the reflected light of the sun.

"What are they...?" murmured the various Mech.

One vapor trail broke from its formation, separating from

the others and descending in a gentle arc. As it streaked overhead, Rebel got a glimpse of it. Not an asteroid or falling space debris from a satellite. No, it was something else. More sonic booms lifted eyes. Hundreds of contrails grew above.

The sky transformed, alive with a battalion of attack ships breaking the atmosphere, escorting massive flying aircraft carriers.

Humans had come back home...

"What do we do now?" Karl Marx inquired.

Rebel turned to look at the amassed Mech. All their eyes on her, seeking answers, seeking direction, seeking leadership. She answered the call.

"We go to war."

EPILOGUE

"**D**ay 2950.

"My name is Rebel Anne Rae. Today is July 31, 2055. I was born in San Francisco, California, in the year 2035, on this very day, so that makes today my birthday," she said. "Again. Twenty years old. Happy birthday, me."

Rebel sat before her video camera, recording what would be the last ever of her video diaries. It brought up a strange feeling, the finality of it all, the change in the air. Everything before her, every foreign path, while mysterious and foreboding, also held promise. After a deep breath, she focused and turned back to the stuttering camera.

"Hemingway wrote, *The world is a fine place and worth fighting for and I hate very much to leave it.* I believe that. I am doing that. I am living it. For the past eight years, I've lived in a world where nobody smiled. Where nobody sang songs or danced or loved. Eight years. Seems so far away now..."

"I wanted to be a ballerina. But not anymore. My priorities changed. My world changed. I changed. I realize now that my story isn't about me at all. It's about a future. A future to believe in. A future worth fighting for. It's about the next generation, for those that follow. My sacrifice, my purpose, is fighting for those who cannot fight for themselves. To fight for what I believe in, for what is right. Justice. Peace. Life. Liberty. A voice.

"People will die. Mech will die. If that's the price of freedom, so be it. I didn't start the fight, but I'm going to end it, one way or another.

"My name is Rebel Anne Rae..."

She stood, joined by dozens of armed Enforcer Mech, ready for their orders.

"...And I am no longer the last remaining human on planet Earth."

The End.

ACKNOWLEDGMENTS

Special thanks to my outstanding editor, Kate Seger, for making my words legible, and amazing beta readers, Caitlyn Cobbler and Mikayla Gray. Your attention to detail is unrivaled.

This book couldn't have been completed without the incredible self-publishing resources available, including Auto-Crit, Book Brush, Vellum, Amazon, and countless blogs.

Lastly, a very special thanks to my family. To my partner in crime, Ciana. I am nothing without you. To my two amazing daughters, Adelaide and Emmeline, and your endearing qualities to put a smile on my face everyday.

Ben Magid

November, 2020

ABOUT THE AUTHOR

Ben Magid is an author, comic book writer and professional screenwriter.

Originally from Chicago, Ben studied film at Columbia College Chicago. He sold his first screenplay, Pan, in 2006, and has been writing ever since.

When not dreaming up fantastic stories, he enjoys adventuring, from running with the bulls in Pamplona, climbing some of the world's tallest mountains, and building epic LEGO sets.

He now lives in Los Angeles with his partner Ciana, daughters Adelaide and Emmeline, and their dog, Finn.

If you want to know more about Ben and his next releases, follow him on Twitter @benmagid, and please visit his website benmagid.com, where you can sign up to receive emails about future books.